This Thing Called Love

SEAGULL
BOOKS
•
CELEBRATING
40 YEARS

THE ARAB LIST

ALSO BY
ALAWIYA SOBH

Maryam
Keeper of Stories
Translated by Nirvana Tanoukhi

RECENT TITLES IN
THE ARAB LIST

HUSSEIN BARGHOUTHI
The Blue Light
Translated by Fady Joudah

JABBOUR DOUAIHY
Firefly
Translated by Paula Haydar and Nadine Sinno

SONALLAH IBRAHIM
The Turban and the Hat
Translated by Bruce Fudge

RAMY AL-ASHEQ
Ever Since I Did Not Die
Translated by Isis Nusair

AKRAM MUSALLAM
The Dance of the Deep-Blue Scorpion
Translated by Sawad Hussain

SALIM BARAKAT
Come, Take a Gentle Stab
Selected Poems
Translated by Huda Fakhreddine and Jayson Iwen

ALAWIYA SOBH

This Thing Called Love

Translated by
MAX WEISS

LONDON NEW YORK CALCUTTA

THE ARAB LIST
Series Editor: Hosam Aboul-Ela

Seagull Books, 2023

Originally published in Arabic as *Ismuhu Al-Gharam*
© Alawiya Sobh, 2009

First published in English translation by Seagull Books, 2023
English translation © Max Weiss, 2023

ISBN 978 1 80309 0 788

British Library Cataloguing-in-Publication Data
A catalogue record for this book is available from the British Library

Typeset at Seagull Books, Calcutta, India
Printed and bound by Hyam Enterprises, Calcutta, India

This Thing Called Love

1

She nudged me gently.

I thought I was out cold. This always seems to happen to me. She'd show up and do things like this, especially after the July War broke out. I started to fall back asleep.

Once again I sensed her hand shaking me more roughly this time. While it didn't stir up much feeling, it did occur to me at that point that I should get up to call Suad and let her know that Nahla was back. When she asked how she was doing, it seemed as if all the anxiety in the whole wide world was contained within her voice.

I thought about how things like this don't typically happen while I'm asleep, like the last time she nudged me gently and I drifted right back off.

I didn't even have to lift my head and look her in the face in order to know that it was her. I could tell by the sound of her voice. 'Get up, dear,' she said firmly. 'Just write it down and let's be done with it. Do I have to be dead before you'll actually write it down? Write it however you like, you can always revise the story later, you know.'

The timbre of her voice was pleasant in my ear, scratchy, raspy in a way that used to turn on Hani, flooding his chest with a warm current of passionate love.

I braced myself, then tossed onto my left side, turning my back to her.

Pen and paper lay right there in front of me on the table but my hand wouldn't obey the way it once did when she'd come over and encourage me to write. I began talking to myself instead.

'All right then, what should I write? I don't know you that well. All I know is whatever they've told me about you, but that isn't enough for me to chronicle your entire life story.'

'What makes you think that even if you knew me for a long time you'd be able to write about me like that?' she shot back sarcastically. 'Come on, just start writing. You'll get inspired once you get going. Maybe you'll even wind up getting to know me. Don't forget: writing is always incomplete.'

The tone of her voice was flecked with sadness. When she fell silent, it was surreal, it hardly even seemed like silence to me because my head was full of roaring thoughts.

I tried to calm myself. Once I had successfully commanded my mind to stop jumping and dancing and all its other nonsense, I forced my body to lay flat in bed. For a moment I wondered what might have happened. This was no dream. I definitely wasn't asleep but couldn't understand why I should be lying in bed with my clothes and shoes still on. I became certain this was no waking dream either. Writing is nothing like that. I don't believe in demons. Writing only comes to me in moments of deep thought and concentration, even if I might occasionally manage to imagine characters in my dreams or have dreams that I'm writing at other times. I was absolutely not in that kind of state. I don't know exactly how to describe what happened.

I got out of bed and headed for my desk, where I rested my elbows and shut my eyes in front of the blank page. My fingers pressed into my temples as I started to think about

Nahla. Instinctively I put my right hand on my shoulder in the exact location where I had felt her nudge me when she asked me to get writing.

I tried to start writing down her story but couldn't. There was no way I would be able to write. I was too tired, delirious from the exhaustion. I hadn't been able to sleep since the outbreak of the July War. That day there were clashes between the resistance and the Israeli army in Wadi al-Hujayr and several other villages. I had spent weeks in front of the television screen flipping between channels, as if my eyes had rolled back inside my head, blood red, leaving me blinded. Just keeping up with the news paralysed my body and my mind. It felt as if my skin could no longer hold my body together. My entrails were disembowelled in front of me just like those casualties I witnessed on screen. My brain was pummelled by the newscast, by the scenes of children fluttering like scraps of paper as they were carted off and transformed into names on body bags that were carefully lined up in rows, covering the earth. I could feel my own body reduced to remains beneath the debris, waiting for someone to collect them, like everyone who met their demise under their own homes.

Everything became unclear to me when I tried to start writing. I could no longer be completely sure if I ever actually knew a woman named Nahla who told me her story so that I would write it down or if I was confecting the life of a woman from among those I watched being pulled from the rubble.

Another devastating war ripped me out of my solitude and my papers and my characters, tore me away from the universe of writing the same way it evicts people from their homes. It forced me back into reality, demolished the alternative world I had built, as if war can raze the foundations of the novel and not just the physical structures in which human beings actually live. It was difficult to get back inside my own head, to catch hold of my thoughts and confront them. War flattens everything—obliterates, pulverizes. It was as if my hand had been severed, like the hand of that little girl I saw on screen. I didn't have the strength to write when Nahla urged me to record her story.

But I have no choice but to obey her—to stave off my own death through writing—so that my novel won't be reduced to a title with blank pages. Besides, if I don't put her life down in words, won't that diminish her to a name on a body bag just like all those little girls and other innocent victims?

I found myself obligated to write, to become embedded in Nahla's life story, one that was filled with love and vitality. I was stunned to hear from Suad that Nahla had disappeared. It aroused an urgent desire in me to trace her life and track her fate.

Nahla never called me when she got back from Paris. She had gone there to visit her boyfriend Hani. After the war broke out the two of them struggled to figure out the future of their relationship. I called her mobile several times to check in on her but I always received an automated message saying her line wasn't yet back in service; or the phone would ring and ring but nobody would pick up. The strange thing was that I had two missed calls from her on my phone. I hadn't noticed them at first because I had a bad habit of not hearing my phone ring. When I called her back later, there was no answer. For a while I expected her to call me back but I don't think she ever did. Even stranger than that were the few times I bumped into her girlfriends Azizeh and Hoda and Nadine at the cafe without her or Suad being there: I noticed how they tried to avoid looking at me, which made it all the more confusing when they started following me around, asking whether I knew anything about what had happened to her.

Suad was the one who messed up my papers.

It never occurred to me that she might come visit while the war was still raging in order to ask if I knew where Nahla was. The first time she came over to my house, Suad didn't ask me about that, though. She was more of the silent type.

One day during the war my doorbell rang at 8 a.m. I was startled and surprised. It was unusual to have visitors so early in the morning. I was particularly worried it might be bad news about someone in my family or one of my friends because the war was harvesting more and more casualties and martyrs all the time. I hurried to the door and asked, 'Who's there?'

'It's me,' a muffled voice replied.

'Me who?'

'Suad. Nahla's friend.'

I opened the door, surprised to find her standing there. She was a frightful sight, it seemed she hadn't slept for some time. Her face was duskier than usual. Her eyes seemed to have no lashes. I took her hand, guided her inside to sit down on the couch, and invited her to make herself comfortable while I made some coffee. She was revived by the aroma and the sound of my footsteps as I came back from the kitchen carrying the serving tray, the coffee pot, and two cups. She regained her composure and turned her dark and droopy eyes away from the blank wall. As soon as I sat down on the couch next to her she asked me if Nahla had called. When I told her she hadn't she clutched at her purse, tears in her eyes, and quickly blurted out more questions: Where has she gone? Where could she be? When is she going to call? Her questions flustered me, piqued my curiosity. At the same time they also made me suspicious. It's inconceivable that Suad wouldn't know where Nahla was. The two of them were inseparable. Nahla didn't keep any secrets from her. Why wouldn't Suad know where her soul sister had gone? I was also confused about why Suad would ask me, of all people. I didn't know her that well. We'd only met a few times, through Nahla, when she told me fragments of her stories.

Not even a full week had passed after she came over to my house when Suad called me on the phone to ask if we could meet. I was concerned. It must have been something serious. I suggested Lina's Café in Hamra and she agreed immediately.

I headed out for the cafe at 5 p.m., as we had agreed. The street was almost entirely deserted, unlike normal daytime hours when the crush of cars and hordes of displaced people transformed the appearance of everyday life. The shelling of Beirut's southern suburbs shook the air and everything else.

At Lina's, Suad told me she still couldn't find Nahla, that she had been searching for her for days.

'I'm devastated,' she said with tears in her eyes. 'Nahla would never disappear like this. I can't take it. I don't know what could have happened to her. It's driving me mad.'

She swallowed her tears, then her words. As long as I was writing her story she asked me to help her find out what had happened to Nahla and to let her know if she called.

I tried calming her down, to soothe her by saying there was nothing to be worried about. Despite my sense that she was hiding something from me that I would discover later on, I also had the feeling Nahla was going to resurface before the end of the novel; I didn't know when or how, though. I reread what I had written down when she told me her story. Maybe those papers would reveal something to me. Perhaps I'd be able to glean her fate from the story. My conviction that she was going to come back increased even though I couldn't know when or under what circumstances. But doubts and questions swept me away once again when Suad and her girlfriends called me in order to ask, 'What if something horrible has happened to her in the war? Or what if she was caught under the bombs and nobody can identify her remains? Could she have gone back to her village in the south before the war started, only to get stuck there and then get killed? Didn't the news from the front report that her village had been completely destroyed? Or what if her husband Saleem had killed her and hidden the body after finding out about her and Hani, about her visit to Paris to see him? Or what if she ran off with Hani, what if she wanted to grow old with him, as she would often playfully tell him she would?

Then wicked thoughts started to nag at me. I asked myself: Could Suad be mixed up in her death somehow? Maybe now she's experiencing remorse over what she did? This dark scenario drifted through my mind as I recalled how Nahla once laughed when she told me she felt like Suad was more jealous of her because of Hani and Saleem than she was of her own cheating husband Sulayman. Whenever Nahla received an intimate text from Hani and disappeared into her room to be alone and chat with him, she could sense Suad's resentment. She couldn't really be sure whether she was jealous of him or her, though.

All I could do was start writing in order to try and get some answers, to clarify her life and her fate. I comforted myself by saying she wouldn't be gone for long. The most important thing was that she not die in this war.

Nahla had called me before leaving for Paris to meet Hani. She asked me when I would be finished with the novel. I couldn't tell whether it was her upcoming trip or something else that was making her nervous. She wasn't speaking in complete sentences. She mispronounced my name on the phone more than once. Then she vanished and never called me again.

Before I started writing down the little she had told me to familiarize me with her life, I recalled what she had said to me the last time we met: 'When we write about another, we gain power over their life, as if the writer can determine the date of their birth and their death.'

If only I knew where to start.

Should I begin with the first time she reconnected with Hani after getting married? Or how she saw him more than once before getting back together with him again in her mid-fifties? Or shall I begin by talking about her childhood and those of her girlfriends Suad and Nadine and Azizeh and her brother Jawad? Or should I tell the story of her body in love and motherhood and all the other stages of her life? Or should I begin with what happened to her and her girlfriends?

I didn't want to play the game of beginnings.

Beginnings belong whenever and wherever we decide to put them. What we believe is a beginning may turn out to be the middle of the road or just short of the ending because writing isn't anything like speech. In speech Nahla yielded to the pleasure of storytelling. I could only begin once writing itself would cooperate with me. Writing links us to beginnings, shows all of us where we can find them, where they end, if they even want to end. In speech we can follow the thread from beginning to end. We can change things and revise them. This is something we can't do in writing because in the end speech is governed by erasure, by the fear of forgetting that so terrified Nahla. From the moment I met her, I noticed how connected she was to her own body, sensing it in the way she walked, the way her body moved, the way she sat and the way she spoke while telling me her story.

The first thing Nahla ever said to me was about forgetting.

She told me straight away the first time we met, flicking her head and her eyes in the same direction, about how she got out of bed one morning and hopped to the bathroom. She would stand under the shower with her eyes shut tight, remembering her dream from the night before, vigorously lathering her hair with shampoo and water as if she were scrubbing the memories from her brain, but it was all in vain, as if her hands were scratching against her bony skull and there was nothing inside but a white cloud where her dreams had sunk in and then drifted away. She opened her eyes and thought about how the steam filling the bathroom resembled brilliant morning sunlight compared with the dense fog clouding her mind.

'I can't understand why I'm so forgetful. My memory no longer feels as active as my body. At this age I feel as though a person comes into being with a blank memory and leaves the same way, just as we arrive on our knees and get carried out the same way. We deposit our memories in the world and depart without them. I'd consider myself lucky to be given a writer who could record mine, so that they won't be isolated and then vanish, so that they'll receive the same fate as a body and a skeleton. And what about you? Have you also started forgetting?'

I nodded at her and smiled knowingly in order to confirm that, unfortunately, I too had started to forget. She took a long drag on her cigarette, then lifted the side of her eyelid that got stuck to her temple because of how sweaty she was.

'Doesn't life scare you?' she asked me. 'Especially as a writer. How can you write at all once your memory starts to betray you?'

She was afraid I would forget the story of her life that she was going to tell me, which would only be whatever she was able to remember. She asked me to write down not only her biography but also the story of her eternal love for Hani, about the surprising twists and turns brought about by the passing of time. She said that time had a scent, the same way a place did. She could smell it in the odour of fermenting old age, in the fresh and delicious smell of her grandchildren, in all bodies and in all things. She interrupted herself in order to ask me, after taking a deep breath, 'Does love end when the story is over?'

She asked a lot of questions the first time she had me over for coffee. I was surprised by the invitation because I didn't know her too well but I didn't hesitate to pay her a visit. Her earnest desire to see me was plain in her warm voice that was marked by distinct yet somehow tender raspiness. When I asked her why she didn't want to write her own story she was slightly taken aback, lost, searching for the right words until her voice crept back out. She told me she couldn't write the story of her love for Hani because she was married. She also said that women have secrets that aren't so easy for them to talk about openly.

Then she told me she was a poet, not a novelist, that she had held onto some diaries from her childhood and ended up burying them along with her poems in the family garden when she was a little girl.

She told me these included stories and confessions but that I wouldn't be able to tell whether she had written them and stashed them with Suad or whether it was her friend who had written them. After a moment of hesitation and silence, she told me how she had always dreamt of telling someone her story so that her life could be rediscovered one day.

Her eyes flashed, regaining their luminescence as she talked about her body, about how she had discovered it in middle age the way she rediscovered it at every age, how it was her private possession, the way it had always been, and not the property of the fear she had combatted and hidden away inside of herself for her entire life.

I don't understand why she talked so much about forgetting. After comparing it to whiteness, she asked, 'Why do they insult whiteness by comparing it to forgetting? How can it be an indicator of death when there's nothing I love more than crushing fresh snow between my teeth? I take indescribable pleasure in doing that. Snow revitalizes the spirit. Fire is extinguished in white. The light of dawn, its first threads, is also white. The smell of soap is white. Why don't we talk about the blackness of memory instead, a scorched black camera reel, for example? Why don't we refer to the blackness of memory, or some other colour? Why do people simply parrot what other people say?

'Names are what I've started to forget most of all. The same thing happened to my mother,' she told me.

In middle age, when Nahla was no longer that young, she couldn't understand why she always had to rattle off the names of her aunts in order to eventually guide her tongue to recall her own name. The whole thing puzzled her, made her feel that if she truly loved herself she wouldn't forget her own name, as if she were a stranger to herself. It occurred to her yesterday, standing naked in front of the mirror, that she could see her mother in her own body, that she was discovering her at this age in particular.

'Nothing resists old age quite like love is what Hani used to say,' she said with a smile on her face. Then she lowered her voice, which was cloaked in sadness, as she said, 'But love wants health, love needs a body, and the body is bound to time, unfortunately. It's an apparatus with mysterious secrets. We don't know when its clock is going to grind to a halt.

'I'll tell you all about this love. Hani is my world and my love. When I don't see him in my dreams, I'm heartsick.

Don't change a thing when you write down the story. You writers lie by putting your own imagination into the story. I know that you changed Dunya's fate in your earlier novel, *Dunya*. No, I like my story just the way it is. And believe me, when you write my story, you'll find out what's true, not what's novelistic, what it is for us to experience our love for all eternity inside the story.'

Before starting to tell me her story she added that there were a lot of things Hani was going to read about for the first time. 'There's still so much I never told him.'

2

I'm confused.

I forget so many things and then remember them unexpectedly. I'll remember Hani, then forget all about him, even though he never leaves my side. He's always somewhere inside of me—silent sometimes, making noise at other times—which is one reason why I still love him.

I may have married another man but still I love him so.

It's as if our love had been born before us.

I immersed myself in the muck of poetry and promiscuity and desire for lots of other men, but I still love him. Many people were born, even more people died, but still I love him. It's been said that millions of human beings fall in love every second, that millions of betrayals are committed every moment, but still I love him. I had a son and a daughter, grandsons and granddaughters . . . but I never stopped loving him.

There were times when Hani was absent from me. What I mean is that I would forget about him from time to time. I wouldn't think of him for days or weeks, sometimes months even. But he would always come back to me as though he had never left. He would appear in front of me and my body would heave, quivering feverishly with desire, overwhelmed. His breath lacerated me, as if it were seeping out all of his pores. My heart folded in on itself, rolled up like a cigarette, and for an instant I was stripped bare, caught in delicious and pleasurable astonishment, like the moment when a son comes back to see his mother after being away for a long time.

I feel like his mother, as if I was the woman who gave birth to him, who raised him and watched him grow up, who loved him as though he were a part of her own body. Hani isn't a part of me, though: he is my totality, the sum of all of my parts. He isn't just my lover: he's my friend and my soulmate, my son, and something else besides, something I can't name or describe, this thing called love. Just the thought of him can make me tremble, the same way I do whenever I lay eyes on him, whether or not he touches me. My heart swells with all kinds of love, each one with its own flavour and smell and voice.

Every time he takes me in his arms my soul is rejuvenated; it feels like the first time our bodies embraced. I wish I had held on much longer than I actually did. I wished I had got my fill of hugging so that I wouldn't have to go through the kind of pain I now feel. I wish I had run away with him, or that he had kidnapped me, that it was no longer possible for us to be apart.

Reclaiming the love I had lost granted me a kind of happiness I wasn't going to let anybody take away from me, not ever again, not a third time . . . not a tenth time. I wasn't going to fall in love with anyone else for the rest of my life. Those few meaningless relationships I'd had taught me that sex without love is a waste of the body, its abandonment, whereas love is what allows us to discover our bodies. I don't want to waste this body I've been given, or the words I have, to lose anything at all on purpose. I cling to the last crusts of bread, the outer edges of everything.

At least that's what I told Suad once. I tell her everything. Her and her alone. If not for her I would wind up talking to the flowerpots on my balcony. Last week I went to the village to recite the Fatiha over the graves of my mother and father. I passed by our house. The two pomegranate trees that stand side by side next to the fountain, one of which bears sour fruit, the other sweet, called out to me. I was gripped with the desire to speak to their leaves, as if I would be able to confide in them because pomegranate leaves are curled, not flat like the leaves of other trees. The poems I wrote when I was younger and so afraid of my mother and my brother Jawad were buried under a tree. They contained all the feelings I had for Hassan on the day I fell in love with him. Now I felt as though all of my previous feelings were little more than a dry run for the way I would feel about Hani.

I'm not going to lose him, not this time. I don't care if my husband Saleem divorces me or even kills me. Nothing is going to stand in my way any more. My two children are married, which means my life and my body are my own once again. My relationship with Saleem has been a facade for a long time, even before his body started to sink and then drown in the seas of old age. Eventually he's going to find out about my upcoming rendezvous with Hani in Paris. Who can predict what's going to happen between us there. Maybe we'll arrive at some decisions, maybe we'll upend our lives altogether. It shouldn't matter that we've reached middle age.

Before he called me two days ago, it had been about twenty days since I last saw him. He needed to have some tests done after being released from the hospital. I would sit on the balcony by myself and gaze out at the water, wondering, How old is the sea? Does it age the same way we do? I've changed so much. I've witnessed the end of my fifties. I can no longer deal with noise or being around too many people. I'm no longer capable of compromise. I've figured out what pleases me and what annoys me. But the more Suad prattles on, the more I remember my grandmother and her friend Jameela, whom I used to watch as a little girl while they gossiped and laughed with one another. Their shoulders would shake without making a sound. I could never understand what they were talking about. Their voices would melt into the stillness and the silence, punctuated only by the sounds of cicadas. On the balcony I would sketch the inquisitive faces of lonely women sitting on benches in the village square. What was left for them now that their children had all been married and their husbands were all dead? I'm not sure what made me think of the shepherd's wife who used to visit us when I was a child. She was all alone after her husband's death and the marriage of all her children. I remember how she used to sit on the ottoman beside my mother and stretch out her legs, rubbing them and then saying, 'Aach, aach,' before falling silent once again. She'd do that several times before heading home. One time I asked my mother why she would come all the way from her house on the other side of town to do that. She told me that people crave the familiar smell of others. She came over so she could smell other people and then went home with a fresh supply of human odours.

The sketches of those women in front of me beckoned. I was afraid of the way this desire to withdraw from the world and hole up in isolation had crept over me at this age, and that this was nothing other than the slippery slope towards death. I became even more anxious whenever the feeling washed over me that neither my memory nor my body would obey me any longer. All of a sudden I would notice how they might have still been with me but that I couldn't grab hold of them. I have no idea whether old age will be more merciful, but the burden of middle age is sometimes terrifying. I reminisce about my younger days in order to beat back the terror. I try to inhabit my earlier body, to put it on once again, although I now feel it's no longer possible for me to recover the original. I become a pale shadow, the shadow I used to see cast by the sun when I was a little girl playing with boundless joy. I would watch it grow longer and then shorter, as skinny as a thread if I moved my body in the right direction. I wasn't sure what kind of shadow I wanted to be, sometimes I'd ask myself if it was possible to possess an unlimited number of shadow forms or whether my shadow would always retain the same shape.

Sometimes I feel as though youth is a shell that expands and contracts until all that remains are memories, which also fade. Reagrdless, I don't ever feel like I resemble dead flowers or that the world is false and evil and harsh and selfish, which is what Suad would always say. I feel a kinship with the fresh flower petals I used to pick out in the valleys when I was a little girl, their sweet fragrance filling the air. Anyway, I've come to terms with my body the same way I have done at every stage of my life, perhaps even more so now.

My body that I love so fiercely, my love for life—I believed they were chaste and generous for me and for Hani. Even when I was in short-term relationships I felt as though I was being tested. I would often try and explain that to Suad, telling her, 'From time to time I'm tested, I experience it, and I submit.' I used to believe that my body was a Pandora's Box, a big, full box. The more I get to know it now in middle age, the more surprised I am by it.

My intimate familiarity with my own body became so deep that I came to believe in it, to believe that it would never end. Now I know better. Now I know what I want, too, and I'm satisfied with what I want. These are feelings I was never aware of during my youth, though there are still times when

I have the desire to relive my younger days, when I stand in front of the mirror, for example, but that's only for a few passing moments.

All of my thoughts flew out of my head when the telephone rang. Hani told me he had decided to go to Paris. A close friend of his who lived there, a doctor who works in a hospital, asked him to come have some tests done. He asked if I would be able to meet him there.

My body cooed like a bird. Life flowed through my limbs and I nearly lifted off the ground from joy. I agreed straight away, not only because I wanted to be there and make sure Hani was okay, but also because we were going to figure out the future of our relationship. There was no way to know in advance what decisions we were going to make. Plus I'd be able to see my son at the same time. I missed him so much. Ahmad had been living in Paris ever since he got married. He worked for a company that was owned by his father-in-law, a friend of Saleem's who had immigrated to Paris in 1975, at the start of the civil war, who had become a French citizen, and who owned a large shipping company.

Packing my suitcase took a long time; its contents alerted me to just how old I had become: half of it was filled with medication, vitamins, anti-wrinkle cream, and other things I would never have needed when I was younger.

This time I also focused on my underwear and sleepwear. Hani gave me the name and address of the hotel where I was going to meet him.

I had meant to go shopping with Hoda, whose femininity was peaking. At this age she was prioritizing her body, giving it all the life she had left in her. She told me she was no longer going to make any concessions. She wasn't going to let herself feel anything but good. She stopped wearing cotton underwear and chose instead whatever would accentuate her femininity, believing that was more suitable despite the fact that her body wasn't as firm as it once was and that she had put on some weight. She came to know her body better, though, took more interest in its specific details. She wasn't stingy in slathering on aromatic creams, having become so obsessed with maintaining the softness of her skin that she tried to cover every centimetre of her back with it. She hunted for the best underwear, even in the wintertime. She became more comfortable in her own skin. When she started to get heavier, she avoided taking off her skirt and underwear in front of her husband Tarek before having sex. She would leave all of her clothes on until their desire became uncontrollable, the lights were off, their bodies were both concealed in darkness. When he approached her in a new way, she didn't know whether it was because he had seen it in the movies or learnt it from another woman. It didn't matter much to her, she didn't care why, she told me. All that mattered to her was that he knelt down in front of her, took off her panties and started to softly caress her between her thighs, first with his hands, then his mouth, moving up higher and higher. She melted, fluttered like a leaf. From that point she discovered she not only had feelings in the attractive parts of her body. She learnt to love her thighs, giggling whenever Tarek slapped them on the sides and asked her, 'How do those ham hocks feel, nice?'

Hoda went to the store with me to buy black lace and chiffon lingerie that I liked to wear and that Hani loved to see me in. It took us some time. The women in the shop were staring at me and smiling as I tried on different designs and sizes, telling me there was no doubt my husband was going to love it. I smiled back at her and asked if she really thought so.

The truth is that I wasn't only buying new intimate apparel to turn him on. I knew full well that I also attracted Hani with the feelings I was increasingly having at this age. My body has had particular significance for me my entire life: I lavish attention on it, I adore its beautiful and its less beautiful parts. The only times I have ever neglected it were during those years I was busy taking care of Ahmad and Faten. I would shower quickly so I could get back out to be with the two of them. I would eat in a hurry so I'd be able to feed them.

Now that I'm older my body is my own again. Sensation has returned to my being. I don't care how old this body might be. I'm as happy with it now as I was in every other phase of my life. Sometimes, when I'm singing, I feel as if my body is chirping and singing along with me. I can't understand why Suad sometimes stares at me so sullenly when I spread my arms like a soaring bird and sing and dance. She did that on several occasions. She would become distant and get angry if I talked to her about my body and my relationship with Hani. One time she even complained to me that I didn't seem to care about what was happening to her. She felt as though she had grown smaller, become weaker, that her body had shrunk down to a grain of wheat, a lentil, a bean. She detested her body. It made her feel as though she were much smaller than she really was, like it wouldn't obey her because she had been silent towards it, allowed it to be belittled. After my relationship with Hani resumed, she came over and I told her about our meeting and then started humming and singing. Her lips moved a little as if to sing along with me but then she froze. When I looked at her sallow face she turned into a bird perched on a tree branch that was covered in snow amidst unbearable cold, silent and still, not daring to make a peep out of fear that its song would be frozen solid.

Hani was the first person to truly introduce me to my own body, to help me become familiar with all of its particularities. The first time he touched me, the first time his breath brushed against my ear, I shivered and squealed. 'You're a devilish handful,' he joked. Hani made me feel better about my ass, which had started to sag a bit, about my ample thighs; God didn't skimp when he created those, granting me instead a beautiful face, a slim waist, and shapely breasts, which were the most attractive and expressive parts of my body. Throughout our life, every time we saw one another, I would experience feelings I never knew before, feelings I would never have had without him. Only now, in middle age, did I begin to discover these incredible sensations.

I tried on my underwear before packing it in my suitcase. I smacked my head and shouted, 'My God! How can I indulge my body this way while Hani has to take medication and sedatives for the irregular electrical activity in his heart and his brain, to calm his nerves and firm up his resolve, to tame his temperamental enthusiasm that could make him rant about the heart attack he already suffered?!'

I was besieged by negative thoughts, beset with dark ideas that had started to plague me. My fear of something else striking him down was overwhelming. What if Hani's heart stopped beating, God forbid, while he was having sex with me? Or what if he had another heart attack or something like that?

I thought about his hands and feet holding up his body while he was on top of me, shuddering until he fell down on me as his heart stopped. I froze where I was on the couch and asked myself: Would I kill myself right then and there if something were to happen to him? I love him to the point of worship. Or would I call reception immediately and ask for an ambulance and allow us to be found out? No, before doing that, I would first put his clothes back on. But how was I going

21

to be able to move his body all by myself? Would fear cause me to instinctively flee his room and run down the corridor back to my room, to abandon him there, naked and laid out on the bed? No, I would certainly have regrets if I did that. I'd come running back to his room from the other end of the hallway and call reception. But what would I do if his door was locked? Would I go back and call reception from my room? Would I flee the hotel altogether? Or would I kill myself in my room immediately?

My God, what diabolical thoughts! Can fear really over-shadow love to this extent? And how am I supposed to think about such things, about Hani, about my life, and even more important things?

I shied away from these thoughts in order to think about his warm body, to visualize the beautiful moment when we would be reunited. Then I cursed myself as I thought about how love always generates negative thoughts and fear for the ones we love. I had thought so much about losing my two children, dreamt so often of them lost and alone, even dead, and I would wake up in a panic, tears gushing from my eyes, thanking God it had only been a dream.

No, Hani's fine. The doctor assured him that the condition was temporary. Our meeting was going to be amazing, and fundamental decisions concerning our relationship were going to be made. I became even more calm as I remembered that he had asked the doctor when they were alone together after his wife and children had left the hospital room if he was going to be able to have sex.

'Sure thing, no problem,' the doctor replied. 'But not too much. Anyway, go ahead and try, but I think the medication you're on will inhibit your libido somewhat, or maybe it'll all be fine. The important thing is that you not take Viagra or anything like it.'

I was finally able to relax when I remembered how lovely and intimate our meeting had been when he first got out of the hospital. He didn't pucker up in the moment I kissed him because his lips had become somewhat palsied after the stroke. I started kissing him along one flaccid corner, the thing I desired then with all of my love and passion and tenderness. I helped to moisten his dry throat with my own saliva. His mouth smelt of medicine; I breathed in the smell as though it were the delightful aroma of flowers and incense. Then I kissed the slackened skin of his cheeks. If Hani gets tired while we're in Paris together, I'll just sit on his lap so we can touch and hold each other as we talk. I'll tell him about things I don't disclose to anyone except my best friend Suad. In getting back together with Hani at this age, I have discovered that love is defined by its duration. The playing is what matters, not the musical instrument. In love everyone has their own beautiful way of playing. If I taste his kisses at this age, I'd want to taste them in old age as well. My husband stopped kissing me when he got old, before he got there even. I wasn't sad about it. Just the opposite. I don't know if I dreamt about the taste of a loving kiss from Hani in old age in order to better appreciate its taste at this age or to reassure myself that our love would last forever.

All through my journey to the airport I kept feeling that I might have forgotten things I couldn't even name. This strange feeling of having forgotten something unknowable bewildered me and saddled me with a sense of loss. I tried the best I could to think, but for the life of me I couldn't remember anything. In that moment I lost some measure of happiness. I was stricken with fear, I became obsessed. But I managed to get a hold of myself once I realized that I was headed in the direction that would lead me straight to Hani, the destination that had come back to rule over my every direction, over my very ability to keep moving forward at all.

On the plane I started to reminisce about our relationship, about taking back my whole life, really. It's amazing how the smallest memory can bring years together . . . an entire lifetime even.

3

We reunited across the vast distance of many years spent apart. Thirty years scratched against my skin as our relationship started back up again about a year ago, that is, in the spring of 2005. I was like a famished wolf, desperate to see him, for him to see me, for us to touch one another and hold each other, for those warm feelings to flow back into my hands, for my hands themselves to come back to me.

Over the past few days I've woken up in the morning with his name on my lips, as if my saliva could quench his thirst.

Strange things were happening to me, feelings that alerted me I was about to see him, feelings that were never wrong when it came to him or my two children.

His disappearance left wounds that cut close to the bone and wouldn't stop bleeding.

The house was empty that morning but the emptiness I felt inside of me was even greater. It was damp and cold in my bones. I could feel it in the air, on the furniture. My feelings of being adrift in the void would only increase. My desire to hear their footsteps and their voices ringing out in the house caused me to break down into tears. I wept aloud, nonstop, until my chest was able to purge all of its sadness, then I got up to wash my face and wished for their success in their marital lives.

Faten and Ahmad got married and absconded with more than thirty years of my life. When Ahmad returned from Paris last summer the house was filled with life once again. During the entire month he spent here Faten, her husband and their daughter would come over for lunch every day. My children would always sit in the exact same seats at the table where they had done before getting married, joking around and giggling the way they used to do when they were little. I nearly burst into tears, I had missed them so much, overjoyed to have them near me now, by the presence of my granddaughter who would cause mayhem around the house whenever she came along with her mother. The place roared back to life. I used to always tell Suad that I'd be a liar if I didn't admit the only time I was able to stop thinking about Hani was while playing with my granddaughter. Chasing her around the house my heart would be flooded with a sort of happiness I hadn't felt in a long time. I remember how difficult it had been to get used to my two children's absence. After they got married and moved out of the house I felt as though someone had ripped them from my womb and taken them far, far away, leaving behind just me and Saleem in the house. Saleem wouldn't talk about anything but health food, wouldn't read about anything else either ever since he had been diagnosed with high cholesterol, diabetes, prostate problems and high blood pressure.

This morning I put on classical music in the living room, as usual, and turned it up loud enough for my numerous plants to hear before going out onto the balcony to water them so that it would be taken care of before Suad arrived. The university is closed over the weekend and on Saturdays she comes knocking on my door so we can have coffee together.

Staring closely at my two lovebirds in their cage on the balcony brought a smile to my face. I had got them the week before in order to amuse my granddaughter. I never had anything to do with birds except for the ones I used to watch fly through the village when I was a little girl, flitting around and warbling in the fields, on branches of trees and shrubs. I had started talking to my plants when I watered them, caressing them from time to time, but only if I wasn't watering them. I serenaded every last shoot, telling them what I believed they wanted to hear, giving them all the love they could possibly need. I addressed the pinkish and greenish azaleas and their petals, 'My sweetheart, there's nothing sweeter than you, I wish you would come closer to me, I love you so.' The wilting gardenia saddened me, and I tried to console it by saying, 'My heart, who's made you so upset? What's the matter? Come on. Laugh a bit, refresh yourself, open up your petals like the moon. If you don't like where you are I can move you. Maybe you'd be more comfortable next to a different plant.'

I picked up the plant and moved it, scrutinizing its planter. My plants seemed to grow and bloom if I held them. Other times it felt like touching them could cause them to close in on themselves. This reminded me of something Hani said when he held me, something about the moment I curl up against his chest. It isn't shyness so much as the feeling that my fragments are being put back together in his embrace. The scent of basil wafted towards me as I approached the plant to water it. In those moments the scents of flowers and plants were something like peace or a greeting, kisses blown to love and welcome them. I had a particular affection for basil and always made sure its pot was near the couch on the balcony. I often wondered why I loved that smell so much. Was it because the basil plant next to the pomegranate tree in our village reminded me of where I had buried my writings and my poems when I was little? Or because the scent of my grandmother and her girlfriend Jameela always seemed to be mixed up with the smell of basil reaching deep inside my nose whenever I sat on one of their laps, leading me to associate the smell of basil with the odour of their bodies?

It made me happy to water those new perennials that can live for such a long time.

All this despite my long-standing love for seasonal flowering plants and beautiful but short-lived ones as well. But I don't need to have them around any more. At this age I can no longer stand the thought of loss and death, especially as there has been so much death all around me since the passing of my mother, my father, and my grandmother who I loved so much, to say nothing of so many other relatives and friends. Yesterday Nadine broke my heart when she showed up in tears, in distress because her girlfriend was dying of cancer. For months she had been sitting at her bedside, rubbing her beloved's feet as though she could breathe life back into her body through touch alone. Then she'd stand up, still holding onto her feet, afraid that letting go would cause her to depart from this life. Loss frightened me constantly because of how frequently it seemed to be happening to me at this age. Despite my love of cats I didn't get a new one after my cat of more than ten years passed away. It used to make me so happy to wake up in the morning and see that the two lovebirds I had got in order to make my granddaughter happy were still alive. Then I would get short of breath as the ubiquitous presence of death weighed on my mind. I became deeply concerned for my husband, who used to get distraught whenever he heard about the death of a relative or friend, more frightened than sad really. The feeling of being besieged by death and loss is intensified at this age. I don't know whether I'll fear losing my loved ones as intensely when I get old or if I'll wind up like the elderly women I see all over my village, their eyes without any sadness, seemingly unaffected when they come out of mourning, maybe on account of feelings that the angel of death had delayed taking their souls, or possibly because preparing for death makes one more accepting of the idea of it, more at peace. When I was younger death wasn't part of my mental landscape. It was beyond my comprehension. I believed it was far off, something that befell others but wouldn't afflict me. It simply didn't have a presence in my life then, despite its ubiquity throughout the war. Now I can feel it is close by, very much present in my life, and the circle of besiegement is closing in. Whenever someone close to me dies I say goodbye to a piece of myself. Now it feels like coming out of my mother's womb was only a transition from floating inside of her to swimming through the sea of life. And what is life if not a swim towards death? We do this without even realizing that our arrival there is inevitable, distracted by the pleasure of swimming, racing and splashing in the sea of life. But we don't fully realize that we're headed there until we can touch its edges, the same way that someone climbing stairs doesn't realize they've reached the roof until their foot lands on the last step. It's as if death has been knocking on our door from the beginning, but we somehow believe this strange visitor has come to the wrong place, that we couldn't possibly be the one he's looking for, that we have nothing to do with him, so we don't open the door. In time we come to recognize his knock, or else we start to feel malaise if he is late to arrive. When we open up for him, we discover that he's the true master of our own bodies and not just the world around us, making us strangers to ourselves, strangers in life. We are stripped of our ages and our bodies. The bodies of all the people that he takes become alike, there is no difference between them and their stenches as they rot all the same.

That's what I heard my father's father say one day, my grandfather who lived to be a hundred and four. Life didn't mean a thing to him after growing bored of the loneliness he experienced since all his friends had died. He felt as though he had already taken leave of this life when they had, that he belonged with them. Often I would hear him talking to God, pleading with Him, 'God, when are you going to take my soul and bring me to Heaven? When is that stairway going to be ready?'

The strange thing was that, in the final moments of his life, which seemed rather pointless to him, he realized he had finally arrived.

My father informed me that he performed his ablutions and prayed, sat down to drink a glass of laban, then put on a death shroud and read his last rites before covering his own face and falling into eternal sleep.

When the basil and the azaleas died they were the only plants I would ever replace, if only to remind myself there was something in my life that I still loved. Once I had finished watering them, I switched off the classical music and went inside, singing to myself, 'Where Will I Find Someone Like You, Ali,' the song I used to overhear my mother singing when she was alone. She would blush from embarrassment if I came inside the house and heard her. She hated getting caught in the act. For her, singing was shameful, forbidden, she had no right to sing, only crying and sadness were allowed. At the exact moment when I started to sing Suad knocked on the door. She came inside with that devilish smile, handed me the morning paper, and said, 'Here, take this, woman. There's some news on the culture page.'

It was Hani. He was leading a discussion along with two other sociologists at the cultural centre about young people and the Lebanese civil war.

Suad and I decided to attend the roundtable together. I had to call him right away, and we agreed to meet up afterwards. My urgent desire to see him reminded me of what Hoda had said about how feelings never age, how desire doesn't get old the same way the soul does. Maybe they get weaker, like memory, like everything, but they don't leave the body until it departs this life.

Hani and I couldn't resist the desire to get back together this time, following our most recent separation of nearly fifteen years, throughout which time I had scrupulously avoided the places we used to go together and never returned his phone calls that came from time to time, especially when I published a new poem, text or novel.

I didn't know whether it was the case that his desire simply hadn't been extinguished yet, just like me, or whether one of us wouldn't occasionally project feelings onto the other, at times failing to notice the size or proportions of the other's true feelings, or whether it had something to do with his fear of endings and loss that made his heart bleed after his wife got breast cancer. I cried alongside him when the doctor decided to perform a full mastectomy. In the face of his unbridled desire towards me I wondered whether death had stirred up his interest in sex, and whether it fomented desire at the same time.

I was certain that his feelings towards me hadn't changed. Still I kept asking myself the same questions. I asked Suad, too, whenever I saw her, but she always looked confused when she tried to answer. Suad was the only person I could ever really share my secrets with.

She had always been closer to me than to Nadine, Azizeh and Hoda. It was as if she had four ears with which she could lovingly listen to me. Whenever I talked to her I would discover new things about myself.

'Talk is cheap. You have to fight fire with fire,' I'd often say to her.

The truth of the matter is that I had no idea what Suad was thinking when she left my house. I often wondered if her colour changed when she got to my place, if she loved me more, if she was jealous of me, if she hated me or if she hated her own condition after she heard what I had to say.

I know full well that my relationship with her is her only space of freedom. But why wouldn't she talk more? What kind of secrets was she hiding? It seemed as though the real secret was the history of the two of us, that wicked things alone were what truly defined our lives, what made us feel alive. When that secret was gone our lives would be over.

Often I thought about whether I would ever be able to divine her thoughts. If only I could become invisible and find out what she said in private about me to Azizeh or Nadine or Hoda . . . or what she herself thought about me. Sometimes I wished she would call me by mistake and leave the line open so that I could listen in on what she was saying. Mine was a constant desire to spy, not only on others' lives but on their thoughts as well, especially when it came to someone as quiet and mysterious while at the same time as close and dear to me as Suad.

I know Suad doesn't love anyone the way she loves me. Even her children interact with her out of obligation more than love. Those children need to understand that love always takes two.

* * *

After two or three meetings in the cafe with Suad present, Hani and I planned a date for just the two of us. Before heading out to meet him I found myself pacing from room to room in a daze. I find some task to occupy myself, then drift off to some other thing. I open the closet, take out a dress or some perfume, then put it right back. I go into the kitchen for some reason, then all of a sudden forget what I had gone in there to do. It wasn't confusion but more like some kind of disability that had befallen me. Should I call it forgetfulness? And why do I feel such emptiness whenever this disability recurs?

The feeling of emptiness I get whenever I forget something is the same way I would feel whenever Hani left me.

Recently, when I told Suad about this disability, I found myself confessing to her about forgetfulness. I interrupted myself and left her there in the living room, riveted, as I ran down the hallway. I stood in front of the large mirror bolted to the wall and began inspecting my body, measuring its height and width, convinced that memory is like bones, that it hollows out and shrinks with the passage of time, weakening all the while, making all the things inside of it smaller and fewer, possibly obliterated. In that moment I felt emaciated despite the weight I had put on, but those feelings evaporated a few minutes later when I could see that I wasn't actually hollowing out. I giggled to myself as I walked back into the living room where Suad was still at a loss. 'It's a song,' I shouted at her. 'It's just a song. I've sung it to you before. *The more and more I forgot, the smaller and weaker I got.*'

Once I had regained my composure I told her how when I forget something I feel as though I have fallen into a well . . . an empty, endlessly deep space. That's also the way I felt the first time Hani left me. When he broke up with me that time I felt alone despite the constant chatter that surrounded me, in spite of all the people who seemed to always be there.

Neither my beau Saleem nor all the other noise could rescue me from the disorienting feeling that I was about to fall. I acted out Hani's forgetting about me, feeling as though he had abandoned me in a vacant space, on the edge of an abyss, and that I was totally inadequate. In brief, I felt like he had forgotten about me entirely.

That feeling of inadequacy stuck with me the whole time he was away, or broken up with me, that is. It felt like I had lost him forever. This feeling didn't overwhelm either one of us, and neither one of us truly believed it was actually happening unless it became tactile, bound up with the weakness of our senses or their loss altogether. When he left I felt as though I was losing a part of myself, as if my vision had lost some of its perspicacity, as if my hearing had been impaired, as if my gait was no longer as graceful and that I couldn't walk with the same control I once had. Sometimes I would become particularly sensitive to my body and my hands and test out my capacity to feel. While listening to sounds outside I would experiment with my ability to identify their various sources.

Separation is like forgetting, I told Suad.

When I first met Hani and he brought up old friends from university, I felt as though I wouldn't be able to remember any of their names. In that moment those feelings of inadequacy that used to scare me half to death came rushing back, making me wish I could just vanish into oblivion. Whenever I was around Hani I felt as if I had lost something, that this man whom I loved would notice I had changed somehow, that I had become inadequate.

Such feelings of inadequacy are hellish torture for someone who is in love. She always longs to be in the presence of her beloved, who is a consummate and tyrannical presence in her life.

Reuniting in middle age gave me back the feeling of being satiated once again. The day we ran into each other all of my senses seemed to regain their memory. Hani was present all throughout me and I was present in everything he touched. He was I and I was he. The memory of his body was no longer detached from me, it became all-encompassing, shaped by the trace of my hands, breath, whispers and scent . . . in the memory of my entire body.

* * *

I recounted to Suad how I had fallen down naked in front of the mirror in order to inspect my body before going out to meet him. I'm not sure why but it occurred to me that she might do the same thing when she went home. She never told me whether she ended her day naked in front of the mirror staring at her body, her sickly skin, biting her foamy lips the way she always used to do, or allowing silence to cover her body, draping herself in it. She never disclosed to me what those cocoons of silence would do to her body.

I felt as though Hani's eyes were able to see my naked body in the mirror. He remembers it from our younger days, knows every inch of it despite the fact that he hadn't laid eyes on me in fifteen years. But he doesn't know everything that has happened. I'm in my fifties now.

I believe my body is still attractive even if my muscles have gone somewhat flabby and my breasts have begun to sag a bit. There are small fat deposits under my skin all over my body, down to the tips of my toes. My thighs arch outward some-what at this age despite their shapeliness, I have become bow-legged, the bones in my legs protrude slightly. My hips are more ample, my slender waist fatter, and some swelling has settled in around the top of my belly. My arms have mostly lost their tone, they are no longer solid or taut. The hair on my legs and under my arms has thinned, I have become smoother, the space between one hair and the next has grown larger. Soft folds appear on my lower abdomen, just above my pubis, which has become fleshier, possibly because of the slackening of my stomach muscles. I place my hands along the small of my back, which has become weaker because of how much my rear end has grown. Then I look at the creases that have mushroomed under my armpits and the wrinkles on my elbows, the flesh gathered around them, how they have turned black. I grab hold of the floppy skin dangling around my neck, pull it upwards and then let go. I stare myself in the face, at the few crow's feet around my eyes, but not for long. My lips are no longer as full as he once knew them to be, their muscles have gone soft, their thin, long, straight lines more pronounced. My nose seems longer to me, the holes wider as the nostrils grow softer. I realize that I no longer conceive of my body as a single organism, the way I did when I was a young woman. Instead I have begun to think about my hands, my stomach, my thighs and my breasts, everything on its own terms. I like some parts more than others. But when I touch my skin the glint in my eyes starts to shimmer. It seems to me to still be as silken as it used to be when he touched me. It's strange but I feel like these are his hands touching me. I fondle my breasts whenever I miss him. That long finger examines the spaces between my toes, the ones he used to adore and kiss.

I grab a little mirror in order to examine my vagina and remember how he looked at it the day we got back together in the late nineties, how he said, 'Your pussy's beautiful. It hasn't changed a bit.' I laughed because I had never considered the possibility that there could be beautiful vaginas and unattractive ones. That's when I realized that his penis was beautiful too—its shape and its soft skin; it was different from my husband's, wide on top and skinny on the bottom; the colour made it seem like it was being strangulated, maybe because of the bulging veins that left dark blue streaks all over.

I am startled to notice a grey hair around my pubis. Dying my hair had helped me to forget about the passing of time but white in that intimate space reminded me of my age. The muscles of my labia have also become flabby. I feel as though my clitoris has lost some of its solidity, that it has descended a bit lower, at least that's what I thought.

These feelings of bitterness don't last long. My sense of femininity and my awareness of my body are much more powerful than they had been in my youth. My desire for Hani hasn't abated. When I see him today I'm going to discover a raft of new feelings specific to this age. At this point any shame about the appearance of my vagina, which still throbs with life, will disappear: I wasn't ashamed of it during childhood and I'm not going to be ashamed of it now. I can remember one day when I was a little girl how I went into the bathroom with a small mirror in order to see what my sex looked like. I thought it resembled a closed oyster. I didn't know whether there was a pearl inside or nothing at all. Everything changed when I hit puberty. It was now sheltered by a thick forest of hair. I would examine its nooks and crannies in front of the mirror as if I were sending a search party into a deep cave or a dark well, to travel to a strange world in order to discover its oceans and its secrets.

One time when we were talking about vaginas I told Suad about the birth of my son Ahmad, about how there can be neither motherhood nor love without them. Whenever I stand naked and look at my own I see it as the source of my maternity, the source of love . . . the source of light, warmth, feelings. Why do people say that only the heart beats? Doesn't the vagina beat as well? It's the abode of happiness and sensation,

Suad, you should think of it as a wellspring for love and not as a place of hardship, as a place that isn't weighed down or violated, not a place of torments and abortion. It's the coordinator of every bodily organ. Tremors throughout the entire body work together with its vibrations. Sometimes you feel as though it is you, a creature that listens and hears and speaks, something that both feels and inflicts pain, both refuses and accepts, both fits in and stands out.

In its moments of contraction and withdrawal, you feel as though it is eventually going to open up and embrace you, kissing you at the same time. You feel as though it is as tender as two hands cradling you in their lap. It holds women back by way of a dominant ideology founded upon a violent logic even as the sex organ itself keeps them in their place, an organ that can only be moistened or flooded with fluid in moments of true infatuation. When I first spread my legs early in my marriage to Saleem, it was as if I wanted to open up a mine shaft in order to gaze out upon life, but love is what truly introduced me to my body. Over the years I discovered the importance of what my mother would say about it being a source of shame, ordering me to never touch it, to not let anything come into contact with it.

My vagina's true home is inside of me, with feelings I can conceal, unlike a man, who can't control his urges the instant he gets hard. I'm the master of my own desires, I can hide them. Hani introduced me to them, helped awaken me to them, but when I experimented with my husband I treated it like a matter of liberation from the destiny of the hymen, the barrier against all desires. It felt like it had become liberated, that it was the sum total of all the noble things in this world, governed by the binary of acceptance and rejection, longing and ecstasy, pain and pleasure, reaction and aversion. It participates in all these activities. Why do we deny it whatever we are afraid of? And why, too, this fear of saying that the world had emerged from it?

The mirror abducted me, spun me around.

I was somewhat disappointed to discover the transformations in my body, which I hadn't examined this carefully for a long time, not since before my relationship with Hani had ended, since I cut off the casual relationships that had been meant to eliminate any trace of Hani from my body and my mind. Those were meaningless affairs that my body hadn't even been fully present for. It had probably been my mind that drove me towards them in the first place.

I shook off the feelings of disappointment that enwrapped me as I gazed at myself in the mirror, wondering, isn't Hani inside my entire body whether it's flabby or fit? And hasn't his body gotten flabby, too? I still have feelings for him anyway.

Then I told myself that when I see Hani today he's going to give his body to mine like a gift. And those feelings will curl inwards even if the light keeps us company, as it usually does. I can't remember whether our bodies had ever touched before . . . in the darkness . . . maybe a long time ago.

4

It's pouring rain. From time to time I steal a glance outside through the kitchen window that looks out over the sea. My hands are busy stripping cilantro so that I can prepare a big bowl of the tabbouleh that Suad loves so much. After zoning out for a while, I have no idea what had just come over me. I press the base of my palms against my temples. Time seems all jumbled together. Now here is the same unpredicted rain falling from the sky—punctuated by thunder and lightning—that drenched me once when I was lugging my backpack on my way back home, or else . . . out in the jackal's den where I used to get lost among my mother's sheep, trying to do my homework at the same time, or else . . . out in the field with my mother while she inspected the seasonal harvest. The same burst of cold scratched at my body, the one that caused me to hurry my steps so that I could get home and cosy up next to the heater, to get a quick fix of warmth that would reanimate my tiny frozen body.

All of a sudden I'm overwhelmed by strange feelings of old age and exhaustion, I'm seduced by the dark sense that my life is turning into something slow and meaningless and heavy, that my fifty-something-year-old body is at risk of becoming as decrepit as that dilapidated building on the corner, the same beautiful structure that had once enchanted me to the point that I asked Saleem if we could buy it, repair all the damage it had been through, and live there after we got married, but he refused, mocking my hare-brained scheme.

'It would cost us too much, much more to fix it up than the price of our brand-new apartment,' he snapped at me one day. I started to fantasize about living there with Hani. In the fantasy it felt like I had never lived anywhere else.

I leave the plucked cilantro on the wooden counter and go wait in the living room for Suad to arrive for lunch. The burden of time weighs upon my mind again, immobilizes me. In fear and trepidation I feel out my body, close my eyes, shut them tight and plunge deep into the time gone by. I'm not sure what has happened to me or why I have begun rummaging around in my memory, my memory that I fear is going to be erased, wiped out, to disappear with every last trace of the little girl I had been more than forty years ago. In the blackness of my reverie those feelings of slowness, meaning-lessness and old age gradually lift. For a moment I feel that my heaviness is lightening, too, that my childhood has flashed up all of a sudden to attack me like a tornado.

I can smell the scents of its spaces and alleyways wafting here and there, its valleys and fields, its sun and moon. I relive the joys, hardships and sorrows. The scent overwhelms me, turns into a flying carpet that wraps the present moment in an enchantment, takes me back to watching my mother's face as she combs my hair, her voice ringing out, 'Just down the block and back. Take Azizeh with you if you and Suad want but you'd better be back before your brother Jawad gets here and starts making trouble for me.'

My mother's voice becomes an echo, then fades away. Her face shines and disappears. With my eyes shut, I wonder to myself: Many things have slipped my mind while other things are still shimmering. Now my memory is starting to betray

41

me, as if time gets younger once again as memory ages, as the present recedes and melts away, as the past becomes present, as if it is the current moment, as though we don't believe that there are many things hidden within us, things we carry with us for a long time, things we get over and then forget about, like a road we find by chance, in a rush, and to which we never return. Many things we think we have left behind and that have left us behind return unexpectedly all of a sudden, awaken and surprise us in the prime of our mid-life, amidst the ashes of incinerated memory. Is it because our steps grow heavier and slower and we no longer have the stamina of those spry legs that in our youth we had to try and keep up with by nonstop walking? Or does the incineration of our present memory help disabuse us of the fear of oblivion, dragging us along through our waking life and in our dreams where we awaken as children? Or . . . or do our feelings have a memory that targets the right moment, even after forty years, to come out of their slumber or their lair in order to chastise us and remind us how forgetful we are, when it is no longer in our power to turn back time and relive the past or even simply remember it?

Pictures of my childhood are spread out on the couch in the living room. I'm gripped by the sensation that I am on a ship rocking me back and forth. My mother's voice fades away and my own voice grows louder with endless chatter that snaps me to attention. I open my eyes, wrap myself up tight. Suad is nowhere to be seen. It's almost three o'clock. Could she have already come over, sat down to listen to me in silence, and then departed without having lunch because I had bored her to death with a childish monologue? But kind and patient Suad doesn't ever get bored of me. She's never late for one of our lunch dates. And she would never leave before 4.30.

What's happening to me? I don't even know whether I've been talking to myself this whole time or whether Suad had actually come over and I told her the same thing I thought I was saying to myself before she left. I'm hardly certain of anything at all, to be honest.

My memory takes me back to the ship. I glide through the darkness, shivering, but a strange happiness washes over me as I listen to the sound of thunder booming outside, which makes me believe that the mountains and the trees and magical creatures are howling and shouting. Then I hear the crack of the rain as it smacks against the windowpane. The voice in my head despairs, pounds away. My attention drifts to the meandering water droplets slapping against the grimy glass and the warm steam emanating from the heater. I am happy to be in love with the dancing rain.

I've always loved the rainy season, even when my feet got dirty in the muddy fields or got soaked in a puddle on my way to school. My drenched clothes would cling to my body and I would burst out laughing. In those moments I would imagine that my body had been shaped by the water. I love the rain limitlessly. The way it flows is like a volcano of love to me. I feel as though it divulges secrets to me that it does not share with anybody else, that it's telling me things it will tell nobody else, not my Aunt Ruqaya, not even my girlfriends. It feels as though my beloved is washing me as I let down my hair, allowing it to fall down so that he can luxuriate in every last strand. Sometimes I even imagine that it pines for me, that the rain is especially for me and me alone.

Ever since becoming a conscious person I have been passionate about everything that is at all like love. Stormy wind and gentle breezes, trees that are full of leaves and those that are bare. I imagine trees that had once been in love getting naked over the sorrow of their leaves having run away. The long convoy of ants scurrying towards the cracks in the wall entertains me, takes my mind off my transient sadness. I try to repay the favour by dropping some wheat kernels in their path that they immediately carry away. Wheat stalks embrace one another as the insects sway. The face of the moon dips behind the clouds, then reappears, laughing. Tobacco seedlings in the neighbours' fields wink at me in the dewy morning. The small pomegranate fruit grows round and globular, like my breasts. Butterflies hover atop a flower vase. The hum of golden cicadas draws attention to tiny bugs alighting on the thistles. Birdsong. A rainbow appears just as the bosom of the sky grows colourful, greeting me in a special way during the month of Ramadan, just the way I had always dreamt of.

It was late in the month of Ramadan, the same year my younger cousin Yusuf died. My brother Jawad, who is two years older than me, asked me to stay up all night with him so that we could look up at the crescent moon on the Night of Power, to see with our own eyes how everything falls down prostrate, everything. The entire village didn't sleep that night. The sound of prayers and supplication constantly boomed from the village mosque, from the plazas and the houses. The rain had stopped that morning. We watched the moon beam its light through the window. I sat there, clinging to Jawad, straining my eyes with all my might so that I wouldn't miss a single detail.

My bismallahs blended together with Jawad's. He scolded me but I didn't care. The joy of just being able to watch gave me great satisfaction. Maybe I was happy about my good fortune that the Night of Power had transpired with the gates of the sky opening up, making my wish come true. I spent the first part of the night wide awake, my face plastered to the windowpane so I could see how the light bathed the earth, bringing the Night of Power down upon it. God answered my prayers. I became a bird of paradise. There was no need for a second wish. I was betting on the fact that my father's concern and persistence would be enough to hold back my mother and convince her to accept me continuing my education.

My death was going to arrive the way I wanted it to. I would live on in paradise as a bird, just like all the other little children, according to what I heard from the women who gathered around my uncle's wife on the day Yusuf passed away: 'Shame on you. There's no point in crying. Every tear that falls from your eye becomes a lump of hot coal that will scorch you in Hell. Your son is a little angel. A sparrow among birds in Paradise. One day you'll see your son standing with the Prophet and his family, and they'll intercede on behalf of you and his father. A child dies without sin, my dear. That's why he's a bird of Paradise now.'

'God, my dream has come true. I don't want to be kept out of paradise. I'll go there pure, without sin, that way I can intercede on behalf of my mother and father and Jawad, too. I can guarantee Heaven for them,' I thought to myself as I stared up into space throughout the night.

That night I fiercely resisted sleep, even though it got the better of me several times, until dawn came without anything being all that different. The pomegranate tree at our house didn't bow down, neither did the neighbour's trees in the fields stretching out beyond their houses. The clotheslines on their roofs were still up, they hadn't moved or sagged. The night had passed without the Night of Power taking place the way I wished it would have that year and in the years that fol-lowed; I stopped waiting for it to happen, ultimately forgetting about it altogether. There were many other forms of happiness to distract me, especially those bestowed by nature, which treated me more kindly than my little body had the strength to endure: the joys and pleasures I received from my relationship with all of its creation nearly drove me mad. Wildflowers in all shapes and colours. Plants and herbs in the fields of all kinds and varieties: sweet or bitter to the taste, I sampled them all. The taste of thistle—I husk it and strip its stalk clean, humming *you're sweeter than sugar*, as if to console it. Most people think of it as a superfluous plant without any benefit. The taste of fennel—its dark green colour entices me the way it stands out against the bright green of other herbs. Barefoot I scamper up the high escarpment at the edge of the field, pick one and waft it near my nose, inhaling the scent deep into my lungs, rhapsodically muttering, 'You're the most delicious of all tastes, fennel, nothing can hold a candle to you as far as I'm concerned. Forget the citrus that Suad and Azizeh prefer.' I tasted and gave my own name to all the herbs I didn't know the names of. My mother found the names I gave them strange and just smiled. Nadine would laugh at me, derisively sometimes, impressed at others. I made nature into my own private heaven. It revealed all of its secrets to me, introduced me to myself. Through nature I came to understand how things that disappear can come back again. Through nature I came to discover all the things about my body that had been hidden from me. Cold guided me towards warmth and to the feel of wool, cotton and velvet. Warmth taught me the pleasure of exploring my own nakedness. I would caress my forearms, my thighs, and the space between my breasts, slowly wiping away the beads of sweat from my skin, which funnelled through my pores a delightful tremor that I only later realized was the trembling of my nascent desire that had yet to be realized alongside my maturing body. Back in that time I used to think that the sex everyone said was forbidden was something exclusively for grown-ups. I envied them and I would fight off that repressed sensation of pleasure, waiting stoically. What's so wrong about that sensation? I would ask myself. If it comes from my own body and makes my heart sing, makes it throb like mad, if it sends me far out into the stratosphere? When I look up and see the face of God in the sky, I become afraid that He'll be angry with me, I'm wracked with shame, so I cover myself up and claim that I'm only experimenting with that forbidden desire, swearing to Him that I'm going to stamp it out once and for all.

All that was left to console my body was nature, which presented things right in front of me that could stimulate my desire, could make me believe. With my eyes closed I began to touch my vagina, bowing my head low so that God wouldn't be able to see me.

I'd pick wildflowers, make them into a crown on my head, press a red daisy against my lips, cheeks and fingers as I lie down among the wheat stalks. I imagine myself as a bride awaiting the groom whom I would love and who would awaken my body, causing pleasure to surge inside me, drenching me in its downpour. I'm panting . . . panting, drowning in a sea of ecstasy. When I wake up I'm all sweaty, but without any feeling of shame. I pull those leggy wheat stalks in close, kissing them, then slice some off with my fingernails, shove them in my mouth, quenching myself with the sweet taste of their nectar. Before standing up once again I examine the bee flower in my bouquet and I encounter the same wonder as the day I first discovered this flower, fascinated by the uncanny resemblance it bears to a real bee. I reach out my hand, convinced there is a bee attached to the crown of these short-stalked plants that are thick with leaves. Touching it reminds me how a plant can sometimes take on the appearance of flying insects, and not just insects but also shapes of other crops. In the field I once saw a plant twisted around the arm of a beanstalk, coated with blobs that looked like beans but tasted different, a combination of beans and some other pleasant taste I couldn't quite place. And the broomrape, which mimics plants, is extremely deceptive, infiltrating the rows of tobacco, tomato and squash, or even lentils and chickpeas. My mother would attack it, yanking it out by the root, cursing its sneakiness and how much damage it had done. She used to say that this invader sucks out all the nutrients from the soil, steals it away, allowing it to blossom before the crops that are more useful to us. It pained me to watch what happened to the broomrape, saddened by what my mother did to it, because she not only prevented it from existing but also denied me the chance to observe its astonishing capacity to infiltrate and mimic, as though my mother was ripping the questions out of me, forcing my eyes to remain shut to all the surprises, mysteries and visions of the natural world that brought me so much joy. My mother snatched away what I loved most about nature, despite its cruelty. The broomrape and other plants like it demonstrated just how savage nature could be, I would often tell myself, but she would never be able to steal away from me the insights I acquired by plunging into the wheat fields when they had turned bright green mixed with yellow as sunlight shone upon them. I once believed that the light was literally hoisting up the wheat, stretching it out and causing its green to deepen. Eventually the wheat no longer had any need for light, departing for other places in order to seed a fresh crop and provide it with whatever energy it needed to grow. I used to believe that this light was independent of the sun, that it came and went of its own accord. The very thought of vanishing struck terror in my heart. I'm

48

afraid of things going away and not coming back, like a spring gone dry that causes crops to suffer during a scorching-hot summer that follows, that is until life returns to flow through the area, replenishing the white lilies that adorn the surrounding earth. My eyes happily fell shut as I discovered that not everything goes away forever. Still, death continued to keep me up at night. Gradually I overcame those fears as well, though, coming to believe that good people are born again in Heaven, and that only evil ones die once and for all . . . that life is goodness whereas death is evil itself. There were many things in nature that I considered to be good despite the fact that evil existed in many natural things as well. It made me sad to think about this, especially when the rain became a flood that submerged the village roads, keeping me from getting to school. I would turn to look up at the sky, begging for something to hear the call of the earth, to release the sun once again, as the soil longed to recognize people's footsteps after they had to hole up in their homes for such a long time, not coming outside because they feared the storm. I stared down at the brand-new leather shoes my father had bought for me in Beirut. I would try to comfort the road that had been submerged in the floodwaters, promising it would dry out soon and that Suad, Azizeh and I would walk on it once again, allowing the soil to hear the echo of our absent steps, quenching its thirsty desire.

* * *

The days changed, and so did I. But I never stopped loving nature even if I became less and less romantic about it. I drove out all those thoughts of death and sorrow, kept myself busy by thinking about the tumult but also the sweetness of life, especially once my body began to mature, after I grew taller and my breasts became noticeably fuller. Through my increasingly beautiful and less awkward body, nature revealed secrets to me that I believed no other human being knew at the time, and, as far back as I could remember, I began to rebel against the black mourning clothes my mother dressed me in during Ashura. We would be draped in them, Jawad and I both, from the tops of our heads to the tips of our toes. I had been comfortable enough in them and my brother Jawad was proud of them, declaiming that they symbolized the cry of truth in the face of injustice, which was the phrase my mother had forced him to repeat ever since he was four years old, when my father took him to Nabatiyeh from where he returned with his head shaved and his forehead sliced open with a razor after participating in the Ashura mourning ritual ceremonies for the first time. His skinny little body didn't help him in trying to keep up with the 'hitting' procession and he ended up bleeding a lot and eventually passing out. He had to be rushed back to the village, where my mother greeted him with prayers and incantations now that he had proved himself worthy of his own name—Jawad being the name of one of the Twelve Shiʿi Imams. My Aunt Ruqaya, who had chosen the name for him, didn't have any male children, only daughters, and she kept on fretting until Jawad was born. She was present for his birth, in fact, she was the one who delivered the baby. On that day she shouted at the top of her lungs, 'As of today we have all the names of the imams in the family! We aren't missing a single one. You are merciful to us, God. To You we turn and in You we seek strength,' she said reverentially. It was the same thing my mother would say whenever she was asked why she had chosen the name Jawad. My father would nod in agreement, looking towards me as he smiled with a kind of tenderness that radiated across the room in my direction, before interjecting, 'I'm the one who chose Nahla's beautiful name. Beauty attracts beauty.'

50

My mother was born into an extremely religious family, one armed with religion. Most of the men were clerics, both young and old, whereas my father, despite his faith and piety, was an open-minded and jovial man who wanted to maximize the joy in his life. I used to wait on pins and needles for him to come back from his work in Beirut every week. His presence in the house provided me with the cover I needed in order to say things to my mother I wouldn't dare say while he was away, to disobey her and even refuse to do some things she ordered me to do. Right in front of her I'd tell him how being at home without him was like being alone in a deserted cave. 'There's no fun or warmth.' I'd be a flirt and always sit close to him. I'd watch him come out of the bathroom after he showered, smelling his clean hair and clucking, 'You smell better than anything, Daddy. I love you more than anyone else in the whole world.'

'Stop being cute and messing around, come on, off to bed with you,' my mother would scold me before turning towards my father in frustration, 'God grant me the strength to deal with her. I didn't sign up for this. She's going to be the death of me. Jawad is so much easier.' Even as the words came out of her mouth she realized she was being too harsh on me. Girls, she'd add, 'shouldn't be given an inch, better to be hard on them. Otherwise they'll never grow up.'

The villagers used to refer to my father with the honorific title 'Saeb Bek' and he was always sure to place a carnation in his jacket pocket. My dapper and gentle father used to wear a cologne that smelt like pine trees, smearing it across his moustache as he studied his face in the mirror and hummed a tune by Muhammad Abd al-Wahhab or one by Umm Kulthum, cranking up the volume on the radio whenever Radio Cairo played one of her songs. My mother would quickly voice her opposition, arguing it was sinful to listen to music. My father would lower the volume in order to stave off her ire, pleading with her to calm down and be more understanding. Because she was the daughter of a sayyid who was the son of a sayyid who was the son of a sayyid, her understanding was divinely inspired, though.

My father never refused a request from my mother. But he could become fierce and stern as could be when it came to verse and explicit love poems.

'You're killing me, Alia. You can do whatever you want when it comes to your kids and your home but you must grant me this little bit of poetry and verse. How does it disturb you?'

My father was weak when my mother was around, or maybe he was just predisposed to surrender. He didn't like disagreements, arguing or even the slightest hint of violence. He hated endless bickering, he'd rather sit with a volume of classical poetry, reciting verses about pride and love, or hum the prayers of Zayn al-Abidine as if singing them. I would listen to him raptly, thinking to myself, I'm going to write poetry when I grow up.

He was an only child. Before being with my mother he had been married to Khadijah, who was twelve years older than him, and he loved her so much that he used to spoil her. After nine years of fruitless efforts to have children the doctor dashed his hopes when he told him his sperm was worthless and that medical treatment might not do any good. Right then he resolved to divorce Khadija despite her pleas not to do so. He swore to her that he would never love another woman the way he loved her, but she was nearly forty years old, time was short and was going to prevent her from having children if he didn't divorce her so that she could marry a fertile man. He realized that her wish to have a child was the only thing that continued to motivate her prayers. Day and night she beseeched God to favour her with a son who could make her life worth living, could help her forget about her fear of growing old alone and abandoned. My father left Khadijah a large, valuable piece of property so that she'd be more attractive to suitors. Eventually she gave in and they were divorced, but my father kept going to see her even after she married Ali al-Ghareeb and they moved to the neighbouring village. Khadijah would come rushing at him enthusiastically even though she was remarried, kissing his shoulders and gushing about how much she had missed him, inviting him to take home some kibbeh with yogurt, my father's favourite dish, 'from her village'.

When Khadijah visited us from time to time she would kiss me excitedly, and I can still remember her twitchy palms and smiling eyes. She'd hug me warmly, patting my back, and stroking my hair, then whisper in my ear, 'I missed you, daughter of my beloved.'

My mother didn't complain because she wasn't a jealous woman.

My father had been her second husband. Her father had divorced her from her cousin who had been unable to consummate their marriage because he was impotent.

If she considered her first marriage to be a sign of God's displeasure, her marriage to my father had been a preordained matter that she'd had no say in. It wasn't out of love. She accepted him but didn't love him because of her conviction that she was being watched by the religious sheikh who had been in love with her ever since he showed up in their village to perform the burial rites for the village leader. That sheikh used to visit the village every week, sometimes having to stay overnight. In order to properly honour him in a manner that would please God, some of the village notables would arrange a temporary marriage for him with whichever woman he chose. It wasn't appropriate for the honourable sheikh to sleep alone, as he was a man of God, and honouring him with temporary marriage is an obligation enjoined upon the believers (at least that's what my mother used to call those notables, sometimes referring to them as 'our best').

She had fallen under the spell of the itinerant sheikh with his black cloak and thick beard, his body as slender as a poplar tree, his eyes the colour of almond. When she caught him glancing her way, looking her up and down, she felt a spark strike her heart that made it beat faster. Her eyes grew dusky when they met his. She imagined he was sending her a message about how taken he was by her beauty. The gleam in his eyes was more expressive than any word. As far as she could remember he didn't pay any attention to the other girls.

That night my mother couldn't sleep. She tossed and turned, insomniac, thinking about the sheikh, the man of her dreams. When she thought about the way he had praised her beauty and her smile, that spark would strike her once again, making her feel as though her body had been consecrated to him by God, a treasure chest for which only the sheikh held the key, which nobody else would ever be able to open.

'I haven't loved anybody else since, not even the father of my children' is how my mother ended a long soliloquy to her cousin with whom she was very close, and whom she used to visit all the time until moving to live with her husband in Beirut.

My mother never loved anyone else, not even my father. Her heart hardened at the mention of the sheikh, about whom she hadn't heard a word ever since he stopped visiting the village. Her broken heart would sometimes cause her to burst out crying without any apparent reason, but she would soon pull herself together, regaining her determination and seriousness. My mother could seem like the most severe and inflexible woman, but she could also plant good tidings in even the hardiest soil. She placed us under total supervision, which somehow made our lives better even as she forced us to bear the responsibility of working the fields with her, relying upon Jawad and me and Aunt Ruqaya during the planting, reaping and harvest seasons. That was before we moved in with my father and went to live in Beirut during the early sixties.

Sick Uncle Mahmoud was unable to help us because he had come down with rickets. Some say that was caused by a fever he had contracted when he was little, others blame it on the spirits. They say that a friendly spirit would accompany him at night down the long path to the village well so that he could fetch the family the water they needed. The djinn would light the way with her fingers, illuminating the darkened road in front of my uncle, who would return home bewitched, talking about a woman enhaloed in white, until one night the spirit disappeared and my uncle had trouble finding his way through the dense darkness. Just then a white goat leapt out in front of him. He thought it might have been separated from the village flock, that it had lost its way and stayed there. My uncle turned around and carried the goat back with him after already having made it a long way in the darkness on his own. As soon as he reached the village square, a few metres from our house, the goat slipped away from him lightning quick, speaking in a strange human voice: 'They're all going to laugh at you. They're all going to laugh at you.' My uncle was shocked, remained silent after that. He stopped going to the well and started going to consult with the sheikh in a neighbouring village who worked magic so that he could learn from him the ways of fortune telling that would allow him to conjure djinn but then send them away after acquiring all the information he needed from them.

After that Uncle Mahmoud was never the same. He started performing magic. He'd conjure djinns, giving some of them friendly names and others scary ones. He'd assemble them and then spread them out in spaces all alone or in the company of others, until he lost control over them one rainy evening and wasn't able to get rid of them. They walked him back to the same place where he had come across the goat and beat him until he blacked out. He might have died there all by himself if a farmer hadn't found him the next morning face down in the mud, nearly suffocated, with excruciating pain in both legs that made it impossible for him to move.

'The djinn pummelled him, the bastard,' the farmer spluttered as he slung my uncle over his shoulder and then placed him on the wooden table in the middle of the house.

Still my uncle wouldn't stop playing with djinns. Whenever they visited him, he'd mumble some incomprehensible gibberish, start waving his arms around, his eyes would get all wide, and a hissing sound would come rushing out of his mouth before he was able to calm back down once again, horizontal on that wooden board under a canopy opposite the old China tree, his eyes drifting off to track the movement of birds as they nested on the thick branches. There was a djinn who used to visit him in the form of a strangely shaped bird. It would sit endlessly on a branch, staring down at him and whispering that he ought to masturbate. It visited him early in the evening or sometimes in the morning, whether he was awake or asleep, provoking him, 'Come on, Mahmoud, pick it up and start jerking, just take it and jerk off.' My uncle would grab hold of his penis and jerk it until he gasped and sperm spurted in his hands.

There were numerous occasions when my Aunt Ruqaya would tell my grandmother, 'That bird wouldn't leave him alone. The more he resisted, the harder it pushed. Every day—yes, every day—it would show up and tell him to pick it up and jerk off. He couldn't resist.'

My brother Jawad and his friends were often amused by what my uncle would say. Their laughter pealed out whenever he pointed down at his own penis. He'd act out what my uncle was doing, his eyes fixed on the next-door neighbour's balcony. More than any other boy in the family, my brother Jawad was spoiled by my Aunt Ruqaya's attention, care and flirtation. He often used to spend the night at her house. She would give him money without expecting him to ever pay her back. She wouldn't deny him anything, and he would always respond if she asked him for something. She used to tell him all about things I had done that made her upset, and then he'd come to me with threats and warnings. He'd start kicking at me and my mother would have to shove him away, shouting at him not to be difficult, then when he was gone my mother would shoot steely glares at me, saying that he was the master of the house whenever my father wasn't around and that I was never to defy him. 'He's your support, your back, and your protector,' she would tell me, but were it not for her I might have wound up crippled from being beaten so hard.

I loved Jawad in spite of his brutality. I would have died for him, still would until this day, even after giving birth to my two children, Ahmad and Faten. My heart buckled with fear whenever he was sad or unwell. I'd pray for God to protect him, guide him, and rescue him from evil deeds and calamities, to find a nice young lady for him who could save him from his emotional emptiness and his dangerous dalliances with loose women, whether they were girls from well-known or lesser-known families. My Aunt Ruqaya had a huge impact on him. In her opinion women were a fallen and depraved sex. They were all 'strumpets' according to her and they deserved to be treated harshly.

She would smack her lips and suck her teeth with unmistakable schadenfreude, her eyes shone whenever she came over to our house with a laundry list of other people's problems and scandals, talking about so-and-so who was divorcing her husband such-and-such or about some illicit affair that was going on between a married woman whose husband was working in Beirut and one of the ne'er-do-wells in the neighbourhood. My aunt never tired of gossiping about other people, even making up fake stories about them sometimes.

On the day she found me sitting on the edge of the fountain with Suad reciting my love poems for her, she went berserk and threatened to tell Jawad, concretizing her threat with a few punishing, powerful slaps that bruised my eyes and left my pinkie finger sprained.

They pushed her into an early marriage before she had even passed her twelfth spring.

On the day of her wedding my Aunt Ruqaya stood on the threshold of her marital home, stiff as a board before she started to cry bitterly, begging her mother to take her home so that she could sleep in her own bed.

'Why would I want to stay here all by myself? The wedding's off. Take me home with you, please!' she exclaimed before continuing to sob.

Her sister-in-law took her by the hand and dragged her into the bedroom by force, her voice rising up as sharp as a knife.

'Come along, get inside, get inside for the treatment, an uncommon treatment. Get in there already, quit messing around.'

The father of the groom kept coming and going behind the door, exhaling with a kind of tension that made his sweaty face look sullen and anxious while he waited for his son to come out holding up the proof of his consummated manhood.

Aunt Ruqaya deflated in defeat. She tried to limit what she witnessed with her own eyes, shutting them like someone who doesn't wish to see, then carried on talking about that night, about how she blacked out when the groom breached her hymen, about how she had no idea what was going on until she was awakened by a sharp pain between her legs and saw a pool of blood underneath her . . . yes, a pool of blood . . . that's how she described it.

'How could he just leave me there like that? How could he do something like that? I just don't understand. All I know is that he raped me and left. Did it ever occur to him that I could have died? Men are shameless. They're all savages, Nahla.'

My aunt hated the whole world from that day forward. She became more fierce. She became harsh like men, and like them she also started to hate women. She began scheming against everyone: she might try to sever the caring connection between a husband and his wife, between a boy and his brother or sister. There was no difference, as far as she was concerned—everyone deserved to be punished.

***

I don't understand why I remember certain things from my childhood while forgetting others. These days my grandma Omnia, whom I miss very much, comes to see me in my dreams a lot.

She appears to me the same way she was in the old days, sitting there with Jameela, her neighbour and best friend, in the basement where she lived out her last days all alone, waiting for death to come and spirit her away. I rushed over to her and sat on her lap, breathing in the scent of basil as it wafted off of her. I smelt her handkerchief and said, 'You're basil, Grandma.' Then I turned my head so I could listen to her tell me a beautiful story that she had told my grandmother many times before.

Jameela talked for a long time and my grandmother remained silent. She never interrupted, just nodded her head, sighed, behaving the same way Suad did whenever I talked to her. She rubbed her eyes and batted her eyelashes a lot, swallowing whatever it was she might want to say. Jameela spoke with a lisp. Without pausing, she'd stretch out her legs to touch the stove when it was freezing cold, massaging them with her arthritic hands and relaxing her head. She had told my grandmother many times the story about her love for Musa, which lasted for ten years but ended tragically on the day he asked her to marry him.

Musa's family refused a dowry of wool bedding, and when the wedding was called off Jameela received nothing but disappointment, tears and pain.

My grandma Amineh, who would ordinarily just sit there and listen, had the desire to talk sometimes and she wouldn't deny herself that pleasure. Jameela would sit with my grandmother and listen to her as she told stories that could make tears roll down her cheeks.

I was enchanted by their relationship. I would avidly listen to their conversation without quite understanding what was going on between them until my grandmother went deaf and Jameela stopped visiting her. One day when I ran into her by chance in the village square, I wanted to know why. I addressed her accusingly.

'Long time no see, Auntie. What's going on? I thought you two were best friends!'

'We were never friends, we weren't anything at all. You expect me to pour my heart out to a deaf woman who can't hear a damn word I'm saying? What's the point in that?

I don't need a deaf woman in my life at this point,' Jameela replied.

What she said about my grandmother was hurtful. She didn't seem to have any shame or compassion, as if her emotions had deteriorated just like my grandmother's hearing.

I was always entranced by hearing older people talk. I was particularly captivated by anything they had to say about intimate matters and romantic secrets. I wanted to know more about such things than was being revealed to me at that tender age. In fifth grade I fell in with this group of girls, listening intently to whatever they whispered to one another about crushes and love. Their conversations fired my imagination. During school vacations I'd take advantage of my father's presence at home and turn up the volume on the radio playing Abd al-Halim Hafez, quickly getting overcome with the desire to write down my feelings and romantic fantasies. I'd tear out a piece of paper from my prayer book and begin scratching out fiery words about my imaginary lover. At night, when my father and mother would disappear, my curiosity would be piqued and I'd try to eavesdrop on them. I could hear my father's gentle hums as my mother scolded him in a dry tone, 'May God show you the way, you moron. We shouldn't be talking about this. Anyway, I don't love anyone but the Lord.'

'May He be praised. You're so pious, woman. But can't a man love his wife?'

'I'm the mother of your children, that's all.'

'And where did those children come from, you idiot?'

The two of them shook the bed. I could hear it squeaking, then silence.

How did they ever have me? I wondered. Did they have me because they used to be in love?

I once believed that children who came into this world without love suffered from some kind of deficiency. There was something different about them, sadness maybe, frailty or ugliness. This idea frightened me as I shut my eyes and tried to find a clear impression of myself, one that would bring me peace. Everything about me was beautiful, very beautiful. It's true, sometimes I would get sad, but I was more prone to be happy. Whenever I was feeling good I swore I would only have children with a man I loved and who loved me. Now I laugh about it whenever I remember what happened to me after having my first child, the moment the nurse placed my daughter Faten in my arms so she could suckle from my breast. Holding her, I felt as though I was just a pair of arms. My entire body morphed into two arms wrapped around Faten as I tried to measure the size of the love that was washing over me at that moment, this limitless adoration, totally untouched by the cold feelings I had for Saleem ever since we got married.

**

As I stare blankly at the sofa I'm sitting on right now, other memories grab hold of me and cause me to slow down for a moment. It feels as if I'm floating on a cloud of memories, blown into a strange kind of disarray, across distant times and places I had completely forgotten about, then shooting me into the midst of ancient faces and events that seem as though they had just happened.

My mother's face hovers over me like a dark cloud. She angrily raises her index finger at me. I stand before her insisting on my desire to continue my education.

'That's enough. We're done here. No more education, no more schools. Don't let there be any doubt in your mind.'

But not even the threat in her voice or her furiously arched eyebrows could break my resolve.

'You have no right to oppress me like this or to treat me this way. You ought to be ashamed of yourself.'

Stubbornness stiffened her tone as she replied, 'Shut up, little girl. You hole yourself up in this house, not in school. Anyway, you're the only oppressor here.'

It takes one to know one, I told myself, as my mind flitted to the image of that vile sheikh who detested little girls, making house calls throughout the village . . . house by house, in order to convince people to keep their daughters from getting an education, raising his finger in the air as he said, 'It would be too much for one of them to even be able to decipher a letter.'

On the day he visited our house, my mother attended to him while my father stood there behind her for a long stretch before asking coldly, 'Everything good with you, sheikh?'

'Everything's good, Abu Jawad.' Then, turning his eyes towards my mother, he said, 'Your daughter has received her diploma. Religiously speaking now, she must be kept at home. Just like my daughter. I kept her home and she was still able to receive her diploma. You know there's no place that's truly safe for girls. Some will go to Hell, but especially those who receive an education. They get their heads full of ideas about romance and love. God forbid. God forbid you'd want to educate your daughter, forget about it.'

'My daughter is a human being and I want her to be educated. Besides, there's going to come a day when my daughter will fall in love with a boy and talk to him. If we keep her at home and she tends to the sheep, she'll become a shepherd who'll want to be with a shepherd. And he'll treat her like garbage. Isn't it be better for her to stay in school so that she can grow up and marry a young man who understands her, whom she understands, whom she loves and who loves her?'

My father didn't convince him of anything, though. The sheikh tilted his turban backwards in agitation and said, with disgust, 'So you mean both you and your daughter want to go straight to Hell.' Then he turned towards my mother and bellowed, 'And you, how you'll suffer God's wrath! You're going to hang by your hair in Hell and burn for all eternity!'

Despite her fear of the flames of Hell, my mother finally yielded to my demand because of my own persistence and my father's support. She was terrified by my threat to drown myself. But my own fear of Hell also kept me up at night. And feelings that the sin I had committed might expose my mother to the torturous fires of Hell also kept me awake, making me feel guilty until they gradually disappeared and evaporated with the passage of time, especially after I transferred to my new school in Beirut.

The will to live burst in me like a flood. I threw myself into this new life with vigour and passion, without fear. I did many things that drove my mother crazy. Laughing out loud was forbidden and a shame. Loving the life my mother was so afraid of was a sin and therefore unacceptable. Humming songs was apostasy and witchcraft, as the sheikh once told her. During Ashura she forbade me from chewing the sugary gum I used to love, from the pleasure of blowing translucent bubbles until they got big and then popped in my face, making me laugh before I did the same thing all over again. As she washed out my mouth with soap she'd rail, 'What are you doing, you demon? You think you're an angel with the protection of Husayn and the Prophet's entire family. May God rescue me from you. Isn't it enough that I'm going to Hell because of you?'

The difference between my father and my mother bewildered me. My happy-go-lucky father who loved life to the fullest was the most beautiful person in the whole world: from his proud stature, brown eyes, warm voice and tender heart all the way to his gentle tone, the kindness of his expressions and his poetic manner I found so wonderful. Even though he had been sent to a religious seminary for two years and never finished school, he knew how to read and write and had memorized many poems and quotations. Sometimes I'd find him furiously scribbling on a piece of paper and I'd ask him if he was copying down verse but he would correct me. 'Actually I'm writing my memoirs, Nahoul,' he would say, calling me by my nickname.

'I'm becoming just like you. I love to write,' I would tell him as though returning a favour for his having stood by me and helping me finish my studies. My mother was pretty much the opposite in every way possible. She memorized the Quran by listening to it being recited. Her fate was to be no more than average looking. Nothing about her was particularly noteworthy except for her stubbornness, solidity and steadfastness in the face of hardship, her capacity to withstand Jawad's misbehaviour. Her sweet sentimental voice was the only thing that could make me happy to the point of tears. I would beg for her to speak up, to sing to me. Her face would turn red and her eyes would flicker with a strange glow, as if she were in a photograph or a memory. She would mumble some love poetry she had learnt by heart, but only after shutting the door and making sure the place was empty so that nobody else would be able to hear her.

My mother's incredible memory had always astounded me. She would repeat verse that I recited out loud in front of her as part of my homework, poems by Abu Nuwwas or Umar bin Abi Rabi'a, Abu Firas al-Hamadani or al-Mutanabbi. She'd memorize them exactly the same way that I did. One time she quoted a line by al-Mutanabbi, and when I asked her who had written that verse she confidently replied, 'Definitely Imam Ali.'

My mother never loved my father the way a woman loves a man. But she always remembered him, and after he passed away she didn't stop wearing black until she herself was dead and gone.

I was enthralled with poetry and loved to read novels and *One Thousand and One Nights*. Books were a daily habit for me. I always had one on me, even when I was going out into the grassy parklands to be with my mother's sheep while I did my homework. Reading was like nature for me: it sharpened my senses, my imagination, my mind; both stoked my desire for love and romance, ripened my emotions and my feelings. A reservoir of enthusiasm pooled and then blended with the blood flowing through my veins. My body would heave, my soul would be healed, and I would be primed for love. Passion announced my feminine maturity, I used to tell myself, arriving at the same time as letters from my neighbour Hassan, who was a few years older than me and who would write me things that reminded me of the things that lovers express in novels and poems.

I became infatuated with my neighbour, falling totally in love with him at the tender age of thirteen. Just the thought of seeing him left me short of breath. I'd come up with all kinds of excuses, even make up lies in order to do so, claiming that Suad wasn't feeling well, for example, and that I needed to bring over her homework and explain the lessons she had missed. My longing for Hassan provided me with the creative energy necessary to play the role. My mother fell for it, letting me go see my sick friend just as long as I didn't come home too late.

My desire to be alone with him gave me an astonishing amount of nerve, led me to lose sight of everything else, and drove me to secretly slip out into the countryside with him to hunt birds.

On the day Hassan taught me about hunting he also taught me about something else.

Standing behind me he started to instruct me with both his hands and his words how to hold the gun properly, how to point the barrel at the bird, how to take aim the moment it landed on the fig tree and then to quickly pull the trigger. Suddenly his voice began to quiver and his lean body that was pressed up against me started to undulate and rub against my body, his arms wrapped around my waist, his lips planting kisses in the space between my shoulders and my neck. My desire was inflamed, incandescent. My whole body trembled. For a moment I was overwhelmed with irrepressible ecstasy, moaning in pleasure until my joints went slack and I collapsed onto the ground in shock, besieged by contradictory feelings that combined the incapacitation of pleasure and the pang of shame.

It all happened so fast.

On the way back I didn't pay much attention to what Hassan was saying. I was in too much of a hurry, my thoughts were racing ahead of me. I was afraid that my mother would get there sooner and send Jawad over to Suad's house to look for me. But there was one unsettling question that continued to gnaw at me: Did my body fall on the ground from pleasure or shame?

Both scenarios frightened me. Either way a huge change came over me after that encounter. I started to understand my body better, to write down my thoughts, and to write poetry.

I wrote down thoughts that came to me after all the various things I saw. I restricted myself to love poetry. I had always loved the rhetoric of poetry, and my thoughts expressed everything else. I collected everything I wrote into a special notebook that I stashed among my books and school notebooks to be safe.

* * *

My God, how the past gazes upon me now, calling me back to those days.

I stretch out the fingers on my right hand in front me, slowly caressing them with my left hand as I reminisce. I remember the deep burn scars Jawad left behind on the day he dragged me by the hair over to where my mother was sitting by the boiler. He took my right hand and smashed my fingers into the metal like a monster, swearing to cut off my hand the next time. My mother leapt up like a mad woman to shove him off of me, barking, 'You're going to cripple your sister. What's the matter with you?!'

'So let her be crippled. Look at this filth she's written down in her journal. Woman, your daughter is a total strumpet. Why don't you listen? Just listen to what she's saying. "Her lips yearn for his".'

Jawad groaned, his eyes open wide as his hands clutched the boiler poker.

I collapsed onto the ottoman in front of them as excruciating pain shredded my hand and my arm, paralysing me even as I listened to my mother's acid voice unleashing violent words that were more hurtful than stones, until she broke down into a fit of bitter crying, lamenting her misfortune.

That was Wednesday night, before my father got back from Beirut. I didn't sleep a wink that night, anxiously waiting for my father to arrive so I could complain to him about what had happened, so that I could tell him that what I had written was nothing but imagination, pure fantasy. By the time my father finally got home, I had fallen asleep. I woke up to throbbing pain and the sound of the muezzin calling out for afternoon prayer. As I rubbed my eyes I heard my mother talking to my father on the other side of the wall between my bedroom and the courtyard.

'That it's, time's up. Our eternal afterlife is in danger because of your daughter. Congratulations to us for all the knowledge she's acquiring. It's going to lead us straight to Hell. But this is all going to stop right now. Your daughter is writing filthy things. How do you expect me to hide my shame in front of everyone? Are you happy now? Are you willing to send us all to Hell for the sake of her education?'

I gaze at my fingers once again and smile. I can see them the way they were forty years ago, how I used to plunge them into the soil, digging with extraordinary focus in order to open up a pit large enough to stash the new pages on which I had written my poems and thoughts, all together this time. This way only the djinn would be able to find my writings and expose my secrets. Standing beside the mint plants and sending signals to the neighbour's daughter, Jawad would never suspect that he was just a few steps away from my secret that was buried where the roots of the flowering pomegranate tree dug down.

I smiled at my fingers after carrying out my mission on that day the same way I smile at them today. Then I picked a stalk of mint and leisurely plucked its leaves, counting out 'He loves me . . . he loves me not.' The leaf of love made me happy. I would sigh with satisfaction and saunter back inside without any fear.

Whatever happened to my papers? Had they disintegrated into dirt? I whisper to myself as if an entire lifetime hadn't gone by since they were buried.

I had always been good at pushing away fear whenever it attacked or snuck up on me. I could fight back and overcome it every time. The teacher who scolded me and sent me home after calling what I had done idiocy and insolence, the one who called me ignorant, was only able to scare me for a few seconds.

I was ten years old, impatient to grow up and for my femininity to blossom. I tried to copy the other girls by putting on makeup in secret. We didn't have any in our house so I had to equip myself at Azizeh's. I goaded her into daring me to try on my older sister's clothes. When I told her I couldn't wait to grow up, her cheeks flushed and she burst out laughing, then guided me to the closet that contained her engaged sister's dresses and underwear. I tried on an ivory bra. When Azizeh wasn't looking I stole it. The next morning I walked the three kilometres between our village and the neighbouring village school, showing off my breasts, which the bra gave a kind of lift they had never had before. On the playground I wasn't disheartened by the snickering of Suad, Nadine, Azizeh or any other girl. I went to class and sat down at my desk in the front of the room, coughing and clearing my throat in an attempt to attract the teacher's attention to my prodigious chest. That was a big mistake.

My breasts were a constant anxiety. I monitored them daily in the sanctuary of the bathroom. In the bathtub I would touch the insignificant protrusions. I balled up my right fist as a measure of their envisioned growth, then closed my eyes, imagining they had swelled, which filled me with happiness. At that age I stopped letting my mother bathe me, insisting that I was a big girl and capable of washing my own body, scrubbing my own back, without her help. When I was alone my hands would explore every last part of my body. I found the touch of my skin pleasurable. I chanted out loud to myself: 'Allah, Allah, it's like silk, Nahla, like silk.'

Just then I hear the roar of the crowd shouting out praise for Umm Kulthum's singing, all using the same word in unison: 'Allah.'

My chest eventually grew. And even though I got what I had always dreamt of, I was still jealous of Azizeh's breasts. She was two years older than me. I looked back and forth at her breasts and Suad's, which were basically flat despite the fact that she had hit puberty. I was relieved to be perfectly average.

I have taken good care of my body ever since I was little. If my breasts grew one centimetre I'd give them a new name. First they were cherries, then apricots, then pomegranates. When I would joke with Suad by asking about her chickpeas, she'd turn away from me without saying a word. Suad was frail, exceptionally intelligent and exceedingly reserved despite the fact that she enjoyed a margin of freedom I could only dream of, coming as she did from a more progressive family, especially her mother, who was kind, refined and educated. She let Suad do whatever she wanted, within reason of course, dressing up in beautiful clothes like some of the girls from Beirut who came to the village during the summer; her brothers were nice to her, too, they didn't judge her or beat her the way Jawad did with me. Suad never complained about her family or her body, talking about it only if I pressed her, stating plainly that it was normal and natural, and that she was in no hurry to grow up.

***

I can still recall her slender body, how it developed later on, filled out, acquired a striking level of proportion, and started turning heads during our first year in university, she in the philosophy department and me in Arabic literature. I can still recall it, as the memory waves at me, sends me flying towards details from my childhood and adolescence at times, towards images from my youth and early adulthood at other times. But

71

some obstacle, some kind of stubborn barrier always muffled my memory about the present and the recent past, as if a thick black curtain protected them from me or as though I had been afflicted with a kind of blindness that prevented them from finding their way into my memory.

No, I wasn't blind or deaf, and I certainly wasn't a horn-dog who gave in to my impulses either, the way Azizeh is now. At the outset she had been ashamed of her vivid imagination and her fascination with the love poets, whom she was constantly defending and describing as 'God's beloved'. This was before she had to drop out of school when her family moved to Beirut. She got married for the first time but divorced after a while.

Azizeh adored the classical poet Jamil Buthayna. She used to cry whenever one of the boys would pinch her or if Jawad harassed her, retorting that he was a . . . but she never had the heart to utter any insults, leaving them suspended in her throat, then saying piteously, 'I feel sorry for anyone who expressed love through his body and not his soul.'

On the day she got her period she was mortified, believing she had been injured somehow. She was wracked with horrendous feelings of fear and terror. She washed away whatever she could from between her legs and scurried back to bed, where she lay down and lifted her legs high in the air, imploring God to stop the bleeding. When she got up after a while she was terrified to find that the blood was still flowing and staining her bedsheets. She decided to use her teeth to tear them into scraps, some of which she stuffed inside her underpants and the rest she hid away. Then she drifted off to sleep, pretending to have a headache. Her simpleminded provincial mother didn't seem to notice something was wrong and knew nothing about what had happened until a long time afterwards. On that day she muttered something incomprehensible and turned her back on her daughter, abandoning her to figure things out for herself.

When I hit puberty it was a different sort of event altogether.

Before it happened I used to ask my mother, 'What's a tampon?'

With feigned innocence I would bait her into telling me what I already knew from girls in the upper grades. But my mother would remain silent. Just then the voice of my aunt Ruqaya, who had started spending a lot of time with us, boomed, 'It means a disgusting and shameful day. Shut up. Just shut up, girl. Thank God you haven't seen it yet, thank God you aren't there yet.'

Secretly I was rushing to get there so that I could become a real woman. The day my underwear was stained blood red and I hit puberty, I ran to tell my mother the good news.

'Starting today you have a bride-to-be in the house, mother,' I chirped.

But my mother understood all too well what I meant and refused to look at me. Her eyes darkened, she furrowed her eyebrows in disgust or reproach, perhaps a combination of the two. Then she pursed her lips together solemnly and said, 'Come on, get up and go look in the middle drawer. Take out a tampon and shove it where it needs to go.'

I still needed a bra that would fit my breasts. I had prepared for this eventuality by saving up a modest amount of my own money. I went to the store and came back with an ivory bra embroidered with lace. As soon as I got home I hurried into my room, got undressed and tried it on, then regarded myself in the mirror on the outside of the armoire and whistled at myself approvingly. I threw my head backwards, raised my arms to tie back my hair, and caught a glimpse of the soft and faint strands of hair under my armpits.

I looked down at my pubis, where the hairs were thicker and longer. It's magic, I whispered to myself, feeling as if I were soaring high up in the air.

My mother considered my nudity scandalous, and her outraged voice, quavering with rage, stopped me in my tracks, terrified me, hurled me back down to earth.

'What are you doing, you demon? You've been possessed by a djinn, for sure. May God curse the day I had you. You'll be the death of me. You're never going to learn.'

My mother slammed the bedroom door behind her hard. Then I heard the screech of the outer door closing and my mother's footsteps anxiously pacing the floor.

I didn't understand why exactly but just then I was overcome with feelings of pity for her, for whatever it was that made her react so harshly, for whatever was so burdensome for her. I never saw my mother dress up or wear makeup or put on perfume the way Suad's mother did. Her only perfume came from the bay soap she used. She cared about her hygiene and about ours, always intoning that cleanliness is close to godliness. She only ever needed a few pieces of clothing: one winter dress, another for summer, a black abaya to be worn over both of them, of course.

I felt bad for my mother for thinking I had been possessed by a djinn. As far as she was concerned that was what drove me to do things that were inappropriate for pious girls. My mother only approved of good girls, which is why she didn't mind that I hung out with Suad and Azizeh. She let me go over to their houses.

Even though I felt bad for her, I never stopped doing things that upset her. I didn't buy my mother's love and approval by silencing and repressing my body or by despising life and seeking seclusion. I took good care of my body. I wasn't ashamed of my femininity or embarrassed by it. I continued writing

74

poetry, journaling, and reading voraciously. I would read novels and the stories about djinns in *One Thousand and One Nights*. I was so affected by them that one night I dreamt a djinn prince who had fallen in love with me kidnapped me and flew me away to a strange world. I was afraid that he would cast a spell on me and turn me into a djinn like he was, I was afraid, despite whatever pleasure captivated me as he held me, just the way it was in the story, when he started to rub his cheek against mine, his nose against mine . . . until I awoke with a start, jumped out of bed and rushed to examine my naked appearance in the mirror. Then I started to realize that I could drown out all the rambunctious noise in my heart and my body in order to please my mother, so that she would give me her blessing. In one brief instant I imagined myself turning out just like her: frowny, severe, stiff, stubborn, silent.

But the world was too beautiful for me to reject it or shy away from it, it laughed at me, so who was I to receive it with a frown? Life drove me to live it to the fullest, to discover more and more. It was good to me so I aspired to even greater things. My little sorrows were trifles. My hunger for life was never sated and it never left me stranded in the world. My brother Jawad could annoy me, and my mother or Aunt Ruqaya, too, sometimes, and I might get a little upset but my heart never turned black, it kept on beating and loving and dreaming and longing for Jawad to be kinder to me and for my mother to become softer and more loving towards my father. She took care of him but she was always more concerned about praying; she loved prayer more than she loved him. If my father tried flirting with her in front of us she would recoil and make a mockery of him, which would only make him angry, then I would get pissed off and quip that she ought to focus on taking better care of herself and her appearance. Maybe then she wouldn't have to keep repeating the same sad songs to herself and could use her sweet voice instead, singing out loud and clear for the wild birds to hear, to come land near our house, and to sing along with her.

*＊＊＊

My heart yearned for so many things.

Thinking distracted me for the next few days until we finally went to live in Beirut. Azizeh's family had moved there before us. I missed her so much.

A vision of her appeared as I remembered the last time we saw one another in the village. We were talking and wandering around aimlessly until we reached the edge of our village and approached the neighbouring town. All of a sudden I changed the subject, reminding her of how I had always wanted to become a tree. She eyed me suspiciously, then gazed up at the tall trees on both sides of the street, looked them up and down.

'What's got into you, Nahla?' she said sternly, shaking her head. 'What you're saying doesn't make any sense. It's obvious that you've become an unbeliever but you don't even know it. One minute you want to be a little birdie in Heaven and now you want to become a tree. It's too much. Can't you just stay here with me on the ground?'

Azizeh accused me of being an unbeliever, called me crazy, criticized my behaviour in those days for having stirred up the disapproval and derision of other people. She reminded me what had happened with the bra and the hunting trip and lots of other shenanigans. She fell silent for a little bit, then informed me what the girls at school were saying about me. She told me how strange they found my newfound excitement, flirtatiousness and fascination with my own body. They

76

recoiled from this bold behaviour, my straight-talking, and the way I trumpeted the onset of my menstruation right in front of them. Even worse was the fact that I didn't seem surprised or ashamed, that I never batted an eye when the teacher called me up to the blackboard to correct one of the other girl's spelling mistakes. I rushed forward to do so, peacocking about how clever I was until I suddenly heard the sound of stifled laughter and then loud guffawing. When I turned around in bewilderment the teacher pointed to the traces of blood staining the backside of my school uniform.

I didn't cry or get upset, didn't betray even a hint of the shame that had appeared on the other girls' faces when they first got their periods; when it happened to them they looked frail, wizened and afraid. I just stood there in front of them with a smile on my face and said brazenly, 'What? There's nothing funny about this. It's just what happens when our bodies mature and we become young ladies.'

I asked for permission to go to the bathroom and confidently made my way there.

'And what about you Azizeh?'

As she stared back at me, her face turned all red. Something odd in her eyes made me feel that she was holding something back that she really wanted to say to me, even as she receded inside of herself.

Then she spun around all of a sudden, fumbling to say that we should go back because there wasn't much time left.

It was a very long time, many years in fact, until Azizeh confessed to me that when she first got her period it had crushed her, made her feel like she had committed a sin. In addition, her repressed feelings for my brother Jawad made her even more ashamed of her body, which fluttered like a feather whenever he 'bumped into her' or catcalled her.

How could I have been so stupid? At night she would dream about him kissing her and sleeping with her. During the day she would get so violent as to yank my hair in fiercely defending Jamil Buthayna, Kuthayyir Azzah and all the other love poets she used to read about. I bickered with her constantly, insisting that not a single one of them knew the first thing about true love, couldn't appreciate its significance as much as Umar Ibn Abi Rabiah.

Azizeh disclosed many of her secrets to me at her new house, where she had been living ever since getting divorced. 'Oh just shut up, Nahla,' she barked at me before I left. 'What are you even talking about? A woman without a body that she fully possesses, that she loves, that she takes care of, what's the point of her life anyway? She'd be a zombie.'

Among all the girls I had ever known since I was little, I was the only one who ever tested out Azizeh's theory. I knew the answer by instinct before ever confirming it with experimentation or my rational mind. But I was nothing like Azizeh back then. I'm still nothing like her now. From the beginning my body existed in perfect harmony with my mind. I recognized it and made my peace with it, even if it caused me pain sometimes. I owned it proudly, loved every inch of it. I would listen to it, speak to it, I would complain to it, it would complain to me. When my brother badly burned my fingers it took a long time for them to heal, and from that point I started to treat my body tenderly, to go easy on it, encouraging it to bear all of life's torments. I raised my left hand in front of me and deftly wiggled my fingers, as if they were dancing, inciting it to fight back, to pick up a pen and write poetry. Whenever I get cramps while I'm on my period, I simply laugh at it all, saying, 'Anyone who wants to grow up and fall in love and get married and have children has to suffer.' Then I take a sip from my warm cup of herbal tea and my stomach begins to feel better.

I like to classify every organ in my body according to its role in matters of love: my mouth is for kissing my lover; I can smell his musk whether or not he's there with me; my arms are for embracing him when I'm awake and when I'm asleep; my chest cradles him in reality and in my fantasies; my ears hear the beating of his heart and the sound of his breathing. My eyes have more than one part to play: they are my lover's bed at night, during the day, and all the time; they're the window I look through in order to consume the sight of him and to know everything there is to know about him, when he loves me, and when he loves me even more.

I'm mystified by the relationship some girls have with their own bodies. I watch how sometimes they interact with them as if they are shrouds, as if they are things that don't belong to them, that have been imposed upon them since birth. On most days they may seem light but as soon as they get their periods they hate them and recoil from them. Aunt Ruqaya calls it 'the time of shame and misfortune'; my mother calls it 'impurity'. Azizeh continued to hide it from her mother and from all of us, as if she'd done something wrong. The first time Suad got hers she received it with a bitter crying fit. But what happened to Nadine surpassed anything we could have imagined. When she sneaked into our house early one morning and violently shook me awake, I shoved her away and reminded her that it was a holiday so I wanted to sleep in. Just then I noticed that she was still in her nightgown, her eyes were like two burning embers, without any tears, smouldering like the flame rising up from the mouth of a volcano in our geography textbook. I laughed when she asked me about the snake venom my mother used to sprinkle along the edges of the animal droppings around our house on hot days, asking her whether she'd like to spray it on herself before breakfast or afterwards. Nadine the volcano immediately erupted in tears. She told me she had started menstruating and that she wanted to die, to be finished with her life lest she turn out just like her mother.

If menstruation frightened Nadine to the point of wanting to die, it caused me to thank the heavens for answering my prayers and granting me the thing I had been waiting for, the very thing I had tried to speed along, something I believed was necessary in order to talk with older girls about romance and love, in order to become a bride, at least, according to what I had heard from upper-class girls at school who were already involved in planning weddings.

I imagined myself as a mermaid on that day even though I had never seen the sea.

My physical maturity turned me into a shining star. That's the way I saw myself anyway, especially when I started to notice flirtatious words zipping all around me, turned-on looks chasing after me. I felt the same kind of satisfaction and happiness when my dress pockets would overflow with choc- olate and caramels during weddings and holidays. I'd hear things that fed my vanity, sang to my soul, and filled my body with grace.

'There, there, Nadine. You're a beautiful young lady and you're only going to get more beautiful. Menstruation isn't some kind of revenge or curse. Your maturity is a blessing, it's good tidings that crown you like a bride,' I told Nadine that day, parroting what Suad's mother had told her on the day she got her period. I nearly confessed that I was jealous of how much taller she was. I consoled her by saying that she was going to be a more beautiful bride than me, then held back my sadness and told her how I had become a woman a year and half before, how our mature bodies complete our femininity and make it possible for us to fall in love and get married. I joked with her that I would authorize her being excused from prayer and fasting, from helping her mother with the cleaning, the sweeping, and any other chores whenever she was on her period. At least during the first few days of it.

I squeezed her shoulder encouragingly and she looked back at me nervously, with a sad calm.

'All right, Nahla. I'll try to accept this but'—and her voice became extremely sad—'but I'm not like you and my mother's nothing like yours. Besides, what goes on in your house isn't anything like what happens in ours,' Nadine said, getting up to go.

My mother was standing by the door like a ghost in her prayer clothes. She made way for Nadine to leave, saying, 'Shame on you, girl, for letting her go on and on about her family's secrets.'

If my mother knew what Suad talked about sometimes she would have taken away my life the way her life had been taken away from her, the way she lost her sweetness ever since her beloved sheikh had disappeared and cut off all contact with her. After that she lived like an ascetic when it came to matters of love and romance, only minimally satisfied by her life with my father. Through ritual, prayer and the fear of God, she expelled her devilish thoughts about the sheikh. Sometimes she would get weak and I would hear her humming soft, dirge-like melodies. I used to think she was singing about how much she missed my father but I would quickly realize that was not the case.

If she truly missed him, why would she keep pushing him away? Why wouldn't she kiss him when he got back from

Beirut? I wondered to myself. Maybe she was embarrassed by him. No, that doesn't make any sense. It's funny, my mother had the capacity to destabilize things that seemed unshakeable.

Then I'd move on to think about something else.

* * *

Lots of things get mixed up for me these days. My mind goes blank all of a sudden. My memory betrays me. I forget where I am and what I'm doing. I clasp my hands and violently shake. I shut my eyes and try to expel the traces of fugitive thoughts, then try to catch hold of them again, but they slip away from me and disappear. My mind is a broken traffic light: the green light disappears before it is ever illuminated. My memory is a shut-in, its door is locked to the present. It's been moved from its road, frightened away by a red light. It is turned back, defeated, and skulks off somewhere else.

My memory is parked in the village streets and I'm parked just behind it. I can hear myself telling Azizeh that God created us with our bodies, and that if He wanted us to hate them or to repress them or to forget about them, He would have created us without them. I try to convince her that it would be apostasy to be frightened of them or disgusted by them or to cause them any pain, that they are a blessing from God and that whoever doesn't recognize or enjoy God's blessings angers God, that this person will be brought to account on Judgement Day. I insist that anyone who isn't happy with her own body, who doesn't enjoy it to the utmost, who doesn't let it live and love and feel passion, on Judgement Day God will hang her by her hair and feed her to the fires of Hell.

I remain silent for a few seconds and then ask Azizeh to think of her mother, my mother and Nadine's mother. I speak of their conquered bodies as though I'm presenting her with definitive proof of my argument. Azizeh recoils, aggressively resisting me by saying, 'My mother and your mother, maybe. But Nadine's? God forbid! What does this have to do with her? However much she may have loved her husband at one point, she stopped before they even got married. Besides, haven't you heard the way she talks about him in public?'

I let my mind wander until my thoughts settle upon Nadine.

Nadine changed a lot during the many years she and her family lived in Beirut. She became a different Nadine altogether. She moved at a faster pace. Her personality changed completely, from a scattered, bashful and introverted young lady into a bold woman who was up for anything, especially things mad and destructive. All the boys in our building, two streets over from where she and her family lived, spread malicious gossip about her. After working for a political party for a while, she threw herself into the leftist struggle, participating in some of the battles during the civil war. We didn't see each other much then, not until Nadine rekindled her friendship with Azizeh, which was how she met back up with our crew and we started getting together once again.

In the old days she would whisper to me that she no longer felt neglected or abandoned, that she had expelled the history of the village and her shameful memories there. I used to remind her about the good times, the happy times, about funny experiences we had together that were also part of that past, but she would scrunch up her forehead, her eyes would cloud over, and she would curse that past and our history, declaring that human history would never be just one thing, even if everyone lived in the exact same place. Nahla, she would say, some of us see the past as a prison, while others see it as paradise. One of us has changed, changed root and branch, has become a new person, as if she has been born again. Doesn't that second birth make you happy? she would say, pointing at herself with confidence and pride.

I glanced over at Nadine, studied the lines on her face, her eyelids, and the glimmer in her eyes, scrutinized the timbre of her voice, her gesticulations, and her curves, every last part of her, traces of the one and only birth that I actually believed in, the birth of love that can heal us from the anxieties of the past, present and future through which time becomes eternal and space becomes infinite and people—each and every one of us—become pure and righteous and loved. I focused on this idea to the point of exhaustion and then started to space out once again.

Through cracks in my memory I can discern the sight of her face drenched in sorrow in the schoolyard as she clutches at my arm, complaining about her womanizing father. He used to beat her mother for some reason or other, or without any reason at all, abuse her by hitting on every woman she hung out with, not even hesitating to harass young girls. She told me how much she hated her father and her mother, who was scandalized by her husband's behaviour and would wind up wailing and crying hysterically. She would smack her hands together and smash her head against the wall until she collapsed in a heap onto the ground. With her head hanging low she would plant her feet on the ground, hike up her skirt and start smacking her vagina with one of her husband's shoes, weepily repeating, 'If it weren't for you, you son of a bitch (referring to her vagina), if you hadn't made me turn my back on my family, what would I have ever wanted with him, why would I still be with him, this motherfucker son-of-a-bitch woman-hater. God curse you, you loser, fuck you, you who saddled me with these children who came out of you.'

Once, maybe twice, I saw Nadine's mother do that with my own eyes. The first time I closed our schoolbooks in a hurry. I was gripped with panic and confusion as Nadine turned her face towards the well and started biting her finger-nails and shivering. My heart broke. The second time I held myself together as best I could before taking her by the hand and guiding her to the door. Once we were outside she let go of my hand and, in a strangulated voice, said, 'Our books are still in there on the floor. I'll just go grab them and then come with you.'

Gentle and oppressed Nadine, whose eyes never stopped racing, as if she had been born with fear, loved school and hated summers. She used to tell me that Hell would be better than having to stay at home, that if it weren't for her older sister Rabia, she would have run away or killed herself.

On the day her sister died by suicide I felt as though Nadine no longer had a refuge or even a leg to stand on.

**

There was no mistaking how excited Rabia had been about her fiancé. Her excitement only seemed to make her more beautiful, luminous, and at the same time kinder and gentler. Her generous heart that offered Nadine love and protection gave her pause the night her fiancé came over to ask her to accompany him to his father's house in Beirut the next morn-ing. Their wedding day was fast approaching and they had to buy furniture for their new home as soon as possible. She knew how much her sister hated for the two of them to be apart, even for one day, but Nadine encouraged her to go ahead, convinced her it would be fine.

Driving along the coastal road she was enchanted by the blue sea. She thought about the magic of Beirut, where she was going to live after they got married, and she smiled, fighting back her exhaustion after a sleepless night. Her obsessing over her wedding dress had kept her up all night. She recognized that she would have to buy a suitable dress for Nadine as well. The touch of her fiancé's arm as she curled around his shoulder in the back seat made her feel strange. Although she liked it very much, Rabia wasn't totally satisfied with her outfit, so when he sneaked into her room that night, she made up her mind to ask him to leave at once.

'What? We're engaged, darling. I'm allowed to sleep with you,' he said lovingly, the echo of his father's words rattling around in his head: Go on and deflower her. That'll break her and her family. Then when she moves in with you she'll be broken in body and spirit, and she won't ever dare to raise her head against you.

Rabia fought back against him fiercely, parried every one of his moves, reminding him of the importance of morality and tradition.

'No way. You can't sleep with me until we move in together. Do you really believe I think so little of myself? That I want to spend the rest of my life broken and ashamed?'

He retreated with his tail between his legs, embarrassed and afraid to come face to face with his father, who pounced on him at the door. He kicked his son hard, shoved him aside and spat, 'Get the fuck out of my way. I'll show you how to be a man. If you can't do it, then I will.'

Then he threw open the door like a raging bull.

Rabia was as spirited as a workhorse when he set her in his sights. She allowed him to get right up next to her and then swiftly kicked him square in the balls, sending him reeling backwards towards the door, yowling in pain. When Rabia jerked her foot at him, threatening to kick once again, he had no choice but to swallow his pride and run away. She locked the door behind him, made up her mind to call off the engagement, and broke down crying, waiting impatiently for the dawn to break.

'I don't want to be with him. We're finished!' Rabia shouted at her mother, who listened to her intently before muttering something and then breathing a sigh of relief when her daughter went on to say, 'He kept apologizing to me the whole way back, swore to me that he would never agree with his father. His father's a monster, may God destroy his monstrousness.'

'Don't give it a second thought. Look, my baby girl, this isn't the way for him to get what he wants from you. Neither him nor his father. If you ask me you should accept his apology. Marry him with your head held high. The elections are coming. Pay attention. His family is powerful and your family could lose the mayoralty.'

Her mother was just afraid that her husband might lose his position, she didn't care about anything else, and she kept trying to persuade her.

'Also, my baby girl, what are people going to say if you leave him? They'll think he assaulted you, and that sin's going to be on your head.'

Rabia bit her cheek, took refuge in silence.

The next morning things had gone back to normal. It was agreed that the marriage would be registered in Nabatiyeh within the next two days. Rabia neither consented nor refused, she remained silent, but she started to show Nadine an unprecedented amount of attention and kindness. During the afternoon of the day after the agreement she got ready to leave, saying she was just going out into the field for a bit and that she wouldn't be long. She promised Nadine she'd bring some of her favourite flowers.

But Rabia was late in coming back. She told her mother she had visited all of her friends' houses, one by one, presenting each of them with a bouquet of flowers. What she didn't tell her mother, though, and what she told me and her sister and all of her friends was, 'Tomorrow I'd like you to toss these at me.'

Nadine ululated in excitement, imagining her sister as a bride with a tiara made out of flowers.

'The sight of you as a bride tomorrow will be the most beautiful picture in the whole world,' she said. 'And whoever said that I'm going to give you up and only see you in that picture. I swear, I swear, I'm going to be right by your side no matter where you go.'

Rabia's lips started trembling, as if she were about to start crying. She stared at Nadine as her eyes shimmered with tears, then she fell against her sister, hugging her and showering her with kisses.

I can't get that image of Rabia out of my head. It stays with me, I'm obsessed with it, it's all I can think about. Her shrouded body in her fiancé's arms, tears streaming down his face and hers as he smothers her and pulls her close, shakes her and coos at her like a little girl, then shouts at her in anguish.

'Why, Rabia?! My heart and my eyes and ohhh . . . my love. Why did you have to die, why? We should have died together.'

He says this and falls silent. Then he repeats the same thing before describing what happened.

He showed up early and she served him a cup of coffee in the living room. She asked him to wait a few minutes so she could fold the sheets and clean up her sister's room, then she got dressed and readied herself to accompany him to the civil registry. She was running late, normally his voice would cause her to hurry up, and when she didn't respond, he called out a second time, then a third, then a fourth. Before taking more than a few steps inside, he saw her lying on the floor in the hallway between the kitchen and the bedroom, as thin, strangely shaped spittle foamed out of her mouth. He shook her gently, then violently, but she didn't wake up, so he hurried out to ask her mother for help.

'The leaves flew out of my hands and I just started running,' her mother continued, slapping her face. 'The horror. I was about to cook mulukhiyah for them in celebration. What a tragedy. My Rabia is gone. Gone. I found her lying on the ground, dry as kindling. What is this Hell . . . '

In the end Rabia revealed what she would never say aloud. She had drunk poison and killed herself, leaving her sister without any support.

I took care of Nadine, helping her to climb the uphill dirt road separating our house from theirs. When we heard the sound of wailing and screaming we knew we were only a few steps away from the door. Nadine got tired of my waiting in the foyer. She threatened to go to school alone, then walked out in a huff without me, and I had to hurry over to grab her by the arm and apologize.

The sound caused us to sit up and take notice, the blood froze in our veins. Nadine's face darkened and her voice quavered as she said, 'That sound is coming from our house.' As she started to run, I ran after, right up to Rabia's shrouded body that was being cradled in the arms of her fiancé, who insisted on carrying her, threatening that he would kill anyone who tried to convince him to put her down. Nadine stood there and cried, pulling out her hair and flopping around like a crazy person until she passed out and fell down on the ground.

The sadness over losing Rabia drove her mother out of her mind. She started saying to anyone she met or who came by to visit her, no matter whether it was a man or a woman, 'Please, you all saw Rabia in a dream. I beg you. What did she say to you? Did she forgive me or didn't she? Woe is me, oh God, woe is me. I'm the reason she's dead. I'm the one who killed her, with my own two hands.'

She was never spared from this madness, these hallucinations, not even after they moved to Beirut. The funny thing was that, at least according to what my mother told some of her cousins, she returned to the same strange happy-sad thing: planting her feet on the ground, lowering her head, hiking up her skirt and picking up whatever shoe was nearby, then going on to beat her vagina and curse it with the same invective.

She used to assiduously cook her husband Abd al-Majid's favourite foods and he would eat everything in sight. He would also call her the foulest names and tell her she was worthless, that she looked like a lunatic, her food was 'over-cooked' or burned, flavourless, he was going to marry some-one else and put an end to the nauseating life he had with her. She would fall down prostrate at his feet, kiss his feet and his hands, and beg him tearfully, 'Forgive me, Abd al-Majid, it won't happen again, I swear to God. Please forgive me.' Then she'd wink at him and promise, 'Do whatever you want, it'll be unlike anything you've ever experienced.'

'All right, get up,' he spat at her. 'Stand up and strip right here in front of me, you filthy woman. God willing you'll do a better job next time.'

***

90

Nadine forgot all about her mother and the sights of her madness, turned away from everything happening around her. Her breathing became difficult. She prepared her skinny body, tall as a cypress tree, for the moment she would be able to enter Mademoiselle Loubna's geography class. Loubna used to keep watch on Nadine, especially when we were all gathered in the schoolyard. Her face would turn beet-red when she noticed her staring at her, whether it was in the classroom or in the corridors. She would always call on her and check in to see how she was doing. Nadine became obsessed with her. I can still see how she would watch her, following her every move, as though Nadine had been taken by the teacher, kidnapped by something I couldn't name, something that kept her from hearing me or even noticing my presence, as if I weren't sitting right there next to her on the same bench. She was thirteen years old and hadn't yet experienced infatuation or fallen in love, although sometimes she did say that she had feelings for some boys. When she started to feel those mysterious feelings for the geography teacher, she repressed her secret and refused to admit it despite my prodding. She kept her feelings to herself. In her own secret spaces, whether at night or during the daytime, she would talk to herself about the secret passion that had captured her heart, her mind, and her body. She surrendered to her fantasies, dreaming that she could fall asleep in her lap as she held her. In the classroom, on the playground, or in the halls between classes Nadine would stare at Mademoiselle Loubna as if she could ensnare her with her eyes, could make her hers and hers alone. She would fall apart when she found her deep in conversation with another teacher or a student from another class. She would go mad if the teacher didn't call on her more than once in class. She felt like her movements became more beautiful, more refined, and she would become desperate to hear her utter it aloud. She convinced herself that the way she pronounced her name was a clear sign of her particular interest in her. With a glance or a whisper I would communicate to her that she needed to calm down, to get a hold of herself. She would frown at me annoyedly and tell me to shut up.

The real catastrophe was the day Miss Loubna didn't show up. Nadine's face was like a wilted flower. She turned pale and stayed away from everyone. The same thing happened on school holidays. Her greatest sorrow was reserved for the last week of the school year.

Nadine continued to mask her secret, avoided being alone with me, and was cruel to me anytime I tried to bring it up. But I didn't give up, becoming even more steadfast because of my feeling that Rabia's death had only made her more confused and maybe even . . . maybe she was manifesting one of the crises she would go through when her father became violent or her mother's madness got worse . . . until one morning in class she surprised me by shunning, grabbing her school bag, and moving to the seat behind us. Ever since then it had become unable for me to gauge her enthusiasm and her emotions directly, so I began watching the teacher instead. I could see how her gaze would drift off towards Nadine, who insisted on sitting by herself, refusing to share a bench with any of the other girls in class. I would notice the strange significance of those looks, which only increased my curiosity and confusion. I tried to attract her attention, by coughing hard or dropping my heavy bag and then staring right at her, which would cause her to blush, not knowing what to do, and then look the other way. Until one day when she lost her cool altogether.

We were intently watching a student draw a map of Asia on the chalkboard as the teacher leaned her back against the wall beside the rearmost seat to observe her work. Nadine created some space beside her so the teacher sat down, and that's when what happened happened.

The teacher's hand started to caress Nadine's neck from behind, then gently rubbed her back, up and down, before wrapping her arm around her shoulders and grazing—as if unintentionally—the tip of her breast. Nadine's feelings were ignited as ecstasy flooded her veins, caused her eyes to dilate, and her body to go limp and then quiver in pleasure. And she was afraid.

All of a sudden she felt like she was in danger. She sensed there was something forbidden in what her teacher was doing. She tried to give a name to those feelings, but to no avail, she knew deep down inside that it obviously had something to do with sex, which she had no experience with yet; all she knew about it was what she overheard girls and women whispering about. She became even more afraid. The whole thing was strange and unfamiliar to her.

That evening, when she was alone, she wondered why she had responded to the teacher's touches the way she had. She was disgusted by her response and resolved not to let her do that again. The question kept nagging at her. And because she wanted to understand the truth of the matter, she confronted herself, ultimately admitting that she was behaving like someone who was hiding something from herself, a secret she had never wished for or even dreamt of. Now she was afraid of getting further involved in unfamiliar feelings, to slide towards this foreign thing. She thought: maybe the teacher was impersonating a man's hands as she touched her, or maybe she had imagined that her hands were a man's hands. The most likely explanation was that Mademoiselle Loubna was a man dressed up as a woman.

Many different scenarios plagued her, gnawed at her and exhausted her. She chewed over every possibility and its antithesis until she arrived at her decision to cut off all ties with the teacher-man.

Nadine became a different person ever since that moment. She tried to expunge every last trace of that experience and return to her normal self. She had relationships with college guys, had sex with men in the movement who convinced her that women's liberation began first and foremost with sexual freedom.

***

Our gang reunited in the Malla neighbourhood.

We had only been living in Beirut for a few short months. Suad's family came to stay with us and then they rented a house in our neighbourhood, a few blocks away from where Azizeh's family lived, on the edge of the locality where Nadine's family had settled.

My father had arranged for me to go to a state school for girls in Ras Beirut, near the Protestant College School. I'd go there every day, usually on foot. Suad and I would walk arm in arm as we chattered or whispered to one another about a step or two behind Azizeh and Nadine. As soon as we reached the pavement outside the college, Azizeh would slow down and start blinking, gawking at the crush of well-dressed girls, glumly eyeing their short skirts and long hair. She'd get distracted and Nadine and I would have to hurry her along. We'd nudge her to snap out of it and come along so we wouldn't be late for class. I always found this behaviour of hers unbecoming. I stood in judgement of her dejectedness that made her shoulders round inwards, her gaze as pathetic as a beggar. Sometimes I'd scold her gently, other times more severely. She'd lift up her eyes and stare at me with a look that gathered together all the spite in the world. As soon as we were away from the fancy girl's area and turned onto a side street that led to our school, Azizeh would stop again, lower her gaze and begin to stare at her ancient shoes, then bend over to wipe the leather with the palm of her hand and mutter her catchphrase: 'It's not fair, this world's not fair. Some people have nothing, some people have it all.'

Azizeh's sadness infuriated me and I was disgusted by her despair, but what bothered me most was the way she behaved in the store where we used to go during our afternoon recess. Sometimes we would run into other girls from the college there, and she'd poke me in the waist and whisper in a barely audible voice, 'They smell good. Like the kind of soap I could never dream of having.' She'd keep on scratching the tip of her nose until I stomped on her foot and told her to shut up, causing her to tumble backwards, opening the way for them to cut the line in front of her. 'They're girls from good families. I recognize who they are and who I am. Show some respect,' she'd say to me if I objected. Even though I really liked Azizeh, I was always less close to her than I was to Suad. We'd spend lots of time together sharing secrets, but the only one I told all of my romantic secrets was Suad.

Sometimes we'd meet up at one of our houses, the three of us. Suad was the best at maths. Azizeh, no matter how long or hard she worked at them, though, couldn't solve difficult problems. She liked to say that they would never come in handy in real life. I'd chastise her by saying that there wasn't anything in the world she cared about as much as romantic love, and that this would only end up driving her crazy, that she'd lose the chance to experience real love. And the conversation would explode into an argument. Azizeh would lose her cool and raise her voice in opposition, calling me a traitor to the soul. She reminded me in disgust of the impudence of Umar bin Abu Rabia, pointing out that I was one of his dark disciples, and that like him I would never repent. I'd laugh her off and scoff at her prudishness as well as that of Jamil Buthayna, sarcastically whispering to her that he was sexually impotent, and the same was true of Qays al-Majnoun. She'd rush to the defence of her beloveds, as she called them, and I told myself that Azizeh was never going to grow up. I remember another conversation we had about the same topic when I tried to show her how naive she was, derisively asking her: 'Do you really think that's possible, Azizeh? Can you actually believe that Layla or Buthayna didn't sleep with Qays or Jamil? It's all lies, if you ask me. I'm sure they masturbated about them every night. How else could that love remain so explosive? If the body had no stake in it?'

'What does masturbate mean?' she asked in confusion.

Azizeh had changed so much. Eventually she rose up against her naivety, or maybe it was her fear. Today her private dictionary contains the entire lexicon of sex.

And what about me? Haven't I changed, too? I ask myself as I think about what I had done since settling back in Beirut.

I rebelled against the hijab at first, tearing it off despite my mother's insistence. My body rebelled as well, dressing up and strutting around in the most beautiful clothes. I placated my father by telling him how much I liked the headscarf he had bought me.

'Honey, I love my country very much,' he said, spreading it out in front of me. 'And now you're going to wear a headscarf with the Lebanese cedar printed on it.' He wrapped it around my head and smiled.

I couldn't stand the headscarf either. I tore it off as soon as I had slammed the door shut behind me and walked out. I stuffed it in my bag and redid my hair in a chignon, which was the style at the time, until I could get rid of it once and for all. But even that wouldn't be enough.

A yearning for freedom and liberation that would drive me to rebel started to flow through my veins. In those days

Beirut was experiencing a state of intellectual and cultural ferment that was reflected in our social life, every class and every sector of society was affected. It enabled me to dare to clash with my mother, and on the day that I confronted her by saying I was a free woman, that I wasn't going to wear the headscarf if I didn't want to, no matter what she did, she blew up at me and lost her mind.

'A liberated woman? In Arabic liberated means immoral and indecent.'

Then she dragged me out the door by my hair and called for my father, who just looked at me and smiled confusedly.

'Are you sure you want to take off the veil, Nahla?' he asked.

'I am. I'm sure, Papa,' I replied agitatedly.

'All right, as you wish,' he exhaled in surrender.

But I never surrendered.

I took off my veil and started wearing a miniskirt. I would stand in front of the mirror for hours, closely examining how attractive and how beautiful I was, fantasizing about walking down the street stealing hearts and turning heads, gleefully paying close attention to myself, calling out to my own reflection: I'm free . . . free . . . free.

5

In the middle of the hallway leading to my bedroom I was talking to myself in wonder and excitement, slowly returning to my senses as I repeated, 'I'm in love, I'm in love!'

When she finished praying my mother detected the tempest in my eyes. She wrapped her prayer beads around her hands and asked me, 'What's with you today, Nahla? You're not yourself.'

I didn't respond.

His beautiful voice had enchanted me and was still ringing in my ears, as though a warm breeze had swept through my body, searing me. The song 'In Return for Love' by Abdel Halim Hafez seemed to have been written, composed and sung just for me.

When our eyes locked and my desire for him surged, he didn't flinch, staring long and hard at me until I felt as though a reservoir of desire was cascading from his eyes and filling up my own. I paid close attention to his body that was overflowing with desire, a rare scent emanated from him, as he emitted vibrations, raw, pure and unique sensations that altered his voice and its timbre and the way his body moved. His hands trembled when he didn't know what to do.

I presented him with the first love poem I ever wrote for him on the day after we met. When he was done reading it, he laughed and said, 'Stop, stop it, this is all too much.'

'No, take it. It's just a token of my admiration, nothing more. It's nothing,' I replied.

'But how can I just forget about it? No, no, no, stop this, you said what you said, but it's too much.'

I wrote him many poems after that to read when he was alone. In one I waxed romantic about his toes, and he asked me, 'What are you trying to say with this? You're so different from all the other women and girls.'

'Just imagine,' I told Suad once, 'if I die and my children ever found out about these poems, actually got their hands on them. There's incriminating evidence in my room, papers with poems I wrote to him and some of my private diaries.'

Amid the noise and the laughter and the music I grew weary of Suad, who sat there beside me on the day I met him as I poured my voice into her ear, going on and on about how in love I was with him, how I would simply drop dead if I found out he felt the same way. Suad smiled at me, her entire face beaming vitality. I added that I felt as though I had already known him for hundreds of years . . . that my ears were clutching at the sound of his voice, as if it were coming out of my memory and not just his mouth.

On the day we met he wore a long, baggy, broken-in shirt with the sleeves rolled up his slender arms, unbuttoned to reveal a white T-shirt underneath, which fit snugly against his slim body and his flat stomach. It was Azizeh's birthday and she had invited him because he was her brother's good friend from school.

The year was 1973 and we were just heading into the summer break before our senior year. Azizeh had dropped out of school so that she could get ready for her wedding, while Suad, Nadine, Hoda and I had started studying for our final exams.

We couldn't tear our eyes off of each other. I'm not sure exactly why I undid the top two buttons on my shirt when he sat down next to me, but it was probably to draw his attention to my breasts, which I was proud of for being so well shaped. It thrilled me every time I caught him stealing a glance at them as much as he could.

When he began talking to me, the conversation flowed like a raging river. I wished for time to stand still so that he would always be there sitting by my side, speaking to me through his eyes before even uttering a word. When he moved to sit next to Nadine, every time he turned to speak with her I felt as though I could gaze at his profile for eternity. From time to time he would glance back at me, and the rhythm of his looks seemed to skate delicately across my body, down to my ankles, while my gaze was transfixed on the length and breadth of his face, leisurely ambling across it. That day I felt like a bird whose wings had been clipped, but his love nursed me back to health so that I could fly high into the sky and nothing would ever be able to hurt me.

As we left Azizeh's house, I walked shoulder to shoulder with Suad and talked about him as if I were guarding my feelings in a garden full of precious flowers. He started dropping by my school every day, waiting for me outside so that he could walk me home. We started going to Chez Paul together, the cafe in Raouché where I still get a lump in my throat every time I pass by even though it has changed quite a bit since then. It was there that we both confessed our love for each other. At the top of my lungs I exclaimed, 'I love you, I love you!'

The first time I met up with him I asked, 'Where are you from, Hani?'

'From the mountains. What about you?'

'From the south, from a Shiite family, a very religious one. What about you?'

'I'm from a Christian family, we've got religious fundamentalists but we've got leftists, too.'

'Really?'

'Yes, really.'

'Whatever the case, you're the most wonderful sect, the most attractive man I've seen in my whole life, more handsome than an actor, more handsome than Al Pacino or Alain Delon, more handsome than Abdel Halim Hafez or Rushdy Abaza or Clint Eastwood . . . more handsome than all of them . . . all of them.'

He laughed for a long time before responding, 'I'm not very good-looking, but they say that even an ape can seem as beautiful as a gazelle to its mother.'

Suad spoke her mind directly and told me that this is what love is. Love is quick and unyielding, Nahla. When we fall in love, we enter a kind of temporary insanity until we manage to get a hold of ourselves. Infatuation has a time limit, it's as sudden as an earthquake, but the intensity of our passion prevents us from feeling anything. We ourselves become the earthquake and we fail to feel the aftershocks until it's too late.

'I'm sure that Hani's love will be the source of all my earthquakes,' I told her that day. 'A region rocked by temblors and aftershocks that are never going to stop. How can I ever get a hold of myself?'

Years later I told her how Hani proved to me that love never ends. We all have a secret place where we fully understand that we can only truly find ourselves in a certain other person.

***

The paved road seemed to be far behind us by the time we turned down into the valley and headed towards the densely wooded forest. Scattered clouds in the sky played with the sun and filtered the light, leaving some expanses in shadow and others illuminated. A refreshing breeze blew softly through the treetops.

This was during the autumn of 1974, when we took off from the university in a car he had borrowed from a friend and headed up into the mountains so that he could show me his home village. We stared at one another as we stood beneath a large cherry tree, as birds landed on the shrubs all around us as if they were delighted to be so low to the ground. Desire took hold of his appearance and changed his colour. Only his lower lip retained its pinkish hue in spite of his dark olive complexion. The way he looked at me was a lot like how Abdel Halim Hafiz looked in his films whenever he was falling in love; Hani looked just like him: the deep darkness in his eyes, those looks, his colour that was beautifully clear the way lovers' can be, and the delightful manner in which he walked, revealing the humility and restraint of someone in love. Hani's face was chiselled, Pharaonic even, with a particular kind of charm. Maybe at first I had been mesmerized by his dulcet voice and by his resemblance to Abdel Halim Hafez, extremely gentle but in an edgy and bold sort of way. His voice could melt your heart, skewer even the most hardened; it always transported me to a world where people's souls were forged out of the clay of love, a world without conflict, without the hunger for love and its accompanying torments, without mild or scorching desire filled with pain, surrender and burning.

His chest rose and fell as his breath came closer to my own. My face flushed just before he kissed me for the first time. I bolted, running back in the direction of the main road while he chased after me.

'If you were really clever you'd follow me and then tackle me,' I challenged him, giggling.

In the blink of an eye he grabbed my hair from behind and I collapsed on top of him. He embraced me as my back slammed into his chest, my hands thrust against my own. He kissed my neck before swivelling my head around so that he could kiss me on the mouth, leaving a flavour under my tongue I can taste to this day. After that walk we took together, it became his wont to kiss me through the metal bars of our gate, holding my face in his hands, laughing, after walking me home from class.

***

We trudged through the rain for a long time, his hand draped around my neck underneath the umbrella, on our way to the small apartment he had been renting with some college friends.

Our first physical encounter took place in that room.

The storm outside was so violent that when we finally made it to his room my clothes were soaked and I was shivering from that late-fall cold snap.

He gave me his pyjamas to wear until my clothes were dry, then turned his back and watched the water droplets collect on the window, whistling an Abdel Wahab tune—'I love her no matter how much I see her, no matter what people say'. I desperately wanted him to turn around and see me naked, for him to be turned on by me, but he didn't.

To satisfy our hunger we sat down at a small round table and ate two hamburgers we had bought from a tiny restaurant near his house. We looked away from one another for a while, then he lowered his eyes and took my hand. We sat there face to face, both of us having lost the power of speech.

Although he had held me in his arms before, this time when he embraced me I felt as though I had passed out. I'm not sure how long he held me that time. One second? A minute? An hour? A lifetime? Everything around me disappeared, I could no longer tell where I was.

He always had such a gentle touch, he didn't squeeze me too tightly the way most men do. The warmth of his chest was scalding, like hot water in a boiler.

His lips trembled before he kissed me. He closed his eyes and exhaled. Whenever we were together Hani was like this. He'd stand a little back from me, shut his eyes, and take a deep breath. This time while I was kissing him I felt as though I were breathing in the air of the whole world, as if I were feeling the heat that anyone in the world who suffered from cold was craving. I was so warm that it felt as though I were sweating on the inside, not just on the outside of my skin, especially when he placed his hand against the small of my back and guided me to the bed, where my spine yielded.

First he would lie down on his stomach next to me, leaning on his elbows, then unbutton his pyjamas that I was still wearing, kiss my chest over my bra, then place two kisses on my stomach before we made love.

He made me wet without ever penetrating me, because he didn't want to take my virginity, he only wanted to turn me on, as he used to say. Even though I found his behaviour odd, I smiled at him and thought to myself, Anyway, it's my hymen, not just some meaningless flap that causes pain instead of pleasure: the hymen equals pleasure.

Later, I would feel that whenever he slept with me it was as though I wasn't losing my hymen but getting it back. Pleasure was being experienced inside both our bodies, and it was through this pleasure that our bodies got to know one another.

That's the way I got to know my own body, actualizing everything I loved about it, I wasn't afraid of or hiding anything, this body I always wished would hurry up and mature when I was younger, which I would watch grow with boundless love. I never felt mistreated when I was with Hani. And I never felt as though I was insulting him by having sex with my husband, just that Saleem's body was shameful, ignorant and less than my body. Still, I never hated him, didn't think of him as an aggressor. The only weapon he had was a thin veneer of masculinity.

***

My dream was for us to get married the same way that so many young men and women, both Muslims and Christians, got married before the war, for all of my desires to come true just like theirs did, but then the war came along and ruined everything.

When the fighting broke out Hani moved to East Beirut out of fear of sectarian killing. The front lines were becoming more violent and crowded. I would wait impatiently for him to show up when the roads and then the tunnels were opened back up during a ceasefire.

When my brother Jawad found out about our relationship he went ballistic. He was the only person I was truly afraid of: he could be peevish despite his good looks and he was full of himself because most of my girlfriends worshipped him, including Azizeh. When he sat down at the table we would all sit down around him, unable to take a bite before he was finished eating. When I dared to stand up to him, he lunged to hit me, but my father cried bitterly that day out of sympathy for me, while my mother just shrugged her shoulders and told him, 'That's just the way men are, seriously. If people knew that a girl had been hit by her brother and didn't raise her voice to challenge him, they'd respect her even more, they'd call her decent, say that she's not immoral.'

Jawad could never understand why I loved Hani or how the flower of my feelings and my desire could blossom whenever I was with him. He was so vehement as to argue that I was a woman who didn't need a desiring body or a loving heart as long as I was his sister and the repository of his honour.

In the eyes of my mother and my aunt he was the man of the house. Sex for him always involved prostitutes. More than experiencing pleasure with them, he discovered pleasure for himself in their company.

The way he smelt seemed to change when he hit puberty. There was a masculine scent around the house that smelt of fatherhood in a way there never had been when my father was around. My mother often hung his bedding out in the sun to dry at that time in order to combat the dampness in his room, but because he had no self-control he continued to soil his bed whenever he jacked off. My mother mostly wasn't disgusted by this, except for that time when she went into the bathroom and froze at the sight of some of his pubic hair. She came out of the bathroom in shock, shut the door behind her, her face all gloomy, as if thick dark clouds were about to start raining from her. The strange thing was that, even though Jawad had become the man of the house, I heard my mother tell my aunt, 'I don't know what's come over me, Ruqaya, but when I went into the bathroom and saw his pubic hairs I was sickened. Now there's a man in the house after there had only been a little boy scampering around me the way a little chick follows after his mother.'

The pungent scent of a popular cologne that he bought in a nearby shop wafted through the house, and I felt dizzy until he went out to al-Mutanabbi Street, which had been down-town before the civil war, where a friend of his encouraged him to have sex with prostitutes.

He stood out on that street, looking right and left, reading the names of prostitutes, unsure of what to do. Then he noticed a long line of men of all body types and ages waiting their turn in front of one particular building to see this phenomenon: The Heartbreaker. He got in that line to wait his turn, then asked the man standing in front of him why there was such a long queue.

'People say this *artiste* gets so much business because she's really fast and the johns have a crazy good time, that she has a very unusual style, that there's nobody else like her here in the market.'

Jawad nodded, carried away by his imagination as he stood in line and waited his turn.

Her space was like a medical clinic, divided into two halves, one for receiving clients and the other with men scattered in chairs who had already been inside and had their turn. Between the two rooms there was a door that led to a bathroom where she took a shower after she had finished with the john she had just seen.

When she saw Jawad come inside, the Heartbreaker got to work, shaking her ass up and down, as he imagined someone underneath her was making her move like that. He stood there, agape, staring at her large behind, and trembling as if he were witnessing a mysterious new world he knew nothing about. She spun her head around, turned to look at him, and called out, 'Why are you just standing there, boy? Come closer, don't be scared.' But he remained frozen in place, unable to move. She got up and started to move towards him, took him by the hand and pulled him along, then invited him to take off his pants, to not be afraid, and he rolled on top of her after

107

she came back, bounced and started shaking her ass. He would never forget what she taught him, how she instructed him to hold himself together and not come so fast so that the women who agreed to have sex with him wouldn't make fun of him or denigrate his masculinity. He did exactly as she said and penetrated her, discovering pleasure for the first time with her, an overwhelming pleasure beyond anything he had experienced before, which constantly brought him back to the prostitute market.

***

My brother prevented me from moving out and going to college despite the fact that he used to speak at political meetings about secularism, the need to abolish sectarianism, and other grandiose slogans he didn't understand at all.

I didn't put any stock in what Jawad said, though, attributing it to excessive emotion more than anything else. I know that he loved me very much. He cried and held me after once trying to hit me. I called Hani and we met at a cafe in Hamra. I told him he could do whatever he wanted but that if he really loved me then we should be together.

I never thought that my family would reject him once he had discussed the matter with Jawad. I had always believed that I was their precious little girl. They would shower me with extraordinary affection, praise my beauty and my intelligence. I'd listen to their arguments, especially my father's, who I always thought would be able to stand up to my mother and my brother, not only because he himself knew what losing love felt like, but he turned out to be the weakest link in the house, even if he were also the most gentle, civilized and humane. My father sympathized with me, was enthusiastic about my marriage to Hani, but my brother got in his face and insulted him, which caused him to curl up in bed and start crying in shame. When I heard they had refused Hani I just stood there in astonishment. Their eyes seemed empty. My mother's blue irises looked black to me. My brother's eyes were thick with lies. The way all of them looked at me had changed. I would have had to fight if I wanted to convince them about him and to convince Hani not to break off our relationship.

They had forbidden me from leaving. I was starting to feel besieged and exhausted, as though I had come to a dead end. I started scheming about how to escape from the house so that I could see Hani and he could see me, so that we could run away together, or do anything at all that would force them to accept the reality of the situation. But Hani surprised me after one ceasefire took hold when I ran into him at a cafe in Hamra, where he told me, 'I've been thinking, Nahla. How are we supposed to get married? I'm still a student, my father's a poor man who sells vegetables from a cart. I wish you would wait until I graduate so that we can find jobs and be together on our own.'

Hani didn't want me to run away with him, he didn't want to just take my virginity, he didn't want to hurt me, as he put it, despite all my efforts while we were together at his friend's place in Ashrafiyyeh, after I had braved the danger outside to sneak over there one day. 'What's wrong with you, Nahla?' he went on to say. 'Your brother's crazy, your whole family's lost it. In these shitty times people are as worthless as Kleenex. They could kill you and me both.'

***

'Get your clothes tailored and go to the salon,' my mother told me sternly and deliberately one day when Saleem, the suitor who wished to become my husband, came by. Hani's words echoed in my ears as I went back into my room to get ready to meet this caller, carrying with me my lifelong feelings of guilt for having been unable to defend my love, for having not waited for him. On that day I had no choice but to put on the most hideous dress I owned.

A forty-year old man—almost twenty years older than me—was waiting for me in the living room. By the look of him he appeared to come from a wealthy family. I was struck by the fact that he was wearing Habit Rouge cologne, which I really liked. I'm very fond of colognes and I can tell them apart. This man's mother and sister were watching me intently, as if they were on the verge of devouring me.

Once they were gone my mother barged into my room in excitement, raised her arms towards the sky thanking God, and said, 'You must be so happy, my little girl. The gates of Heaven have opened up for us, it's as if the Day of Judgement has arrived when a man like that asks to marry you. A famous lawyer who lived in Africa for a long time, who made a whole pile of money. And all his properties, oh my. You see, not all men are unbearable. This one's easy on the eyes. And this kind of guy doesn't come along every day. Thank God, all praise and thanks to You.'

It all happened so fast. There was a huge lump in my throat. My heart was pounding when the marital bed had been made and decorated with a coverlet for the wedding night. I dreamt of a single pillow that would bring me and Hani together, just to sleep beside him in the same bed more than I wanted to have sex with him.

On our wedding night when my husband took my virginity, I was overwhelmed with pity for him. I felt as though I hadn't actually given him my body. I was completely dissociated from myself, as if the body he was clinging to belonged to some other woman. What should have been a simple matter of pleasurable penetration, even if it could only be physical, turned into torture. I was truly confounded that night when we entered the bedroom, he took of his clothes, and got into the bed before me, covering his body with a sheet that rose up into the air around his midsection, as if he were pitching a tent. In reality, the thing that was sticking up underneath the sheet was his fist holding onto his dick in order to make it look it was sticking straight up and to make me believe he had some kind of extraordinary manhood.

That night he told me he had a very strong libido, that like a bear he could detect the scent of a she-bear in the snow even from a great distance, and that his ass would thrust just like a bear's, the only difference being that his strength would never flag whereas a bear's erection snaps like a twig as soon as it penetrates the she-bear and he has to retreat with his powers sapped.

He also told me there were some people in the village who referred to the men in his family as bulls because of the size and strength of their penises, while others called his family bears. He made up a story about one of his relatives who broke his dick on his wedding night when he penetrated his wife, just like a bear, because of how hard he was and for the power of his desire, but he still didn't pull out until he was completely spent, which caused him to collapse in exhaustion as he tried to walk away.

After collapsing on top of me, the flaccidness of his dick compared with how hard I knew they could get was an embarrassment. He made a valiant effort, though, and I played along despite the fact that I had been evacuated of any emotion, my body now merely a tool that I had to help him use.

What might have appeared to be responsive gestures and moaning was nothing more than my attempt to turn him on so that this formality could be over and done with. When he finally succeeded in getting it up, as he bounced up and down on top of me, I did my best to make him feel like he was making me feel good. I did that for him and for me. It's strange how capable a woman is of satisfying herself and her partner at the same time, without really needing him there at all. Women have such wondrous power. Perhaps masturbation gives women more pleasure than men because they care more about penetrating a vagina—or anything at all, really—than the pleasure that might be experienced in the process.

The blood that symbolized my torn hymen seemed to delight him. I had always heard from my mother, my aunt and other girls in the village how painful it was when the hymen broke, all they ever talked about was pain and suffering, nothing about pleasure. I never heard a woman talk about losing her virginity as a pleasurable experience. But on my own wedding night the hymen wasn't all that interesting to me. I had never paid much attention to mine, though I always wished Hani would be the one to break it before I got married, but he wouldn't, saying that was for my own protection. My hymen had always made me afraid of my own body, not to be afraid on its behalf. When I was just a little girl my mother used to warn me constantly not to fall down so that my vagina wouldn't smash into something hard that could rupture my hymen. I can still remember one time when I fell off a wall in the backyard of our house in the village. I blacked out for a few moments without anyone knowing what had happened to me. When I came to and went back inside the house I told my mother I was dizzy and in pain.

'Where did you fall, you idiot?' she shouted in my face. 'On your head? On your back? Tell me, where? Hurry up, tell

112

me. Fall on your head, your back, fall wherever you want, whatever you do just don't fall on *it*.'

I resented being a virgin, was spiteful about it, unlike Azizeh, who would always say that virginity was a debt women owed to men. When we were in school she would complain to me about her fear of losing her hymen, knowing full well that no man had ever touched her. Even the pink colour that she would notice when she got her period used to make her think it was hymenal blood, and her face would turn yellow as she asked me what to do.

'You should quit masturbating if you're so scared,' I told her.

'Yeah, I don't know why I do it when innocent love is so attractive to me.'

'So, do you put your finger inside?'

'No, never.'

'All right, forget about it then, you've got nothing to worry about.'

Azizeh was the first one of us to get married. When we went to congratulate her I was surprised by how much she had changed. She was no longer the shy, weak girl who didn't talk very much, and even when she did she would only talk about chaste love. It was confusing to me that marriage had given her this kind of strength and self-confidence even though she still didn't know the meaning of pleasure with her husband, didn't know much of anything at all. She walked over to me with a cup of coffee on the serving tray and whispered in my ear, a rosy smile on her face as if she had just survived an exam, just discovered she was virtuous and unbroken, and said, 'Turns out I'm a virgin, Nahla. You can't believe how happy I am!'

Azizeh celebrated losing her virginity but also told me how much it hurt.

The pain that I experienced on my own wedding night was partly from my thinking about how religion helped me to endure it, even diminished it somewhat, but in those moments I felt sorry for the man who was mounting me the way he would mount a beast of burden, struggling to jam his penis inside me and achieve victory.

That's the way my husband seemed to me on our wedding night.

After he was finished with me I fantasized about Hani's hand reaching out to caress my body and help me fall asleep. Bit by bit I recalled his scent, rising up with it to sleep, but falling asleep alongside my husband instead.

When Hani learnt that I had got married he left for Paris. He had had enough of the war that seemed like it was going to last for a long time.

In late 1975 Hani took off in an old beat-up Volkswagen, travelling overland, without even calling me to say goodbye. On their journey they stopped in many different cities and saw a lot of different things. All that he took with him was a small suitcase packed with clothes and the audiocassettes that we together used to listen to, with songs by Abdel Halim Hafez, Fairouz, Warda, Abdel Wahab and Umm Kulthum, especially her song 'Memories'.

Passing through those cities he thought about all the time he had spent with me, the image of my face was never far from his mind, as he told me later. He would imagine I was right there in front of him: my smile, my hair, my devilishness, and even the way I sounded, my affection for him. Whenever he and his friend stopped somewhere to rest and have something to eat he felt like a film actor, as if everyone around him was watching.

He talked with his friend, the one who was driving, about how devastated he was on my wedding night. He spent days

114

wandering the streets muttering to himself and when he came home he shut his bedroom door behind him, he didn't want anyone to bother him by asking what was wrong.

By the time the car had left the Lebanese border behind, he felt an emptiness in his chest, not simply that he had no heart, but no ribs, no ribcage at all. He felt an absence in that part of his body; he only felt like he had all his ribs intact when we were together.

6

'I'm no martyr for love, Suad,' I told her one day at the City Café. She was my other half, independent of me yet always prepared to offer a consoling hand. Suad smiled like someone who knew me well but her eyes soon locked onto the waiter who greeted us and then took particular interest in her, which caused her eyes to shine, her hunched shoulders to straighten up in a way they hadn't for a long time.

Suad turned back towards me after realizing that I was referring to a sixty-year-old man sitting at a nearby table who had caught my eye. I had seen him a few days earlier sitting at a table just inside the main entrance, a pipe in his mouth, some newspapers and magazines in front of him, everyone entering and leaving the cafe was saying hello to him. I left without looking at him even though he was staring right at me from behind his glasses, didn't pay him any mind that day because I was still so hung up on what an idiot I had been when I met a young man at Hoda's house, a relative of hers who was many years younger than me. I had been very bored, my eyes were distant and hollow. My desire to shock my body back to life had gotten the better of me, convinced me to stop thinking about Hani. During the long time he had been away all I could think about was a phantom dancing against my lips, like poetry I used to read to Suad and then hide away inside me once again. Only poetry could bring me back to life. It seemed as if I had lost all my bones, my body was desiccated by yearning for him, hardly able to absorb the acidity of silly little things that happened but that I gulped down along with my saliva. I was afraid of my desire for him that pulsed inside me like a mute beam of light when I lay in bed alongside my husband.

Still I don't know why I agreed so quickly to go home with that young man. When we got there he left me to wait in the living room while he went to the bathroom, took a shower, and came out wearing a white terrycloth robe that exposed his penis, the smirk on his face suggesting that he thought this would turn me on. The sight of him was appalling and nauseating. I picked up my purse and started to leave, intending never to return his calls. What he said to me before I could even open the door was even more revolting.

'Where do you think you're going? You were so quick to come over, hold on now, why don't you get me off real quick.'

I had the same feeling at the City Café with Suad when I caught the eye of this sixty-something man. I placed my book of poetry down on the table in a way that would attract his attention, then told Suad not to move it until I got back from the bathroom. Smiling to myself I started to spin out the conversation we might have. When I came back to the table, making like I was getting ready to leave, he came over to us, stared right at me, and said, 'That book has a beautiful title.'

'Well, please, why don't you take this copy.'

'Aren't you going to inscribe it for me?' he asked as he picked it up. 'Actually, just write down your phone number because I'm leaving the country, and as soon as I get back I'll give you a call. You'll have to excuse me for being so direct.'

I hesitantly wrote down my number on the last page, telling him, 'You should know, I'm married.'

We saw each other several times. My repressed feelings of love towards Hani flared up, something inside me had been ignited. The strange thing was that as soon as I started to write a poem, Hani would immediately come to mind, as if it was through poetry that I was trying to kickstart my feelings for him, as if I was trying to conjure him every time I put my hands on another man.

When I published a poem in the paper, Suad told me this man would find out that it wasn't for him as soon as he read it, that it had nothing to do with him whatsoever.

I told Suad many times that I'm no martyr for love. Often she would inquire about the secret of my intermittent dalliances.

It's true that I would tell her how I wanted my body to be rejuvenated, to be as free as possible, and I wasn't lying when I said that, but the secret of my clandestine encounters remained opaque to me. Was I being led around by my desire, unable to say no to my body, even though it had disobeyed me since adolescence? Was I retreating inside in order to resist my desire for Hani? Or was I trying to exact revenge from a relationship that was inevitably going to end?

Now that I had fallen back in love with Hani in middle age, the answer wasn't all that clear to me either. Was it because I was clinging to a passing desire now that death had become a constant visitor? Or because in middle age we come to realize what our bodies actually want, these bodies that are no longer capable of lying, that they no longer yield to us because they have become capable of refusing what they don't want, loyal instead to their own mood, choices, voice and feelings?

I repeatedly told Suad about my casual relationships, about how I got to know more than a few men in my life. To me they were misguided experiments, just flings, really. But those relationships made my body even more drawn to Hani, made my connection to him even stronger, because our knowledge of the body is only accomplished with the help of the people we love, which is why, even though I felt another, different kind of love for those other men (no relationship resembles any other), they were nothing but visitors to my body. Hani, by contrast, was its only resident.

My body wasn't free with those other men, it didn't get very far with their bodies, the way that it vibrated with Hani was different, its pleasure was real because of the depth of our love, which allowed my body to truly know his, for his body to truly know mine. Hani also told me that he had been with many different women without discovering his own body, that the only way he could find affection for it was through his relationship with me, which had a different flavour altogether when we fell back in love with each other in middle age.

The last time we saw each other he told me that he had started to feel like his hands were actually present, and that ever since I had described to him how beautiful his large hands and long fingers were he started to care about clipping his fingernails often and carefully. Sometimes he would just start staring at them while he was at home, observing the details of those fleshy rolls sagging under his belly as he grew soft and old. He wasn't ashamed because I would kiss him all over and say nice things about his body. He'd gaze into the mirror at his flabby pecs even as I passionately rubbed them.

My relationship with Saleem was totally different.

***

Saleem's phone conversation with my brother Jawad lasted a long time, as he paced back and forth in the living room in his sweaty white T-shirt and shorts. The two of them were discussing the results of their medical examinations, exchanging the names of the medicines each was taking for their prostrate and diabetes and blood pressure and cholesterol and so on, as I looked the other way watching the nightly news broadcast, waiting for Suad to come over for dinner.

I stole a glance at him from behind, burrowing my eyes into his broad back and the fleshy masses bunched around his waist, his skinny legs with flaccid muscles. I was gripped by the feeling that his body was beat-up, not because he had lived in it but from the amount he had used it.

The same feelings came over me when he was in bed sleeping next to me, before I moved to my own private bedroom after my children got married.

The truth is I never hated Saleem nor felt any malice towards him. I did feel spite for him when I believed that he had raped me while I was pregnant with Faten. The sense that there was a life growing inside of me interrupted my willingness to take things lying down. The most difficult side effects were strange cravings, nausea, lack of desire, and feelings of disgust. I don't know why I detested his scent so much, for it wasn't a vile odour, it had never put me off in normal times. Throughout my pregnancy, I would go nuts as soon as he set foot in the house, I would feel the urge to throw up whenever he came near me or opened his dresser or if I got near one of his shirts. Not only did I avoid going into his room but I would no longer sit with him in any room at all. He constantly took showers to try to satisfy me, but it was in vain because I still couldn't stand the smell of him when he came close. Throughout my pregnancy the feeling in me grew that this man was playing with my body whenever he got near me, that his looks could reach inside me, penetrate me and turn me into an object just by looking at me. Even as my face turned angelic and I became more beautiful, I also got very skinny. My body started to look like a skeleton.

I'll never forget this one time when we were talking about the pain that only women can experience and I told Suad that everything in our bodies has something to do with pain and timing: from puberty, periods and hymens to childbirth, abortion, craving certain foods during pregnancy, breastfeeding and menopause, even sexual intercourse becomes part of the pain, as if it were one of its limbs, as if there was no love and no life without pain. I'd add to that list my love for Hani, which became part of the pain in my body.

I never felt, not for one day, any kind of intimacy with Saleem's body. I would always say that he doesn't lack anything as far as I'm concerned, except when it comes to his body, his boxy frame, and his big head that sits on his fat and strikingly short neck.

Even before he began to suffer from chronic sexual dysfunction, it didn't feel like there was another body there when I slept with him. Sometimes it seemed like he had borrowed his body from another man, it looked odd on him, he was perplexed by it, couldn't comprehend its sensations, nevertheless he wanted to enjoy it however he could for as long as he had it.

Sometimes it would occur to me that I loved him because of his kindness and generosity, especially the way he always helped my family financially, paying for my mother and my grandmother Amina's medical bills before they died. He also promised to pay for Jawad's children's education. But now I feel differently and would say this wasn't love between a man and a woman in the conventional sense.

It never felt like I was betraying Saleem even though I was constantly doing so. Instead, whenever I came home after having seen Hani I felt like I had stolen money from him, as if I had opened up his briefcase and pilfered whatever I could find, maybe because of my perpetual feeling that there was capital to be spent. But I still don't know why my eyes would spontaneously well up with tears that would then stream down my face as I became overwhelmed by the thought that he knew about my relationship with Hani, or at least that he had some suspicions. And yet, I don't know why I would continuously refuse to call my feelings for him love.

'What are you talking about?' Suad asked. 'You know there isn't a single Arab man in the world who knows that his wife's cheating on him and remains silent.'

I nodded and returned to the matter at hand, telling her that love can't last long when there's uncertainty or suspicion, love makes us cry like nothing else, makes us cry from its own abundance. My crying out of fear for my husband differs from the way I cry sometimes from the intensity of my longing for Hani. I don't do that out of weakness. Even if that were the case, it wouldn't diminish my unconditional emotional generosity towards him or any such balance sheet for feelings. I can feel how much I love him when I'm crying, when I let my emotions come washing over me, which makes me feel as though I'm submerged and drowning in them.

Many times I asked her what to call this kind of love that tears me apart inside and makes me feel alive at the same time. Am I meant to be with Hani the same way my mother believed she was consecrated to that sheikh, the way he could look at her and pigeonhole her in the blink of an eye just like any other woman who promised herself to him? My God, what's the name for that kind of love? I ask God all the time, every day when I'm praying, the way all women in love speak to God.

Why do I love him so much? I often asked Suad. Is it because love had long been forbidden to me? Or because our love had been interrupted? Or was it my feeling of guilt for having been unable to defend this love when confronted by my mother and brother? Or had it become a symbol of rebellion

122

against my upbringing and my past? Or was it simply because love existed at all, a warm part of life, and because I didn't believe in anything other than my body, my heart and my desire?

Maybe love is all of that, passion and healing, Suad replied.

That night, while we were having dinner at my house, I told her what I told Hani: we were bound to each other in body and spirit. I asked him if he thought it was a coincidence that my name is Nahla and his Hani. Don't you see how the letter *h* is trying to escape and get ahead of the *n* in mine, don't you see the *h* comes before the *n* in your name, arching its neck? Just look at the difference in the relationship between the letters in our names, it makes me feel that my name is hiding inside yours.

When we saw each other after a long period apart I told him I was hiding inside his name and that he had been hiding inside mine the whole time we didn't see each other. That was the reason I couldn't forget about him, because we never forget about the things we keep hidden inside.

I told Suad, told her all of my secrets. I read out loud what I wrote in my diaries. When I was with her I'd freely share my conflicted, contradictory feelings. Those were the only moments in which I truly felt there was a possibility of Hani being a part of my life, as if all of my wishes could come true.

***

My wish to see Hani came true in 1977, the first time I had seen him since I got married. I was eight months pregnant with my daughter Faten, and crossing between the two Beiruts had once again become possible after a ceasefire between East and West.

When the phone rang that afternoon I was surprised to hear his voice on the line. I was astounded actually, I couldn't believe it, and remained silent for a long time, I didn't have the strength to respond even after he said more than once that it was Hani calling and asked whether I was able to hear him. When I finally did answer he asked me if I was able to meet before he left for Paris, where he was going to continue his studies.

I agreed immediately, eager to see him, especially given that my husband was abroad at the time. Also, it was going to be my first time seeing him since I got married, and perhaps I would never see him again, so I told him, 'Sure, of course.' Then I fell back into silence and stopped listening to whatever he was saying, thinking to myself, what a pity! How could I agree to see him when I was eight months pregnant and my body weighed a ton? How was I going to see him with my belly as testament to my infidelity, to my having given up on him, to my surrender by consenting to marry someone else?

I heard him asking me again whether I could still hear him, if I was still on the line, and I snapped to attention to blurt, 'I've missed you, Hani. I want to meet, I wish we could meet right now, and tomorrow, and the day after, all the time.'

His familiar laugh rang in my ears. It sounded like the laughter of forgiveness and we made a plan to meet.

After hanging up, I started addressing my unborn daughter whom I was going to call Faten, asking for her forgiveness. Her existence in my womb made me think twice, caused me to hesitate before meeting Hani. I was afraid that a foetus was capable of hearing her mother's thoughts. I patted my stomach, starting to tear up, drew my mouth as close as I could to my stomach and whispered, 'Mama, God willing you'll be born and grow up, and then you'll be able to understand my predicament.'

The streets were nearly deserted when he pulled up in front of the popular seaside cafe along the Manara waterfront where we would go sometimes when we were in college, driving a car he had borrowed from his friend.

We didn't say much. He didn't touch my hand. I was having trouble breathing. I was tired and my face looked very puffy. We parked on a dark dirt road off the corniche. The crescent moon cast soft silver light that shone along the surface of the water but wasn't bright enough to illuminate our faces inside the car; the windows were covered with thin foam adhesive.

We were trapped in silence as the voice of Umm Kulthum singing 'Love Story' played in the tape deck, a song we loved listening to together before I got married. Stagnant feelings started to flow and fill me up inside, feelings that were like foreign oceans of intimacy washing over me. I leaned back against the headrest and closed my eyes, wishing I could place my hand in his and tell him it would be impossible for any melody or lyric to express the way I felt towards him. Music and song only help me inasmuch as your love for me can flow more easily and inasmuch as I can incline more and more towards you. I wished for him to tell me that he still loved me the way he used to, which got me all excited that he might say it again. Whenever he used to say that, I would lose my mind, unrestrained by anything other than the desire to hear him say *I love you.*

In that moment I wanted to tell him so many things but I didn't know how. As I sat next to him, touched by the madness of my love for him, I didn't know whether I was feeling comfort or fear, exhilaration or sorrow, the desire to weep or to jump for joy.

But we were frozen in silence under the moonlight until just then, when we were suddenly interrupted by the appearance of Palestinian fighters pointing their weapons in our faces.

Hani shook. He threw the car into reverse to get away from them as they opened fire into the air to try and get him to stop. When he didn't obey their command they shot up the tires. It seemed they might eventually shoot right at us. Fearing for my safety, Hani shoved me down onto the floor in a flash and then covered me with his own body in order to protect me. I couldn't breathe with him on top of me and I squealed in pain but Hani didn't pay any attention until the last bullet aimed at us ricocheted off the steering wheel and grazed his knee, wounding him slightly. They rushed in to interrogate us both. We understood from them that they were monitoring the place because a young woman had been found dead there the night before.

I made it home that night breathless from fright and exhaustion. I hugged and kissed my son Ahmad and then started to weep. What if I had been injured? How would my son be able to survive and grow up without me? My discovery that Hani still loved me as much as before made me cry even more bitterly. His love was more powerful than his fear of death or bullets. He would have given his life to protect me. I'll never forget what he said to me that day: 'If I get hurt, it's no big deal. The important thing is you and your life. Your life has value and must be protected. We got out of there by a thread, by our love I'd say. Now you should go and pray.'

When I got up in the middle of the night to drink some water and saw the militiaman on the calendar that Suad had given me after donating to one of their organizations, I began screaming and crying once again. As I imagined this fedayee opening fire at me, I jumped out of bed, ran over to the wall and tore the calendar down.

Tears were running down my face when Hani left the country. I was afraid but I kept that to myself. It's true I wasn't seeing that much of him, but at least he was still in the country. Now he was being ripped away from me, those Western countries were going to steal him away from me forever. Mean-while, I realized that he was the one who had disappointed me this time, not I him, and this made me feel a little better. But I still couldn't stop crying.

The hero of our encounter was fear. I couldn't seem to get enough of him and he couldn't get enough of me. There were so many things I wanted to say, I'm still not sure why my tongue got all tied into knots. In the car I stared at him intently as he gazed up at the moon, listening to Umm Kulthum, wishing I could devour every last detail and store them somewhere inside me. It felt like years might go by before I would see him again.

7

I switched off the light and lay down on the bed, quickly pulled off my underwear, closed my eyes, and surrendered to his kisses.

His sweat was beady and fresh. It felt hot and sticky against my body, shimmered against both of our bodies like stars in the night.

His warm touch caused the blood to surge through my veins, his kisses ignited my passion, and my body rebelled by giving in to my volcanic desire. He was on top of me with his eyes shut, his large hands scrambling ecstatically all over my body.

He used to appear to me in my dreams but now he was here, flesh and blood, kissing me in my own bedroom, in my marital bed. Now that Saleem had gone I was all alone with him. His hands and his mouth found their way all over my body, activating all my senses. The more I felt as though I was going to collapse underneath him, the more I seemed to soar up into the sky.

I never felt like I was cheating on Saleem. I didn't think about him at all.

All I could smell was Hani, the depression of his clavicle glistening in front of me. I heard the sound of my voice saying,

'My pussy,' repeating it several times as I begged him to enter me so that he would come the way he always asked me to do whenever we were together. A wave of convulsions swept me away before my body's storm abated.

When I opened my eyes there was nobody in the room: night, stillness, silence. My finger was still inside of me. I glanced around the room nervously when I realized I had been masturbating.

Those fantasies didn't go away after I broke off my relationship with Hani and got married. Sometimes, when I was alone, I would close my eyes, purse my lips together in the shape of a gun barrel, hold my breath and then release it as quickly as I could. It felt as though they were his breaths, and the fingers of my right hand would become his fingers. I'd wet them with my saliva and touch my nipples, feeling like he was the one touching me, as if I was on top of him or underneath him, and I would no longer need to shut my eyes. He became my eyes. I aimed my hot breath at his chest, using my hand until the warmth of his flesh spread all over my body.

I had always dreamt of having a child with him.

Once I dreamt I had given birth to him. I was in awe as I began to examine his shape while he was still in the doctor's hands after emerging from my womb.

Another time I dreamt I had given birth to a little blonde girl, that we were living together in a house I had never seen before. I held the baby in my hands and told him, 'Look, Hani, this is your daughter.'

His imposing presence and the sense that he was there with me made me feel good, but this could also make me feel bad if it was all in my mind, which would lead me to banish the thought. That banishment seemed impossible until I saw him again in 1978, when he came back to Beirut for Christmas and

New Year's. Our relationship came roaring back to life, which convinced him to stay in Lebanon for the rest of the year.

Our bodies got to know one another better that year, each one seeming to take up permanent residence inside the other, there was no doubt they were fellow travellers in desire.

I try to remember so many things, but all in vain.

It's as if my memory is at the top of a steep mountain, and every time I try to scale it I fall back down before reaching the top. I pick myself up and try to climb the mountain again. Like dark worms dropping from tree branches I slither back towards the top but to no avail.

There are still memories that float back up to the surface from time to time, but it's impossible for me to remember anything else. Now I can recall how I wrote about that meeting in my diary and read what I had written to Suad. After hearing about the second time we said goodbye she placed her hand against her chest the way she would whenever she was annoyed, as if she were searching for something inside herself, and then she would fall silent. It was always like that. Whenever she got excited she wouldn't say anything, as if she had lost the power of speech, as if she were gradually but fruitlessly trying to compile her own vocabulary.

That morning I was drinking coffee on the balcony. The rain seemed to be speaking, its droplets tapping against the window frame like falling tears, rain that seemed to be reciting light, rhythmic prayers before getting blown and redirected elsewhere by a soft wind. Staring out at the rain I thought about how life reveals the secrets of its moisture, duration and decline. As soon as the rain stopped, my eyes caught sight of a new flash of light, a flash that could only be a sudden lightning strike.

Suad came to see me that morning and I read her the poem I had written the night before. When I was finished, she looked at me with her sparkling black eyes and luminous smile, surprising me when she asked, 'You know Hani's here, right?'

'Here, where?' I asked her, my face turning yellow.

'I saw him yesterday at the Rawda Café. I said hello.'

'What was he doing there? When did he get here? Who was he with?'

Questions tumbled out of me until I couldn't speak any more, and I changed the subject, afraid of hearing something I wouldn't like, and I started rambling about my children, my words as disoriented as my thoughts.

Less than two days later I got a phone call from Hani. He said he had wanted to call but had been unable. How could you be in Beirut and not see me? I asked.

I met him at a little café in the city where none of our acquaintances ever went. Seeing him again after such a long time made me feel like my soul had returned to my body. As soon as I sat down across from him at the table, I felt the blood rushing through my heart. My cheeks turned red, pinkness shone in my ears and on the tip of my nose. We talked about his studies, my children, the war. We were trying to talk about anything but our relationship.

Then we started walking without a destination, without a care, roaming without seeming to remember that both of us were married. I didn't ever want to go home again. The whole time I imagined we were holding hands even though we weren't.

That was the first time I ever came home late without telling my husband why. Before saying goodbye we agreed to meet again soon, or at least to be in touch, although we avoided meeting again right away, both of us coming up with different excuses. A few times I hid behind the fact that one of my children or my husband was sick, while other times he claimed he had meetings he couldn't get out of. The truth of the matter was that during many of our phone calls he was the one who said he couldn't meet.

I was confident that he loved me as much as I loved him. I never doubted that. But I also knew that he was afraid of our relationship going back to the way it had been, to say nothing of my own fear of the same, although I would occasionally ask myself whether he would ever come back to me just to take revenge on my marriage, or on me for having abandoned him when he had wanted me to wait for him. He was never capable of taking that step, never knew for certain whether his feelings towards me were true love or a passing fling, as he would tell me much later.

After weeks of hesitating he gave me the address of his friend in the Sanayeh neighbourhood, a friend who was now living in Paris and had left him a key to the apartment.

On the way to meet him there for the first time, I thought about how he was going to open the door, where I might kiss him, that I could fall asleep on his shoulder, and whether his body would remain in an unnatural state of excitement.

I sat trepidatious in the living room, my body turned inward, my eyes glued to the wall or bouncing around the room without looking right at him. When he came closer and pulled me towards the bedroom, I started to follow him without thinking. But as soon as I reached the bed and sat down on the edge, the warm desire in my hands turned ice cold and I told him I was freezing in spite of the summer heat, pretending to not feel well, and to be turned off by the thought of any sexual encounter between us. After promising to call him soon, I left. Walking home I felt as though I was swallowing broken glass as I choked back my own saliva. I had the overwhelming desire to sleep with him but I hadn't been able to.

What if I wasn't capable of ever giving him up? What about my family? Or what if the sexual encounter was just a feeling that needed to be retrieved so that the whole thing could be over?

As I headed back there the following week I didn't imagine any particular scene for the encounter, expecting that whatever happened was going to be entirely improvised.

My body was in a state of anticipation, without any specific expectations, as if I had been trained to be responsive and hopeful, without any caution or any suspicion.

His eyes were raging like a wildfire, a beacon of desire that made it seem like he was going to consume me, his hunger becoming more pronounced as he got hard as soon as he opened the door and I went inside.

Our time together that year was a storm.

I would peel off my clothes and stand naked in front of the mirror for a long time before going to meet him, examining my once-fit body and my marble skin as if I was going to see him without anything on. During those encounters I noticed how he wouldn't really pay attention to what I was wearing, but sensed that he could somehow see my underwear. Sometimes I would start smiling right there in my car seat when I tried to come up with a good reason why I shouldn't just start taking my clothes off and walk in naked. As soon as I knocked on the door and walked inside he would start taking off my clothes, then begin to undress himself, and I would reach out my hand to start unbuttoning his shirt even as he pulled down my skirt or my pants. Our hands carried out their missions with such great enthusiasm that it became impossible to tell who was taking off whose clothes. As soon as our clothes had been thrown off we would pull back a little in order to see the other one undressed, and then moved to the bed.

It was the first time we had sex.

In the moment I gave him my body it felt as though I was revealing a secret.

On that first day our relationship started back up again, I couldn't tell whether the tears I shed, which he couldn't see in the darkness while he was on top of me, were tears of joy over our being together or tears of sadness because I would have to be apart from him again, or some combination of the two.

It didn't feel as if I was giving him my body or that he was taking something away from me, more like he was introducing me to my own body and I was introducing him to his own. When he got on top of me and told me he desperately wanted to come inside me and get as close as possible to my womb, I gasped deeply and then grinned, tugging hard on his grey whiskers and pulling him towards me.

As he talked to me in bed, his voice became all of my senses. When he touched me, his hand became the whole world.

His chest was warm. I pressed my fingers against the few hairs that had not yet turned white, his whiskers that he used to shave when we were in college in order to please me even though they would just grow back even thicker. His pores were like windows through which I could hear the sound of a loving wind.

It was in those encounters that I came to understand my own feelings, the same way I now know that flowers can never bloom in silence, without making a sound.

I believed that the hairs covering him were proof of his manhood, an indicator of masculinity; they seemed like lilies, their pods blossoming all along the length of his slender body, and because he was so thin I thought of his body as a watery expanse irrigating those lilies, creating a sound for them, as if they were singing. At some point, those hairs became little kamanchehs playing a beautiful melody.

The musicality of the senses astounded me in those moments.

I had always known that fingers can do many things, play musical instruments, for example. But I never realized that they can also play a beautiful, audible melody on the body. I used to believe that the function of the eye is to see, that it might be capable of speaking or being silent, but I never considered the possibility that it could sing, that it could produce sound and melody. I used to believe that ears could hear love coming out of lips, even when closed, but my ears started to hear every-thing, including the ecstasy and susurrations of my body.

That day we were sprawled out in bed when he shared his desire to live inside my womb: the same desire he had been expressing to me for a very long time. He went on to say other things about the womb that I'll never forget. He described it as an empty space where a man can practise the art of build-ing, which includes the pleasurable act of getting a woman pregnant, the place from which a man emerges at birth in order to return there and then occupy it in a different way, granting him both existence and meaning, where he can be an active force and not a weakling. By returning there, he feels like an owner, a sovereign. A human being, Nahla, he said, is fated to relive the experience, but only as a consequence of a submerged desire to be at the scene of the action, which is why the space that he leaves behind in the womb when he departs also becomes his location for rebuilding.

When he revealed to me those feelings about the womb, I said things I would never say to my husband, things I would only ever tell Suad.

135

From the moment my doctor told me I was pregnant and through the entire time I was carrying my daughter Faten, the world faded away. The strange thing, Hani, is that you were the farthest thing from my mind back then, even if you did show up in my dreams. When I went in for my gynaecological exams, monitoring things on the screen in front of me, my womb did look like a wide open space, as if it were the universe of my femininity, the thing that truly made me special, an entire planet inside me, Hani, one that seemed to contain lightning and thunder, atmospheric disturbances, where it could feel as if it were going to rain, I could almost hear the crashing peals of thunder coming out of the monitor.

I thought long and hard about the nature of that mysterious space inside me, if it was a sky and what I was seeing were lights and clouds, or if it was a sea and what I was hearing was the pounding surf. I wondered whether the foetus growing inside of me was comfortable with the sound she was hearing or whether she was annoyed by it considering the fact that her sense of hearing was the most developed at that phase. I was overwhelmed, Hani, with complex feelings as I thought about that bounded and protected aqueous sphere where she was floating.

He hugged me after that conversation, telling me he wanted to have a child with me.

The whole way back I felt as though I was going home without a body or a soul. But from the moment I walked inside the house my face regained its old, composed features, the blankness to which my husband and children had become accustomed. Submission helped me to redraw that noncommittal smile I would tear off whenever I was with Hani, a sign of how happy I was just to be with him, a smile from the heart, a smile that became unfamiliar to me the same way I became a stranger to my own appearance whenever we were apart.

The same smile that would grow taut across my face whenever I was with him would go slack when I was at home. My eyes used to dart around the outside world whenever I was with him but would later turn inwards once again. Without even noticing, I would rub my eyes as if to make sure they were still there, feeling as though they had dropped inside my skull.

***

My happiness with him changed the rhythm of my body, altered my entire appearance.

After the last time we were together that year his face remained suspended in front of my eyes for a long time.

After a long silence he surprised me with the news that while he was at university in Paris he had met a young Lebanese woman named Sawsan, that she and her family had welcomed him, stood by him, and that they were thinking about getting married.

The news hit me like a bolt of lightning. A question drifted across my eyes before my tongue could force it out of my mouth.

'Okay, if that's the case, what do you want with me? And why did you want to see me again? I don't understand what's happening, Hani . . .'

I wasn't able to get out everything I wanted to say. Drowned in my tears, I didn't know quite what to say exactly.

'Come on, Nahla,' he replied. 'We've got to be realistic. You're married. This girl's nice, decent, and she loves me. I think I could be with her.'

'Well, if we're talking about decency, my husband's a decent person, too, he's good to me and to my family. He has a special place in my heart, which is to say, I love him, I don't hate him. But with you it's something different. I can't imagine you getting married, I can't imagine not being with you. I can't bear the thought, it drives me crazy. Anyway, if she loves you ten per cent as much as I do, your mother's sure to bless this marriage. But you know something, Hani? Your mother doesn't love you as much as I do. As they say, though, the love you give comes back around.'

'I do love her. And I dream about being with you. You're the love of my life. You know that. Do you want to go and do something crazy, though, turn your whole life upside down? Could you just leave your husband and your children to be with me? Think about it while I'm here. If not, this'll be the second time you let me go.'

That last sentence plunged into my heart like a knife. I couldn't listen to anything more he had to say, I had to leave the house, so I hopped in the first shared taxi I could find, barely able to spit out the address for the driver. My voice had been throttled.

As soon as the car took off I burst into tears. I couldn't hold back the tears, they unstoppably cascaded down my cheeks, like a salty river. It was terrifying, as if the pressure of the flow was going to burst, as if my tears couldn't dry up until their source was cut off, until I was completely dehydrated. My tears were accompanied by a violent gasp that the driver heard, causing him to look at me in the rear-view mirror and ask, 'Please, miss, is there anything I can do to help? It hurts me to see those pretty eyes crying so much. It's tearing up my heart.'

'Do you have children? They can be such a pain,' I told him, still sobbing.

He told me he had five children but didn't say anything about them.

Stealing glances at me in the rear-view mirror from time to time, he then told me what torture it was to be with his wife.

'What can I tell you, miss. Akhh, akhh. I have a wife who won't let me near her. When she gets into bed she always complains that she's not feeling well. I mean I don't get any you-know-what except maybe once a year. I mean I can smell but I can't taste, not even when I'm nice and try to get close to her. Her heart is closed, I'd say its wooden and all dried out.'

I didn't hear anything more of what the driver said. His voice grew fainter in my ears until I could only hear the sound of my own thoughts instead.

I realized right then that I was going to cut off my relationship with Hani once and for all. How could I just leave my kids behind? Would I ever be able to make a decision like that?

Every moment of Faten and Ahmad's development was etched in my memory. How could they mature any further without my own two eyes bearing witness? Would I even have forearms any more if Ahmad wasn't sleeping on one and Faten wasn't nodding off on the other? The two of them were like dreams on each of my arms. What would happen to my arms without the two of them, when I ceased to embrace them, once they had grown up and moved away, when I too grew up and started sleeping alone, a more restful sleep without my husband's odour and his nauseating habits, perhaps?

Still, how can I live without the scent of their childhood?

In the car I remembered when my daughter took her first step, which was also the moment I grasped the true meaning of fear. When I monitored her, it was as if I were holding onto her with my eyes, as if looking at her was equal to supports that could hold her up and help her take the first few steps without falling down.

139

I remembered the way I would check the children's breathing before they went to sleep in order to make sure they were in good health, tracking their breathing while they slept in order to determine whether the rate increased or slowed down. Knowing they were all right made me feel good.

Even if I allowed myself to forget all of that, how could I forget about the dream my son told me he had had the week before, when he got out of bed and ran over to me, taking shelter in my embrace, unable to stop crying for a long time. When I asked him why he was crying, he could only respond in long gasps until he was finally able to calm down and say, 'Mama, please don't go away, I don't want you to die. I'm afraid of being alone. How can I live all by myself without you?'

I had to recover from my stupefaction before I was able to ask him desperately, 'Why would you say something like that?'

He told me he dreamt I was a candle that was melting and then got extinguished. When he tried to grab hold of the candle there was nothing there. He was just holding his two empty hands. He looked all over the house for me. It was all just a dream but he couldn't find me.

He didn't say another word before breaking into tears once again.

I imagined my son, now a married man, back then, sad and alone. That day it seemed to me, were it not for me, he and his sister would be poor and weak . . . unprotected.

I felt there was a strong rope tethering me to my children that was more powerful than any other bond of love, a rope that was infinitely soft yet stronger than iron. How would I ever be able to untie that?

I cried harder and harder as I sat in the car, contemplating the possibility that I might never see them again. But at the same time I wished the tyres would spin in reverse and take me back to Hani. As the car sped along, I wondered, what if my heart could be the car's GPS?

When I got out of the car the driver shouted at me, 'What about my money, sister?'

I walked back to pay him his fare. Then I went inside, imagining the sight of Hani when he could no longer bear to listen as I told him we had to stop seeing each other. But as I walked away he remembered the mountain he once saw as a little boy when he was out with his father. It was a stormy winter's night and the wind sounded like a shrieking madman. As he gazed up at the mountain beyond their village, he clutched his father's hand in fear and wondered whether the storm could knock the mountain down. That night he dreamt the mountain split open and a chunk of it about to come tumbling down. He moved closer to the mountain, pushed against a stone, and felt the rock crumble into bits. He felt the exact same way in the moment before confronting me, the exact same fear. As I walked away his smile seemed sad and sarcastic, as if he were saying to himself that his fear back then had been childish. My God, those childhood fears have come back, gripping him in this moment, the same fear that led him to believe the mountain was splitting open. The only difference is that now it's him instead of the mountain.

. . . At least that's what he told me much later.

8

I used to read Suad everything I wrote. The look on her face was inscrutable and full of secrets when she listened to me. I'd gaze into her eyes, which got all dry as they sat transfixed in her skull, devoid of light, like two small empty pits. I always wondered why she stared at me like that, so blankly and strangely. I wondered whether she was concealing her own desire to write or whether she really was writing but didn't want to me know about it. What could she have been writing that was so secret that she didn't want me to know, though? Could she have been writing down everything I read to her or was she keeping secrets because silence had become her last refuge? Or did it only seem to me that she had started writing since she turned into a pair of ears that just listened to me? Where was the beauty that used to radiate from her face when we were in college?

I don't know what happened to her, what her husband may have done to her. I find her submission to her husband so odd, it seems to shrink her body and her very existence, something so strange for a college professor, who should be able to handle anything.

She used to complain to me about how he had spoiled her early on in their marriage but no longer said anything more than 'What's the matter with you?' and 'Get out of my face, move it!'

I know that her loyalty to me is unconditional. Azizeh and Nadine and Hoda constantly make fun of her for that. She likes to describe our relationship as having many shades when in fact there is only one colour in the life we share. But I must admit she's extremely important to me. When I think about something as simple as cooking, for example, I don't choose what I like or what my husband and my children like, thinking first and foremost about what she would like instead. What I cook most often are mulukhiya and yoghurt, her favourites.

One day she came to see me before noon, carrying a large bag, her narrow face too small for the broad smile that stretched across it. When I asked her what she had with her, she didn't answer, instead saying hello to Azizeh who had come by to giggle and talk about her relationships. Suad and I listened to her say, 'No, no, no . . . I don't go out with old men for money any more, not even if they're hot, I don't think about them any more. I can't even remember all the men I've slept with recently. When I see one of them, I want to see his cock right away, to know what it looks like. I mean, I tell him to take his clothes off and stand there naked in front of me. If he doesn't look good I send him packing. What really turns me on is a straight penis that stands right up when it gets hard. The other day there was this young guy who really did it for me. I was just feeling horny. But when I saw how thin his dick was, in a way that didn't seem to match his body, forget it, I just wasn't into him any more.'

As I tumbled onto my back in laughter, Suad's face turned all gloomy, like a cloudy sky, neither embarrassed by nor opposed to what she was hearing, but because emptiness had seeped through her ribs while she was in bed the night before, causing her to lock away her desire, transforming it into mummies underneath her splotchy skin.

After we had finished our coffee and Azizeh had got everything off her chest, a smile crept across Suad's face, indicating she had good news to share. She handed me the bag she was holding and then watched me open it in order to see my reaction.

Inside there was a brown envelope that contained a copy of *Love in the Time of Cholera* by Gabriel Garcia Márquez. Thumbing through it I was surprised to find that Hani had written me a note on the first few pages, which were blank except for the title. My hands started to tremble before I even began reading it. What did Hani have to say to me after such a long break from our relationship?

My dearest Nahla,

I just finished reading this novel and I find myself driven to write you a note without even thinking. The novel has given me back some hope that we might yet again sail on a ship of love that I hope will arrive someday. No, I'm sure it will. You were the dream of my youth, and you've remained the dream of all my days since. I wanted you in the past, I want you now and forever. You're my life preserver. Your hands are my life's safety net, the net they put under the tightrope at the circus. I never wanted to hide from you. I know I'll never try to hide from you. You're my water and thirst. You're my fullness and constant hunger. You'll always be my ocean and my ship, in these times, for all time. I want you, before reading this novel and ever after. I want more from you than is humanly possible, from your body and your spirit, because you are my body and my spirit. I want all that's possible from the breaking dawn that is your smile. My dawn and my smile. I want you in your fullness, all of you. I yearn for the years you have already lived and those yet to come. I want to rejuvenate my ancient, eternal desire to live in your womb, to return to myself and to life. My desire, and O how I desire everything about you, you alone with whom I discovered this thing called love. I want to melt into your lips, into the softness of your inner thighs. I want to disappear into the timbre of your voice, your silence and your language, into the colour of your skin, marble, smooth and silky, into the flutter of your heart. I want to rest in the slumber of your lips and the wakefulness of your nipples. My unbridled desire for you is palpable, deep and overflowing, it fills up my heart. I'm jealous of myself for knowing you once upon a time, and I'll envy myself even more upon the arrival of our ship of love, which is going to come and take us far away. I'm so afraid, though, I'm trembling, at the thought of losing you again if it arrives but doesn't find us waiting for it . . .

At the end of the note he told me it was inevitable that we would find each other again, that he had no doubt he was going to take me away on that ship, but in a time without cholera, and that we would sail away together in a time of perpetual happiness.

That was in the early nineties, after the civil war had ended, when Hani had come back from Paris to study sociology at the university.

I had never read the novel before he sent it to me. I was sweating on that freezing-cold winter day as I read those feverish and infatuated words in his letter. My feelings for him had never been fully extinguished but now they came roaring back. Suad tenderly stroked my cat who was sitting comfortably on her lap.

My husband wasn't home. I reread the letter aloud to Suad, who then stood up and melodramatically handed me a tissue so I could wipe my nose that had swollen up from all of my weeping.

Tears came pouring out of me as I cracked a smile and began to read the novel. I had always been fascinated by ships, the cerulean sea underneath them and the blue sky up above. Most of my clothes were blue—my favourite colour. The first dress Hani ever saw me in was blue. In my mind ships always had some connection to love. I imagined that the stories he told were everlasting, carried here and there by ship, until the heroes disembarked.

When I was finished reading the novel, I reread the letters the hero sent to the heroine, then I reread some other passages, as though I were trying to hold on to everything that was reminiscent of Hani and me. I thought about how many years it would be until I reached the heroine's age, wondering whether it was reasonable for me to wait that long before seeing the ship, before we could sail off together into eternity?

When I closed my eyes, I had a vision of Hani and me aboard the ship. I felt whole and happy, having broken all my bonds and all my chains. I no longer felt anything but my own existence, the existence of Hani and me on the ship.

I remembered how vivid my feelings had been after finishing the novel, the resulting sense of certainty that I was eventually going to get him back. I imagined that all the details and the dialogue in the novel were a premonition of my own future, which allowed me to relax, to feel refreshed. And when I looked in the mirror the glimmer in my eyes was back.

After Hani returned from Paris, I avoided all the places we might bump into one another. Something wasn't right and I steered clear of those spots out of fear or so as to prevent any confusion or weakness. My decision to end the relationship was like a covenant I had made with myself.

When I ran into him unexpectedly at the Rawda Café last summer, I felt as though I was in another place altogether, somewhere like Heaven. I wished for all of my prior feelings to come true. But afterwards I felt as if he had picked up an eraser and started to disappear himself. I entertained the possibility that I was no longer in love with him.

All these decisions nagged at me millions of times, any time he tried calling me, every summer when he came back to Beirut and I didn't pick up the phone. But it was impossible for me to deny his existence altogether. He was always present inside of me, he had never really exited my body.

I used to ask Suad all the time: What would I do if he no longer existed?

It was a strange question, but one that recurred millions of times.

I had posed the question in the distant past, asked it again and again more recently, now, and on that day the letter arrived as well.

It was a strange thing, for me to imagine he no longer exists. But from a certain moment I convinced myself I had to seriously consider the possibility.

It was as if he truly hadn't existed for years anyway.

Was I responsible for obliterating his existence throughout those years when I would ask Suad what I was going to do in the solitude I had once so deeply desired, to live by myself, released, far away from him, with my husband and my children?

During that entire time I floated outside the swath of history and memory that had always kept me connected to him. The truth of the matter is that I never really thought about my own existence beyond his, never really thought about my own life beyond his. I violently reduced him to a window onto life. He wasn't just a window, though, sometimes he was life in all its fullness.

What I didn't realize at the time was how much I still loved him, at least, until I told Suad just a little while ago that, to whatever extent we love life, we also create a separate world where we can live again. I asked her whether Heaven and Hell were metaphors that we can actually experience while we're still alive.

'Lemme ask you something, Suad: when I die, will I stop loving Hani?'

'Go ahead and die, sister, give it a shot and let's find out!' Suad said, snickering.

I changed the subject and started talking about how much Nadine had changed, about her madness and how she had gotten caught up with Mirna and Dr Sahar.

After reading the novel I started wandering in and out of the house, buffeted by the desire to call and the instinct to not call him on the private phone line that he had scribbled on the last page of the book. My intense uncertainty paralysed me momentarily but I was impelled to dial the number, and we agreed to meet the next day at an out-of-the-way Beirut cafe.

I couldn't tell exactly when dawn broke or when the sun began to shine. All night I felt as if the darkness was a wall keeping me apart from him, one that I wanted to smash and sweep aside so that I could see him and he could see me.

After I got ready and headed out to meet him the next day I was eerily haunted by the ghost of Garcia Márquez. I found myself sitting behind the wheel, addressing myself or possibly the spirit when I said out loud, to nobody in particular: *Ahh, Garcia Márquez, you have foreseen the return of my love, but my goodness how you failed to describe it in all its detail. You couldn't reveal everything to me because my eyes are not your eyes, and my body reads other things than your body does. Love alone knows how to read properly.*

When I walked into the cafe and saw him sitting there, the feeling I had had on the way over there—that I had grown old, even though I was only in my late thirties and had managed to retain my figure, my looks and my vigour—immediately vanished. The feeling of age is so odd: it has neither logic nor foundation. I can recall when I turned eighteen I felt as if I were already old and washed up. Now I laugh at myself any-time I think of that. I always used to think of people in their forties and fifties as elderly, finding it strange that old people would say they were just kids. Now that's exactly how I see them, as if we carry the sense of youth with us from one age to the next, as if the older we get we forestall old age so that we'll never quite get there. It's strange, too, how my strength has returned ever since menopause, as though a woman who is not me is pushing herself out from inside. I never knew her before, neither man nor djinn had ever seen her, a pure, dif-ferent woman I whom came to know and who came to know me. I made my peace with her, just as I came to terms with myself and my body at every age. But she was somehow dif-ferent from the woman who used to emerge when I got my period every month, and sometimes it even felt like every week because of hormones, on which I had no say. When I told my girlfriends all of this one day as we sat in the Rawda Café, their faces turned to consternation. Hoda started talking about how heavy her period was in order to remind us that she was younger than us, boasting that she still got it every month. A friend of hers in her late sixties was also there with us, who told her it would stop eventually, and then went on to say how she used to get hot flashes whenever she put her hands against her face despite the fact that she had undergone a hysterectomy more than twenty years ago.

Hani was the only one who had been able to find me at every stage of my life, only he was able to help me get to know myself.

As soon as I had sat down across from him, I covered my face and neck with my hands, as though I were still a little girl, now afraid of him seeing how old I had become. The more I tried to avoid his gaze, the more my eyes bugged out of my head. As I chastised myself, telling myself to pull it together: that's enough, that's enough now. For an instant I heard the sound of birdsong in my heart. My face relaxed to the rhythm of those chirps as I saw the way he was looking at me, his handsome smile that he only showed sparingly, a safe and calm child smiling up at me, but one who could also become mischievous and devilish when staring at me with desire.

I stared right back at him. We fell into a silence that lasted for minutes, confusion and uncertainty plain on both of our faces. The way we were looking at one another suggested that each of us was searching for something familiar in the face of the other.

He was wearing a jacket that was too big for him, perhaps to make his shoulders appear broader than they were. His proud nose seemed to have lost some of its stature, falling over slightly. The three beauty marks on his neck were still there, and the arteries in his throat had become even redder. His hands were still as elegant as ever, although the veins had become a little more pronounced, and were meatier and thicker even though he had lost some weight. I couldn't stop looking at his hands, which had always fascinated me. I had a particular affection for them, wished to reach out and hold them, to recover their old, familiar sensation, to remember the goodbye I had said to them. Never again did I find the same warmth that I did in his hands.

I yearned to examine him with my hands the same way I was observing him with my eyes, as if my entire memory of being with him had been conjured in that moment through just those two senses alone.

His forehead was wider, more prominent, a bit puffy now that his hair had thinned. His skinniness and his protruding elbows reminded me of just how delicate he was, inspiring my tenderness and gentle feelings towards him.

He didn't look the way I had expected him to: I had assumed he would have gained weight, grown a paunch, gone flabby the way my husband had. There had once been faint crow's feet around his eyes but his face had never been grooved with wrinkles and lines the way it is today.

When he asked me why I was smiling, I said, 'Because you look exactly the way I imagined you would, how I expected you to be. Just the way I'd visualized.'

Before he had even responded, his gaze jolted me, electrified my body. I was overwhelmed, lost all sense of time. I couldn't regain my focus until I heard him say, 'My God. I never forgot your face, Nahla. I can always see you. But you've gotten older.'

'Of course I have. You have, too. But you men never seem to age that much, no? You know, sometimes I used to feel that your features were slipping away from me, like I no longer had eyes to see.'

'Seriously? Anyway, Nahla, it's true you've aged a bit, but you've only become more beautiful. I can still see that sweet and sad little girl inside of you. And that light in your eyes still shakes me to the core.'

His voice seemed to harbour a trace of love. It was not ancient, musty or rusty, but warm and fiery.

We talked and talked and laughed on that day, as if ten years hadn't come between us, as though it were the continuation of a conversation we'd started the day before.

When he left, I felt exactly the same way I did after he'd left me all those years ago. It felt like he had gathered up the entire conversation and placed it in an unlocked container; anytime I think of him the words come out on their own and zip into my ears, assaulting me, which allows him not only to remain with me but to have some measure of control over me as well. The second time I saw him, I said, 'You rogue, you've always known how to control me. It's as if you never left.'

The relationship we had in our early forties was beautiful beyond description. Nadine, Azizeh, Hoda and all of my girl-friends flattered me by saying that women are more beautiful when they're in love, hoping that I would crack and confess to them that our relationship had been rekindled.

Every time we met I felt that the world had conspired to bring us together. I used to wish our time together could be captured for all eternity in a single photograph.

***

The first time we reconnected physically, our bodies didn't feel like strangers; just the opposite, his body was still at home in mine. His scent generated new feelings deep inside me. His caresses across my back ignited my senses and swept away the cobwebs from my soul and my skin. His warm, pleasant voice was like a tranquillizer, softly guiding me from one state into another. When we were in bed together, I never knew where we might end up.

Our relationship became freer, possibly because we had become more aware of our feelings and our senses, as if we had co-written a book of love, page by page, word by word, letter by letter.

The sound of my voice filled the bed in a way it had never been filled before, like warm steam rising out of my mouth and my nose as I spoke, even if I had been breathing with my mouth closed underneath him at first, unable to swallow the breaths that had accumulated in my chest as it rose and fell. My silence distracted him and he wrapped his arms around me, squeezed me tenderly, asking me what the matter was. My silence frightened him, made him wonder whether I was thinking about my husband or someone else, whether I had drifted off somewhere far away, dreaming about something that had nothing to do with him. Hani never liked it when I was silent. He was more comfortable when my voice touched his body, turned him on, when it was his guide. My mouth and my hands led him. I'd place my hands wherever he wished as I kissed him, and he would do the same. But I asked even more of him—'I want more,' I would cry out, without any shame, realizing that when I owned my own body then I could possess his as well. In our embrace and the union of our bodies, it felt as though my waist, my hands and my neck, truly all the different parts of our bodies, were like letters turning, entwining, wrenching, hungering, yearning to touch and be intertwined, and that my womb was the Arabic letter *noon*—ن—opening its two arms to receive him.

We didn't stop talking after having sex. One time, as he held me, my head on his shoulder, he asked, 'Nahla, do you know how many words there are in Arabic for the male sex organ?'

'No, I don't.'

'A hundred and twenty. All describing its characteristics and its actions. Can you imagine?'

'Oh my goodness. Anyway, professor, the nectar of life comes from there. It's unbelievable how much Arabs glorify sex.'

'There are a lot of words for the female sex organ as well. But you know something, what scares me most is "the biter", the one who's supposed to bite the penis. I've always been terrified of that, and it isn't just me, it's all men.'

'Really? And what do wise men say about that, professor?'

'Well, my good lady, they say that a woman has ninety-nine places of desire in her body. I can't remember the source exactly. But they say that modesty prevents her from showing men how to get there, or even telling them about it.'

'What makes you think women know their bodies well enough to show men the way around them in the first place? Men don't leave them alone enough to explore. Women here have ten children and turn eighty without experiencing any pleasure.'

'I'm just saying, men would love to have the chance to find ninety-nine places of pleasure. They'd go crazy.'

Our relationship picked back up again for a year. I kept it hidden from my girlfriends. Suad was the only one I told everything, even what we did together in bed, until that day when my old friend named Maha returned from a conference in Europe. She told me she had started seeing Hani two months before and that she had strong feelings for him. Her eyes were wide open as she told me all about what it was like to sleep with him. Maha was a college friend of Suad's, a researcher in philosophy who attended a lot of conferences abroad. She was dark-skinned and lustful, with broad brown eyes, her sharp little nose resembled a kitten's, and she didn't smell good or bad, but pungent, in a way that lingered in your nostrils.

It was so odd for her to tell me about her relationship with him and then laugh right in my face.

I couldn't believe what she was saying.

'Who was it, you bitch?!' I demanded, irritated, curt and irrational.

'I'm telling you, with Hani. What's the big deal? I thought you two broke up.'

'But I still love him. And you're my friend. I told you this.'

'If you love him, then he belongs to you, even if he's still married?'

After throwing her out of my house, I cried bitterly and smacked my face mindlessly.

Suad tried to calm me down, saying, 'Come on, why are you being like this. She's a flirt, her whole life she's been so hot and sexy.'

When I confronted Hani the next day about his relationship with her, I didn't give him the chance to respond. My speech was like a spray of gunfire. He tried to cut me off by saying, 'Fine, what do you want from me, she took off her clothes, it was a meaningless relationship, it was a mistake.'

'But why didn't you tell me? I told you about all of my little affairs. And if it didn't mean anything, you would have told me, for sure there was something there. And if it was just a silly mistake, it wouldn't have happened more than once. And I even told you once how this woman loves to seduce everyone I know. She even tried to get with my husband Saleem. She had a relationship in college with Suad's husband. Besides, I'm not against your little relationships. I'm hurt because you lied to me.'

155

'When did I lie to you?'

'You lied when I was at the Rawda Café with Suad and Mirna and Azizeh and we saw you having coffee together. I asked you on the telephone why you were there with her, and you told me you had bumped into her there by chance.'

As I walked away, I told him I didn't want to control him but that I was going to cut off the relationship because he had been untruthful, because I felt he had started a relationship in secret by not telling me.

'My God, the way men are,' I said. 'Look, Hani, let's just break up. Nothing will harm our love. It's best if we break up and leave our love unsullied. Besides, carrying on like this is only going to hurt me and hurt you, too. You have no idea how much it tortures me to have feelings for you while I still have my life with my husband and my children. Our feelings will never be right. All the signs seem like theft, even though I'm convinced I'm not stealing anything. Besides, what I'm stealing isn't my property, and yet I'm reclaiming something somehow. And you're having affairs and hiding them from me. You're lying to me.'

'Believe me. It was a simple mistake, that's it,' he said, then went silent.

I left him there and walked away. I headed into the street to get a taxi home, feeling like my feet were walking me backwards, back to the chair where he was still sitting in the cafe. Time was messing with me. I felt like cracked earth, splitting open and swelling before erupting with fire and lava.

When I got home, I held my children and started to cry. In a single voice, the two of them asked me, 'Why are you crying, Mama?'

I didn't reply. I wrapped my arms around them, afraid they would fly away without me and that I would lose them forever.

9

I switched on her bedroom light and we stormed inside to find her lying on the bed in darkness, staring towards the window that was totally blacked out by the curtains. Azizeh hurried over and pulled them aside to let in some air. The room was suffocating with heat, humidity and cigarette smoke.

'Why are you doing this to yourself, Suad?!' I shouted. 'Why are you shutting yourself inside in this heat like you're in a tomb? Why are you filling up the room with smoke when you're dying? How many packs have you smoked? Don't you care about yourself at all?'

As soon as she saw us there Suad sat up and cracked a sly smile. I told her to stay in bed, then tried to make her more comfortable by propping her head up on two pillows. Sweat was dripping down her face in the summer heat, she was turning bright yellow, she looked exhausted, there had been a sudden increase in her blood pressure and her heart rate.

I nearly lost it when Azizeh called to tell me Suad was sick. She said she was considering visiting her and I got dressed in a flash, ran down to my car, and rushed over to pick her up so the two of us could go check in on her.

It had been three weeks since I saw Suad. I was unable to convey to her just how concerned I had been.

I rarely fought with her.

She had accused me of trying to seduce Issam, our friend Hoda's husband. She was trembling in agitation as she told me how upset she was that he had been flirting with me, how she caught him staring at my breasts, which were partially visible through my blouse.

The whole thing came as a surprise to me. Suad understood me better than anyone else. She had never in her whole life shouted at me the way she did then. She knew I would never do something like that, that I didn't think about anyone but Hani, that I couldn't imagine seeing any other man in the world than him, especially after we got back together. So why was she spewing such a hateful accusation at me?

Her unexpected behaviour shocked me and made me cry. I calmed down once I had been able to think over her relationship with her husband Sulayman and her perpetual feelings of loneliness. After all, was there anyone dearer to my heart than she? Through those three weeks, the fear of losing her lit a fire inside me that made it hard to breathe. My body wasn't functioning regularly during that entire time, as if it had lost all sense of balance, as if this friend had become part of our weight, flesh and blood, and our entire bodies. We were suddenly emaciated, our souls and our bodies weakened in the moment we lost her. The whole time spent without her I felt like my voice had been severed from my vocal cords, as if it travelled to my mouth at an excruciatingly slow pace, had to cross vast distances to get there, over mountains and valleys, or as if it was unable to leave its place, forced to take long detours, only finally reaching my mouth restrained and completely exhausted.

I kissed her forehead, and she smiled at me as if nothing had happened. I felt better about where I stood with her, but the state of her health concerned me.

Her husband Sulayman didn't pay any attention to us. He came and went outside the door, with his narrow shoulders, distended paunch and stubby legs, chewing on a sandwich as if munching candy, and then left.

As soon as Azizeh had made sure he was out of the house, she shut the door behind him, took off her high-heeled shoes, and knelt on the bed next to Suad, saying, 'Look, you jackass, you're going to kill yourself, you idiot. And when you do, God's not going to give you another chance. That husband of yours still wants to stop your heart from beating. I'm not joking. Come on, get up, sweetie. Only love can unblock the veins of your heart. Seriously, sister, if you felt love even once a month you'd be as strong as a horse. You know that women are often chosen by those whose hearts can no longer feel, by those who can no longer love or have a relationship. Or else what, do you think the whole world starts and stops with Nahla? You think the universe is nothing but eating and drinking and roses? First you want everybody to eat whatever they like, and down to the last you still want to be in love. You jackass.'

Whenever Azizeh talked about how she behaved with men, specifically mentioning how she would pounce on someone she fancied, tearing off his clothes in order to inspect the shape of his penis once he was naked, as if she were playing a role in a play, Suad would smile and reveal hidden aspects of her face. I recalled what a talented actor she had been when we were in school. Her dream was to become a stage actor. I could still remember the sight of her reading aloud the poetry of Jamil Buthayna in a theatrical register, a romantic look on her face as we cheered her on.

I thought about how much Azizeh had changed with the passing days. Her dream of acting evaporated the same way her distant past vanished. She no longer spoke much, and when she did it was only about hedonistic pleasures and the global brands she liked to wear.

Suad watched Azizeh's movement through astonished eyes. She seemed as comfortable as ever with what she was saying. The strange thing was how I was able to see a different side of Suad with her there. Now she was a philosophy professor, choosing her words carefully, speaking in a different language, another language, a vulgar one that she would only speak when Azizeh was around. When we visited her place in the fancy Ras Beirut neighbourhood for a drink, those might have been Suad's happiest times, when her face would turn ruddy, full of life and excitement. From the way she looked I could tell how much she coveted Azizeh's life, to sell her body the way she did, for pleasure and money at the same time, which was much better than selling it in devastated silence and self-destruction.

Azizeh had always been the poorest one among us, also the one most prone to romantic fantasies when we were adolescents. She used to imagine herself in made-up stories. Her blue eyes set against her wheat-coloured face would drift into space as she recited the verse of Jamil Buthayna. One time I asked her directly, 'Why are you so obsessed with that chaste love poetry?'

'Because I think a girl should remain chaste even after her husband has had his fun with her and discover that she's actually human.'

'Do you know how a woman gets off, Azizeh?'

'Are you serious? Why should a woman get off? And what do you mean anyway?' she replied naively, exuding a kind of sexiness she wasn't fully aware of.

We often talked about romantic love and carnal matters, until one day I settled the matter by telling her I didn't want to copy anyone else, that I didn't want to be a duplicate. I wanted to invent my own version of myself, to discover the kind of love I'm driven towards by my heart, my body and my feelings.

When she first revealed her beauty and her coquettishness, Azizeh had been pursued by many suitors, but she turned down all of them because she was in love with my brother Jawad. Her family responded by marrying her off to her cousin Abdelhusayn when she was only seventeen.

On the first day of their marriage, her father-in-law told his son, 'Give her the hard stuff so that she'll know who's boss. That way she won't just come and go however she pleases when you're not around.'

And give her the hard stuff he did. She never left the house when he was in Kuwait for work. He never visited Beirut without giving her a good beating first. One time he broke four of her fingers, two of them are still maimed.

I can remember how stunned I was when she came knocking on my door one day with a black eye he had given her for just asking, 'Seriously, Abdelhusayn? You think a woman gets pleasure when a man comes?'

Before beating her up, he rose up like a raging bull and demanded, 'Who do you think you're talking to?! Tell me who else you're sleeping with! What kind of whores are you hanging out with?! Clearly Nahla or Suad fed you that horseshit!'

'Nobody told me anything. It's just some stuff I heard. Now I'm asking you whether or not a woman can actually come, because I can't feel a thing,' she replied through her tears.

After he was done beating her, he tried to soothe her and convince her that a woman can't experience anything like that, that she sleeps with her husband for his pleasure alone.

Abdelhusayn never wanted her to feel anything. He rarely slept with her anyway, worried that she might get used to having sex and then learn something about it, imagining that if she ever learnt how to feel pleasure she would have no choice but to cheat on him while he was away. She heard him tell his brother who had just married someone he loved, 'Don't sleep with her too often or she'll start to take control of you. If you want to go abroad, then go, the mother of your children should stay at home. She needs to be respectful. If you miss her, you can sleep with someone else every two weeks or so, if you can wait that long. That's it. I'm just giving you my advice.'

Of course, he never did what he advised his brother to do. His love was to be found outside the house. Gambling was a hobby he brought back with him from Kuwait, which is what drove her one day to refuse to have sex with him. He tore her clothes off and raped her, then beat her until blood oozed from her head. After that she snapped, tried to kill herself with a whole vial of tranquillizers, which was when her family stepped in and insisted that he had to divorce her. Anger imbued her with a kind of strength she had never had before. She picked up the television set and other things around the house and threw them at him with full force without even realizing what she was doing. When Suad, Nadine and I went to see her on the day she got divorced, she told us all about how he had treated her.

'He's heartless. You wouldn't believe how he was with me, what I silently put up with. Whatever, I had three daughters with him but I swear to God I didn't came even once. Nahla, how many times did you ask me, But do you come when you sleep with him? I don't even know what it means to come. I never felt anything with him. Everything was for his pleasure. All I ever felt was belittlement. Anyway, after all of that, good riddance.'

'What did you expect, girl? Men only care about them-selves. Even the ones who seem pure will betray their woman, no matter how beautiful she is,' Suad shot back.

Only a few days after her obligatory waiting period Azizeh married a man from a wealthy Beirut family who was thirty years older than her and already had four children.

Azizeh loved her second husband, Bassam, a well-known lawyer, because she was able to live a comfortable life with him. She felt like people began to show her respect and she was able to wash away her feelings of inferiority. She started seeing her own picture on the social pages of women's maga-zines. Wherever she went people would stop to gawp at her. But the one thing she found odd was how her husband's per-sonality would self-destruct whenever he was around his father. She never heard him call him anything other than 'Our Master' or 'Father Sir'. He would bow before him and kiss his hand coming and going from his house. In spite of his tender-ness, though, she never experienced any real pleasure with him either. The first time she felt the sensations of her own body was in 'the hands' of the bathroom, where the hot water stimulated a sensitive spot in her vagina, revealing pleasure to her, which led her to start visiting the bathroom all the time. Sometimes she would stretch out in the bathtub, raise her legs up and spread them wide, point the shower head at her vagina and begin to masturbate. Her husband Bassam knew when she was getting herself off and he would often knock on the bathroom door if she was taking a long time, asking, 'Come on, Miss Azizeh. It's been half an hour. Enough. How many times do you need to come?'

Bassam rarely made Azizeh feel like a woman. Besides his lack of sexual proficiency, he didn't get turned on much by any-one other than maids. He only got near Azizeh intermittently, when he was very drunk or horny and didn't have anyone else to have sex with. Then he stopped having sex with her altogether when he fell in love with a Filipina woman he had been having an affair with at his office after popping a few Viagras. Azizeh lost it. She hired a man to spy on him twenty-four-seven. Often she would go over to his office, fling open the door, and find a used condom on the couch. One day when she tried to initiate something in bed with him, he said, 'Look, Azizeh, I love you, and I respect you, but if you want our life to go on, if you want to hold on to me, there can't be any sex. I have to spit on what is halal and make it haram if I'm going to get any pleasure.'

Azizeh would come to see me in tears, complaining about having to follow Bassam to bed, lie down next to him and masturbate while he just sat there and watched her before grabbing her shoulder and slobbering all over her chest. He would come home late after spending long days at his law office in Ras Beirut, across from the Beirut University College, with his Filipina girlfriend who twice got pregnant and had abortions each time. He cried bitterly because she had ended the pregnancies without asking for his opinion.

It had been a long time since Azizeh talked to Suad and me about chaste romantic love. Throughout that time she refused to believe there was anyone who would ever be as true to her or her body as her own fingers. I can still remember the way she stood in front of us one day and said that her fingers were worth more than the whole world, that they made men irrelevant. 'Don't you know that old expression?' she asked, laughing. 'Whatever makes you wet, let it pour.'

Another time when she came back to see us, and after my husband's sister informed us of her arrival, she laughed as she told us how jealous her husband had become, how he wouldn't let her leave the house without him, 'Men are nuts.

If a woman has to go, no use trying to stop her. What a bunch of jackasses, men who try to slam the door on their women.'

We had forgotten all about Azizeh's life with her first husband; she couldn't really remember anything about him either. But she remembered Bassam fondly and still had feelings for him. She became a widow in her early forties after his sudden death in a gruesome car accident on the Damascus road while he was on his way back from Chtaura with an Ethiopian maid. The car slid off the road on a stormy, grey winter's day. I don't believe I have ever seen such profound sadness in Azizeh's eyes as I did that time from the intense pain of her loss.

✳✳✳

After getting back from the commemoration marking the passage of forty days since Bassam's death, Azizeh got into the tub and let the sadness wash over her, especially after she learnt that Bassam had bequeathed power of attorney over his money and his children to his brother.

As she reminisced about the good and the bad times she had spent with him, her chest rose out of the water in the tub every time she inhaled. From time to time she splashed the water up towards her shoulders, then submerged her arms and closed her eyes, soothed by the sound of water in her ears. Standing beneath the shower she longed for the water sluicing down her body to wash away the feelings of loneliness and devastation that stuck to her like molasses.

Standing naked in front of the mirror beside the tub as she dried herself off, it seemed as if she were seeing her own body for the first time. She squeezed her breasts together, and after twirling around a few times and checking out her slightly raised rear end, she let her gaze drift all over her body. Her beautiful and shiny white skin made her think about how

165

frigid and forlorn she had become. It was disorienting how her body seemed to extend deep inside the mirror, escaping far away from her, to the point of nearly disappearing. She held on to her hips just to make sure they were still with her, still hers, that they were actually in her hands, and still in front of her in the mirror. She hungered for a man's hands instead of her own to ravish her. She intensely yearned to feel the eyes of a man looking at her, for his fingers to touch her beautiful body and smooth skin, to become as warm as her breath. She had grown tired of her own fingers, of her own glances. Azizeh told me in front of Suad that she could feel her body shaking like a bustling beehive waiting for its honey to be harvested. She said that I was right the time I told her there was intensely affecting music, allure and loud noises crashing in my body. She told me she could feel the same music, that she actually heard it, standing in front of the mirror regarding herself. Then she started listening for it, listening to it, and it would speak to her, whereas in the past it had only spoken to her the way my mother would—impassive, unresponsive.

'Nahla,' she said to me, 'There isn't a bone in my body that hasn't chastised me or spoken to me.'

What truly terrified her though, what opened her eyes wide to the world, was a single question: Why hadn't she just lived off Bassam the way her friend Mona would? Why wouldn't she just let things go on that way as long as he was still so handsome and full of life?

For a long time she pushed those questions out of her mind, but then started asking them once again after she met Fadi, who fell in love with her and treated her well.

It was with him that she experienced a different kind of feeling for the first time.

Her body drove Fadi wild. He was ten years younger, and he drove her wild, too. With him she discovered the pleasure of sex. He would snort some cocaine and have sex with her several times in the same night. Still, she wanted more, feeling like her thirst for sex would never be quenched, like her body would never be sated. She couldn't understand why Suad would sometimes come to mind while she lay in bed with Fadi post-coitus. She would smile and think to herself, My God, Suad. Then she'd ask herself whether Suad would have the strength to resist if Fadi ever hit on her. It seemed to her that she might devour him in a single bite, convinced that Suad lived in a state of perpetual hunger, in silence and wolfish contemplation. She could smell the hunger on her body. She thought about whether Nadine would leave Mirna and quit being a lesbian if she were to sleep with Fadi. She often talked to herself, saying things like: Where are you, Nahla? Can you see what love's doing to me? New pores have opened up in my body that I never saw or felt before. You used to tell me not even a needle could make my body feel anything. Now my entire body is on fire.

Azizeh changed when she was with Fadi, became more beautiful. On the weekends she would go up to the mountains with him and when she came back to Beirut her face would glow. When she came to see me, she'd say, 'Look, Nahla. Can't you see how radiant my face is? It's unreal what sex can do for a woman. And can you believe Fadi, it's as if he's got three balls, or ten, not just two!'

Fadi loved her. He was addicted to her the same way he was to cocaine. She would eventually leave him because of drugs and because he got thrown in jail in Dubai, where he was working. Then he tried to kill himself. When he got out and tried to break into her house and force himself on her, she lost it. Her children were a red line and now she feared for their safety. But Fadi loved her so much that he would come once a month just to see her. He wouldn't eat before she did.

Once she hurt her leg at a restaurant where they were having lunch and he crouched down, took off her shoes, and started massaging her toes to help her relax. He was constantly giving money to her and her children. He showered her with gifts. Once he even went to Gemayel Jewellers and bought her a seven-karat solitaire that made her head spin.

Fadi loved her to death. But all she got out of being with him was sexual pleasure, which made her feel that their relationship wasn't worth all that much. Signs of tortured love started to surface in her eyes because of Doctor Jawdat Mahmoud, the thyroid and diabetes specialist who had been treating her mother.

She first noticed his interest in her after a few visits to his office with her mother. She also discovered that she had feelings for him she'd never experienced before. The smile that rose out of his heart when he saw her made her melt, and she accepted his invitation to have a cup of coffee in the southern suburbs. She came to see me right after their date, her eyes awhirl. She flopped down on the couch and just stared out at the sea. Her blue eyes spaced out the way they would when we were young. She rested her head on her hands that were folded underneath her, and told me she was dizzy from happiness, that she was happy, that she felt drunk.

That day she asked me about love, asked me to explain how I feel when I'm with Hani. When I inquired why she was asking, she told me she didn't know if what she was feeling was this thing called love.

When the doctor sat across from her in the cafe gazing deeply into her eyes, her body trembled, her hands and her legs shook, she felt as if fire was shooting out of her head. Her hands were usually as cold as ice but now they were burning up, her palms had turned bright red, her spine seemed to split in half as she stared at his lips and imagined plunging into them with a kiss. Something mysterious was happening in her body, something like pain but not exactly pain, something like joyous tittering but not pure joy. Her eyes were tearing up when she asked me whether what she was feeling was this thing called love.

She told me her desire for him was nothing like what she had felt towards Fadi, clarifying that with Fadi it was a simple matter of sex organs rubbing against each other like flint, sparking and then igniting depending on how horny each one of them was.

'Now my heart's on fire, Nahla,' she said. 'It yearns for him desperately. My desire to be with him is limitless. It's like I want to sleep with him right away, for his body to consume mine. Every nucleus in every cell hungers for him, but I'm afraid that he'll dump me if I try anything. He's observant and a member of a religious political party. I dream about marrying him nonetheless.'

Her voice was delicate, crystalline, steeped in love. Then she looked over at Suad and asked for her opinion.

'I don't know, Azizeh,' she replied. 'Some guys dump a woman as soon as they've slept with her. With other guys, sex puts them on the hook. I would guess, though, that if he's religious and traditional, then you shouldn't sleep with him. Get him to marry you first. But would you start to wear the veil if he asked you to?'

'I'd do even more than put on the veil. Why not? I'd do anything he wants, just so long as he marries me.'

'Just try not to sleep with him. He'll have no choice but to marry you.'

'I can't resist him, though. If you only saw the way I melt when I'm around him. I just fall apart.'

'Oh, get over it, Azizeh. You're such a softie. Pull yourself together.'

'I can't. What am I supposed to do? How can I ever be with him when I always fall apart like this?'

Suad giggled. She had always felt a special affection for Azizeh.

'Listen, sister,' she told her. 'Here's what you do. When you feel the need to be with him, just splash some water on your face. If you really want to marry him, do what you have to do, just don't sleep with him before then.'

Azizeh didn't take Suad's advice. She slept with the doctor but only after he had executed a temporary marriage contract with her, because he's so pious. He refused to touch her, even to look at her or speak with her, without such a contract, telling her, 'If you don't want the contract, we can go our separate ways. I can't just have sex like that. I can't even touch you, or even talk to you on the telephone. If I were to hear your voice on the phone, and feel anything at all, that would be blasphemous and forbidden. I can't speak with a woman unless I know the relationship between us is halal.'

Azizeh honoured the contract, but he dumped her as soon as his desire had been quenched. She was devastated for days, didn't leave the house for months, spending most of her time in bed. When she had managed to get back up on her feet, she told me there was no larger love in the world than what she felt for her children and only they deserved any of her care.

In those days, Azizeh started spending more time with her girlfriend Mona, who made a living off her body, sleeping with men whose money supported her and her children. Azizeh wondered why she shouldn't do the same thing. She was pretty and she and her children had grown accustomed to a life of luxury. She recalled how Fadi used to shower her with money and presents when they were together. It occurred to her that older men could be a goldmine, her path to safeguarding a life for her and her children. At the same time, she would be able to avoid torturing herself again because she would be sure not to fall in love with any of them. Surely older gentlemen would be attracted to my good looks, she told herself.

Azizeh found a way to meet them. She started selling menswear, clothes and ties and such, and then escorted those who turned out to be generous towards her. She told Suad that she hoped one of them would propose to her so that she could serve him and benefit from this position, even if he was bound to a wheelchair, because all that mattered to her was the money. But she gave up on marriage and older men altogether when she found herself embroiled in a scandal with a well-known government official who also happened to be a friend of my husband Saleem. She had met him at a dinner party I threw at my house.

One day she came to see me in tears, saying, 'I was ready to accept shit, but not even shit would have me.'

Suad's round eyes spoke volumes as I asked her, 'Ooof, what happened, Azizeh? Tell me, honey.'

Azizeh got lost in Suad's eyes for a moment before replying by asking her, 'Please, Suad, your eyes are bulging out. Why are they so wide and dilated, like a scorpion's? And with everything else that's going on?'

Suad cracked a crooked smile, saying, 'Well now, what do you care about my eyes? Tell me, what happened with you and the captain?'

The confusion on Azizeh's face vanished. She calmed down, laughed a bit, then said, 'This shit captain I met here at Nahla's, I felt sorry for him, even fantasized about marrying him, although God made him a man who isn't cut out for a serious relationship. I swear on the lives of my children, may I be struck down dead in the street if I'm lying to you. He's got nothing going on down there. Like a little breathing tube, but nothing comes out. I swear it's the most disgusting thing I've ever seen.'

Azizeh told me he didn't make a move on her the first time she went to see him, he didn't buy her anything either, but he did invite her over to his place the next week. After a few more visits at his request, he instructed his driver to leave the two of them alone so they could sit together in the living room. He was wearing shorts, which revealed that his legs were covered with pustules from diabetes, their hard yellow crust making it seem as though he had just come out of surgery and his legs had been bled white. He asked her to escort him to the bathroom so that he could wash his hands. When the two of them got back, he sat down next to her on the sofa, resting his trembling hand on her knee as he said, 'You mean a lot to me, Azizeh. Just seeing you gives me hope for the world. Your love is so pure.'

'Yes, captain, you're very kind. I love with all my heart. For sure I'm pure,' she replied.

He opened the briefcase at his side and handed her five hundred dollars. Then he drew his face in close to kiss her. Between one kiss and the next he gathered his strength and took a breath so that he didn't get winded. Azizeh concealed her feelings of revulsion that washed over her, thinking to herself, Hang in there, Azizeh. If a kiss gets you five hundred bucks, just imagine what sleeping with him could get you . . .

Just as she was thinking that, he closed his eyes and touched her breasts before moving his hand to even more sensitive parts of her body.

'Whose breast is this?'

'Yours, captain.'

'And your thigh, whom does it belong to?'

'To you, captain.'

'And your pussy is whose?'

He shut his eyes as he listened to the sound of her voice answering him, stretched out on the couch, and asked her to unbutton his pyjamas and suckle at his breast.

Azizeh fell backwards laughing as she told me, 'I reached out my hand, Nahla, just to see what he had in mind, what he was on about! There was nothing to it, really. His hair was this short, and his armpits stank. He told me he didn't like to bathe even though he's this big important person. My goodness.'

Azizeh just about threw up as soon as she had done what he asked. Then she left him there and ran into the bathroom to do just that. She tried to convince him to let her bring him into the bathroom so that she could bathe him herself but he refused, saying he hated taking a bath. From that point forward Azizeh never left home without cologne, because nobody knew what kind of condition he might be in.

Azizeh found it even more disgusting that he started boasting to his driver and his personal assistant about his sexual prowess, as if he were afraid he might lose his status and influence around them if they found out he was impotent. He rolled around laughing when he said, 'You temptress, Azizeh. What are you doing to me? You're destroying me, you little devil. More than twice or three times in a row, you naughty girl!'

Azizeh started to change, transformed by the passing days.

She gave up on her dream of becoming a stage actress. All she could think about was the fear of sliding back into the kind of poverty she had experienced before. One day she took a deep breath and told me she had already lived and acted out her stage life, but she didn't know whether it had been written by herself or by others. She wanted to remain the protagonist, but the play would have to end, she would have to fall off the stage.

Azizeh tried to cling to her youth and good looks. She tore off her old veneer of shyness, came to life with a kind of vitality that was mixed with deep cynicism. She wanted to gulp down this life in one shot, to acquire pleasure and money all at once. Her blue eyes were alight with desire, her face even more attractive when her black hair cascaded down over her shoulders. Cosmetic surgery had given her back some radiance. Her bosomy chest was always on display, even in the coldest days of winter. Her body was curvy, as if it harboured the power of a stallion, a kind of strength she never possessed in her youth.

The lust that had been buried deep inside her body, repressed throughout her youth, exploded all at once, and she began to make a living off her body, escorting men who spent money on her and her college-aged children. She came to believe that true love in the life of a woman is meant for her children.

She told me numerous times, 'There's nothing more valuable than a child, and yet women worship men. I wouldn't be able to live with myself if anything ever happened to my children.'

She stopped going out with certain men altogether, choosing instead only those who could satisfy both her body and her pocketbook, because she had a lot less life ahead of her than she had already lived. She came to believe that she would never be attracted to a man who wasn't able to support her, that she wouldn't be able to love or respect such a man.

Suad laughed so hard the day when Azizeh came over to tell us all about it, sitting beside her on the bed, 'What do you mean, is there anyone out there who wants to help a woman out for nothing in return? A woman doesn't even like to put out for her husband for nothing in return. If he doesn't provide for her and spend money on her she'll eventually come to hate him. As for me, my friends, I no longer get anything for free. On the other hand, I no longer have anyone to have a good time with, after that disgusting captain. God hasn't been kind to me. I've even started eyeing men's cocks. If a guy lays a finger on me without any desire I'll bite it off. My pussy is just for me. I have to make myself come or I never will. My God, anyone who saw how disgusting his dick is wouldn't be able to finish. But when I'm comfortable I can finish. I swear to God, even if someone offered me the world and I don't wanna come, I'm not gonna do it, even if I didn't have a dime to my name. How much longer do I have to have a good time anyway?'

Then she looked over at Suad and said, 'You idiot. Let your heart pound from love and not high blood pressure. Come on, go get rid of that bag of bones you call a husband.'

After she made the acquaintance of George Feghaly at a luncheon a friend of hers in Jbeil invited her and Mona to attend, Azizeh stopped seeing anyone else. George was drawn to her and she liked him because he was handsome and wasn't shy about spending money on her.

But Azizeh became afraid that George might leave her when Mona told her about a friend of hers who had been in a five-year relationship but broke it off when she found out her boyfriend was impotent. He then stopped supporting her and wouldn't even return her calls.

One day I went over to her place and found her praying, which was quite unusual. When she was done, I asked her,

'What is this . . . you pray now? Where'd this belief come from all of a sudden? Did God show you the way or something?'

'Shut up, Nahla,' she said, laughing. 'I'm so scared. I prayed to God to help me, to help my children. I said I'd pray as often as necessary to make George stay with me. What would I do if it turned out he had some kind of sexual dysfunction or stopped supporting me or no longer wanted to see me, the same thing that happened to Mona's friend?'

10

Something that morning was calling me to write.

I had been thinking about Hani all night. My desire for him made me feel as if language was extending its hands and inviting me to ladle out for him all the feelings I needed to express, and even more than that.

I opened the window and was met with a cool spring breeze, bracing and sweet-smelling. I took a deep breath, headed over to the study, and sat down at my desk to begin writing as I did every morning. I looked up at the sunlight streaming into half of the room, observing the way it disappeared and re-emerged with the movement of those few clouds floating by overhead. The sun seemed to be playing peek-a-boo with me.

I had only squeezed out a few words when the telephone rang. I was surprised to hear Nadine asking to see me about something urgent. Her voice was raspy, as if her throat had been scraped with a knife. She told me she had just walked alone on the Corniche for two hours, feeling sorry for herself, like she couldn't talk to anyone but me about what was going on with her. I could tell that something was wrong so I invited her over.

She threw her head on my shoulder and burst into tears as soon as I opened the door. I had to ask her several times what was going on before she replied, 'Doctor Sahar is driving me crazy. She's got me hanging on her every move, Nahla. I'm in love with her. I think about her night and day. She's messing with my head.

'Who is Doctor Sahar?'

'Somebody I met. I'm head over heels in love with her.'

'Okay, but didn't you tell me that you and Mirna were . . .'

'Yeah, Mirna's my life and my sweetheart, there's nobody better than her. And she can see how much I'm suffering. But ever since Doctor Sahar and I started seeing each other, she's totally cut me off. She won't answer my calls.'

'God, I'm such an idiot. I never understood that you suffer and struggle with love the same way we do with men?'

'Duh. Even more. What, aren't we human beings too, Nahla?'

'Okay, fine. But if you love Mirna then what are you doing with Doctor Sahar?'

'It's true, I love Mirna, but I feel real passion for the Doctor. It's out of my control. What really set me off was her telling me she has a girlfriend she loves very much, someone she could never leave even if she cheated on her. Then she told me I'm just a passing fling. If you ever saw this girlfriend she claims to love so much you'd be disgusted. She's hideous. You wouldn't be able to look at her. She's short and even skinnier than me. Her hair's cut like a boy. But what really gets me is that I have more experience, I know a lot, I'm capable of doing so many more things than her.'

Nadine's face was drawn as she poured her heart out to me, telling me secrets I had never heard before despite the fact that she had been a dear friend since childhood. All I ever knew about was her relationship with Mirna, and her crush on Loubna ever since we were all in school together, Loubna whose initials she had once inscribed on a heart she drew in order to express her feelings. Nadine liked the drawing, Loubna liked it too, but back then they didn't have a sexual relationship. The whole thing never developed any further than some light touching.

Nadine told me her secrets and her memories as if she were talking about a different woman who had never hurt or wounded her, whose feelings hadn't gone in another direction.

The high bridge of her nose was red from all the crying, and from time to time she swept back her frizzy red hair that fell down on her shoulders behind her ears. This made the freckles scattered all over her face more pronounced, shinier.

That morning she told me that she loved Doctor Sahar, that she felt a kind of passion for her she had never felt for anyone before, not even with her sweetheart Mirna who helped to raise her children after she divorced Ziad.

Doctor Sahar harassed her in her office.

She tore the bandage off of her mouth, allowing her breath to merge with Nadine's, filling her tooth with extreme gentleness and precision even as the soft music numbed her body bit by bit, her eyes closed, laid out in the chair.

Nadine opened her eyes when Doctor Sahar had finished her work. They locked eyes just as Doctor Sahar began to sensitively and deliberately stroke her neck and then remove the hygienic towel wrapped around it. She told her that the two of them were alone in the clinic because her secretary was sick. Doctor Sahar realized from the look on Nadine's face that she had already surrendered herself to her, that her body was limp and didn't wish to get out of the chair. Doctor Sahar reached out and held Nadine's cheeks in her hands, then asked her whether it had been uncomfortable to keep her beautiful and inviting mouth open for nearly an hour. Nadine grabbed hold of her and shook her head in the negative, then closed her eyes once again. In the blink of an eye Doctor Sahar and Nadine found themselves embracing in the chair before they tumbled to the floor and began tearing off each other's clothes and having sex.

Before she left my house that morning, Nadine and I agreed to meet up the next day at Mirna's. Hoda, Suad and I had been invited there for a new year's party. Suad wasn't enthusiastic about it. She wanted to spend the night at my place instead, just the two of us. But she agreed to the plan when she realized how excited I was about the whole thing. Saleem was out of the country and Hani was going to spend the night with his wife and kids.

It was no ordinary evening. We sang and danced deep into the night.

I never saw Suad drink so much. Her eyes were bloodshot, they looked crooked; her face turned many different colours, her red splotches grew even more brilliant. Hoda was relentless with her jokes about impotent men until her eyes got all wide as she watched the way Mirna's body delicately and lithely inclined towards Nadine, who danced with her for a little while before sitting back down on the couch.

Nadine seemed anxious and distracted the whole time. She was busy sending texts, though it seemed as if she wasn't getting a response, and jealousy shone in Mirna's eyes as she watched her while pretending to be busy on her own phone, avoiding eye contact altogether. After we left, Nadine stayed over at Mirna's, but she turned her back on her in bed and tossed and turned throughout the night, sighing audibly, which caused Mirna to get up numerous times to switch on the light, hold Nadine and ask her what was wrong.

Nadine wept as she complained about how Doctor Sahar was avoiding her, about how consumed with jealousy she had become because there was no doubt she was spending new year's with her girlfriend. Mirna was extremely understanding because she felt the sincerity of her pain; her jealousy evaporated as she was overcome with feelings of tenderness that could slice through mountains. She tried to comfort her, secretly wishing that the storm of her desire for Doctor Sahar would pass and that she would come back into her arms.

'Can I tell you something?' she asked, after wiping away her tears.

'What? Tell me.'

'Send her a message that says, Happy New Year, Love.'

'I sent her that a thousand times but she never responded.'

'Send it to her again.'

Nadine retyped the message, stayed awake all night sending text after text, but Doctor Sahar never responded. Mirna continued to stroke her hair until she calmed down and felt safe, until dawn came as she fell asleep in her arms.

Nadine had barely left Mirna's side ever since meeting her except during this infatuation with the doctor. She didn't know what came over her with this woman who loved Westerns while she, Nadine, was a fan of art-house films. Doctor Sahar was just using her to make her girlfriend jealous when she got bored. Meanwhile, Nadine felt something for her she had never felt before. With other women she had always tried to turn them on and give them pleasure; here it was the reverse. She dumped her anyway and got back together with her girlfriend.

Mirna would never forget the way Nadine stood by her side from the moment they met, back in the early nineties when she was in an extremely fragile state after divorcing her husband after she discovered he was having an affair with his secretary, whom he had married in secret. Mirna had converted to Islam so that she could marry him after a long romance that moved her from the extreme right to the left and then to become a partisan of the Palestinian cause just like her husband.

One time Nadine went over to Mirna's, having promised to help her redecorate her house. She was an interior designer but had a real interest in classical Arabic music, which is one of the first things that attracted the attention of Nadine, who, despite her specialization in business administration, had always loved music and cinema, Oriental dance and theatre. Ever since the war ended in the early nineties she had been working at an advertising and marketing company.

For Mirna, the fallout from leaving her husband was brutal. She had lost all confidence in herself when Nadine reached out a hand and started coming over to help her raise her children. Both of them needed the sympathy and tenderness they shared with each other, even though they had been brought together by loss in the war, despite the social differences between them. Mirna came from a well-off Christian family, while Nadine was a Muslim who came from poverty. From the earliest days of their friendship she told her the story of her sister Rabia's suicide when she was a little girl and how her father tortured her mother.

Mirna didn't bat an eye when one night Nadine told her about her sexual tendencies in a forthright and trusting conversation, even if it left her on edge for a few days. Nadine didn't talk about it with her after that, letting things develop naturally instead.

One night they went back to Mirna's after dinner with Suad and Azizeh at my house. The two of them had had a lot to drink, and Mirna acquiesced to her feelings under the influence of alcohol.

The bed was shrouded in darkness and silence, light beamed softly from the television screen, and Nadine's eyes darkened as she stared at Mirna and they lay down in bed, their heads on adjacent pillows.

After gliding her hand along her shoulders and telling her they were cold, Nadine asked Mirna if she felt the same way she did. Mirna smiled and held Nadine's hand, wrapped her arm around her neck. Nadine drew her face in close and kissed her on the cheek, then stroked her hair gently and tenderly. She whispered words in her ear that Mirna couldn't decipher but she could feel her warm breath. After a few moments Nadine reached out to touch Mirna's lips, then she smiled, holding her neck and stroking her body, feeling like she was going to crumble under her fingertips.

That night Mirna struggled to climax because it was her first time. She wasn't used to being with a woman. Even though she was turned on and disoriented and happy, her husband still occupied her body. But their first tempestuous meeting kept Mirna at home for an entire week with her legs spread wide open, as she couldn't even stand up after Nadine bit her hard on the vagina and left a mark in the shape of her teeth. She had the desire to penetrate her but she was unable to do so.

Mirna didn't understand why she delighted in the hairs on Nadine's skin. She would often ask herself whether they reminded her somehow of male characteristics or if there were other reasons she couldn't divine. But she stopped thinking about it after managing to tell herself one day: My God, things get so complicated in our memory, why does anyone want to understand why things happen anyway? It's enough for me to know just one thing and one thing only—that I love her. I don't feel like a freak or a deviant. The feeling that I'm completely abnormal is gone, and goes even further away when I'm with her, or when I see her in bed.

A kiss came to mean Nadine's lips. That same feeling had stayed with her before when a kiss would remind her of her husband, ever since she danced with him at a party long before they got married, when she was still a young woman. On that day she felt warm all over when her lower lip touched the corner of his mouth. That kiss was stamped on her memory for a long time. Another feeling that lasted a long time was the sense of shame that germinated inside of Mirna during the early days of her relationship with Nadine, whose femininity was entrancing. It's true that she was enormous, just like Doctor Sahar, but her feminine qualities weren't restrained in quite the same way. Freely and alluringly, she would flick her long black hair off her wheat-coloured face. Her scent had changed, as if hormones and senses possessed a smell that evolved with her own transformation. Some hairs had sprouted on her chin. Doctor Sahar, by contrast, had short hair, wore glasses, and in the winter always had on jeans and a black leather jacket; and the way she behaved reminded her of Soraya, the wife of a major political leader during the war. In those days, she hadn't only been the source of love but of decision-making as well.

Soraya was the first woman to attract Nadine towards lesbianism at the beginning of the Lebanese Civil War. Nadine was in her early forties, adrift, in despair over men and the war she saw in all its savagery, in the streets, having been pulled behind the barricades. Her experience was in the side streets and on the front lines, where she witnessed the most horrifying sights of kidnapping and identity-based killing, senseless murder and destruction. She witnessed with her own eyes comrades in the movement carry out massacres, which drove her to start snorting cocaine in order to block out everything she had seen. At that time Nadine wasn't the shy little girl I knew from childhood; she had become more inscrutable, crazier, more unreachable. She was always in a fog, as though she were searching inside of herself for something that would allow her to forget, to turn herself into a person without hatred or spite. Her experience in the movement had caused her body to collapse into ruins even as she sought refuge and security. Her comrades during the war had convinced her that having sex with men in the movement was part of the struggle and a form of liberation. The power of that experience sent her racing from one bed to another. She felt depleted and exploited. She had sex with comrades who dumped her immediately afterwards. What really made her mad was when someone she loved and had dreamt of marrying asked her to have sex with a friend of his who was into her.

She realized that she failed to develop a meaningful relationship because of the ugly memories she shared with those comrade-theorists and militiamen she used to have sex with, those men whose bodies and breath and clothes stank of sweat and blood. Even as she was starting to have feelings for women she tried going out with a guy, but she felt nothing for him. So she stopped seeing men altogether and came to loathe penises, became disgusted by them.

Because of the complicated security situation during the war Nadine had no choice but to stay at the military commander's house. If she was unable to go home because of the continuous bombing she would sleep in his wife Soraya's bedroom. When both of them grew tired of the comrades' late-night boasting about the number of martyrs in the organization, Soraya would take her in. Nadine had been growing increasingly disgusted by the way the comrades' faces and their bodies looked as they guffawed, did bumps of cocaine, and sipped the finest whiskey in the country, despite supposedly being the defenders of the poor. She was transfixed by the leader's black shirt and trousers, his white bandolero filled with cartridges, and the silver gun glinting by his side.

In bed Soraya whispered in her ear how much she hated her husband, hated his body and his penis that was like a lethal machine gun. She asked her to touch her because she couldn't fall asleep without the caress of a tender hand. Then she took Nadine's hand and moved it over to sensitive spots all over her body. Then something happened that had happened to her before but which she had tried not to think about for a long time, something that had caused her to run off with men she hated. She once had a casual encounter with her professor Loubna, though it never reached the level of sex, and it wasn't entirely obvious or clear to her how it happened in the first place. She hadn't been able to understand what her body wanted until that night.

The politician's wife was svelte, elegant and beautiful. Although photos of her in women's society magazines often showed her wearing extremely feminine clothes, outfits that showed off her cleavage and her bare shoulders at social galas, Nadine discovered that she wore men's boxer shorts when she was going to make love, that she liked it when her partner wore sexy lingerie and clothes that came off easily. And while she wore a lot of make-up she liked the women she slept with to be au naturel, without any plastic surgery. She often told Nadine she didn't like to be near a face as ugly as her husband's and that she didn't like tomboys either. After she got together with a woman, if she didn't move to her own private room, she would prefer to be in bed with a man.

The first thing she noticed about Nadine was her shape, but what most attracted her attention were Nadine's gauzy eyes and her black or dark-red hair, her lips and her chest. She was turned on by the extremely feminine heels she wore. She would often ask Nadine to get undressed in front of her as the rhythm of beautiful music created an erotic mood, especially when she was hopped up on cocaine. Nadine told me she didn't like to use sex toys, and that she wasn't satisfied with once or twice a night. When she was finally spent she would cry and fall asleep. She used to hate how glum she got because she was, as she would later tell me, sensitive in the bedroom, and any annoying move could elicit an aggressive response from her: she might beat her the way she had beaten many other women. That was why she preferred to come to an agreement before starting to have sex.

Relationships didn't come to Soraya on silver platters. She would cook them up and then wait for the other woman to make the first move. She couldn't stand flirting but she would melt when another woman flirted with her. It was best for that other woman to point out aspects or attributes of her appearance that weren't true or accurate. She would approach a girl who was being nice to her or sociable all of a sudden, cautiously taking her pulse, then invite her to bed or to go out with her, saying things that could be interpreted as flirtatious, and the girl would either respond or she wouldn't. She liked women very much, as much as her husband who was always cheating on her, and like him she also liked to be in control. She became selfish because she had experienced the torture of loving him; she started putting her own needs ahead of everyone else's. She couldn't bear to be with a married woman— the first relationship she ever had with a woman, when she was thirty-two, was with a married woman she had been in love with, but who then dumped her after she had grown attached, feeling things she had never felt with her husband. Nadine broke things off with her on the day she invited her to an orgy when she was fucked up on cocaine. Forgetting about her was torture.

Even with the action going on all around her, Soraya often told Nadine that she was a lonely woman. She was unable to rise above those feelings of loneliness, was tortured by them. Yet somehow she had grown accustomed to it.

Nadine, on the other hand, overcame the hostility she felt towards men and determined the matter of her sexual identity. In time she acquired a lot of friends. They would often spew lewd suggestions about their desire to watch lesbians in action. She was hurt by what she felt was aggression directed against her personally, especially when someone said there was nothing that turned him on more than the sight of two women having sex. Some of them wouldn't hesitate to join her and Mirna in bed. This caused them to mostly avoid men altogether. She complained to me about that more than once.

When she told me that, I don't know what made me think that my brother Jawad would certainly have had no interest in watching two women in action. I can attest that he would find it impossible to project himself into another body somehow cut off from the act, to imagine that he was not the agent and remain distant, as if it had nothing to do with him at all.

11

My phone rang nonstop on the way back from the hospital. I had gone in for a few tests and the crippling traffic was barely moving. Saleem called to tell me he was waiting for me with his friends and my brother Jawad and that I shouldn't be late for lunch. I assured him everything was ready and that the meal could be served minutes after I got back.

But I was annoyed the entire way home. I was bothered by the gynaecological exams that one has to have with utmost regularity at this age, they made me feel like someone had stripped me of all my femininity, all the feelings I had in my intimate parts, and caused me to lose touch with my body altogether. Mammograms depressed me. The nurse would grab hold of my breast, pull on it as hard as she could in order to rest it on the apparatus, and then press down, making me scream from pain. It felt like my breast was being crushed, like someone was flattening it or smashing it on the ground, like it was nothing but hamburger meat mushed into a patty before getting sizzled over a flame. The speculum exam gave me a different feeling of demoralization altogether.

I took off my clothes and put on the white gown, then lay down on the table for the exam, spreading my legs wide. The doctor asked me to scooch down a bit and my feet were placed securely against the stirrups so he could insert the device. I bit my lip and shut my eyes, feeling as though someone had just sunk his teeth into part of my uterus, or even ripped something out of it; like something being cut out of me, like I had just been raped, feelings I never had with my husband, not even when I slept with him just to appease him rather than out of my own desire.

I was still annoyed when I got home. Men's voices boomed around the living room. I was struck by how loud his friends could be, considering how quiet he had always been. I noticed how differently the room smelt when they were around; men's scents changed the same way women's did. When they used to come over a long time ago, their bodies smelt of youth. Now they reeked of sickness and medication.

But I could hear that same old song playing even though their conversations might have changed over the years, and so had I. It's as if you don't only get your work's worth, you reap the worth of your words too, as the saying goes.

The men licked their lips as they surveyed the food being served, especially the most delectable dishes that their doctors had deemed off-limits because most of them struggled with diseases that resulted from being overweight in their old age. My husband Saleem swallowed hard and wiped his eyes that had gone all teary beneath his prescription glasses when one of his friends began to boast of having eaten dozens of fatty lamb kebabs the night before along with sugary sweets. A juvenile grin spread across his friend's face as he rubbed his round belly, proudly holding court about how he didn't need to deny himself the pleasure of eating because his medical records were spotless, thank God.

'Congrats, brother, on this blessing God has bestowed upon you,' my brother Jawad said, daubing his forehead. 'My doctor forbids me from eating anything. Yesterday I treated myself to some cheese kanafeh. Man, I wanted it so bad. And my God! They poured the rose water on there as high as it would go. I got dizzy and nearly fell down. Yeah, is that any way to live? Fuck no, that's no kind of life.'

As they talked about how hungry they all were, I started to think how unjust the world is, about how the pleasure of desires and tastes is forbidden or becomes nearly impossible as we grow older, despite the fact that we never understood this, or never knew how to savour things the way we would later on. It also occurred to me how our delights can become linguistic, as if the mouth takes the place of other erogenous zones, becomes the site of pleasure. I recalled a skinny Suad telling me how much she hated food. But now, at this age, she savours it, recognizing the value of all those delicious fares forbidden to her.

As they yammered on about food, my eyes unconsciously fell on what was between their legs. These friends of my husband, their genitals seemed to be soaking wet or absent altogether, their sagginess plain to see, as the swelling spilled down between their thighs, completely unlike their younger years when their girth was up higher. Some of their penises used to bend towards one side of their trousers, as if this one's dick were hanging its head low or another's was receding inward. Somehow this didn't detract from their masculinity or attractiveness—just the opposite, it had once seemed to me.

Talk about their illnesses continued unabated while we ate lunch. Each of them proceeded to share whatever medication, vitamins and sex enhancers they were currently taking. A long discussion ensued about whether Pharmaton or Centrum vitamins were better, about which sex drugs were more effective: French, American, Canadian or Swiss.

After lunch they started playing cards in the salon and I moved to the living room but couldn't hear a sound coming from the television set. They all laughed when my husband

Saleem told the story of his uncle Ridwan. At the age of eighty he had married a thirty-five-year-old woman. His lifestyle and point of view changed dramatically, his back became unbent and a shine reappeared in his eyes, and he only came out of the house to boast about his manhood, about how happy he was with his life now that he had regained his vitality, about how marrying a younger woman was more effective than any medication. But recently he had started to become senile. All he would talk about was his sexual vigour even though he could barely walk. One day a little girl from the neighbourhood came up to him and said, 'Uncle Ridwan, our neighbour Abu Ali is dying. They want you to come and turn his face towards Mecca and recite the shahada to protect him and make the angels hear that they need to come to his grave.'

Turning his head away from her and waving his hand behind him, he said, thoughtlessly, 'Get out of here. Just let him sleep with a young lady who can give him back some spirit. Sex can bring a person back from the dead.'

This story about my husband's uncle led them to talk about women. One of them said, 'What are we talking about, guys? Even if she's young and a hot catch but still a heartbreaker, what's her body good for? I'd feel bad for anyone who got close to her legs and her incredible chest. I'm telling you, she'd drive you nuts.'

I could smell them just as well as I could hear their snorting waft in towards me. Their laughter grew even louder when they started discussing the wonders of Viagra. Somebody told a story about how long he was able to stay hard during sex with a woman he used to be crazy about who finally slept with him. He went on to describe his powers, her beautiful body, and how much the way she moved turned him on. She started to flutter in his hands like a bird, which nearly drove him out of his mind. He concluded by saying, 'She was on fire, nothing like my wife, who doesn't respond to me at all.'

Saleem nodded along as if this man was expressing exactly what was in his heart.

Jawad pulled back from them, didn't join in the conversation about Viagra, which he refused to admit to taking the same way he denied getting older by dyeing the hair on his head and chest. He basically lied to his doctor after having some tests done.

'How's sex for you?'

'Just great, doctor.'

'Oof, at this age? My word. You mean, I don't need to prescribe anything for you?'

'To tell you the truth, doctor, it's a little complicated,' he replied.

'Why torture yourself? Isn't medicine made to be used? What's Viagra for, after all?'

Jawad couldn't believe what he was hearing. From that point on those blue pills were always in his pocket, just in case. When he was younger, he used to care about the great cause of the Arab people. Now he no longer cared about anything but his cock.

He nearly lost his mind when he started to suffer from erectile dysfunction. Months went by and he was unable to get it up with his wife Samiha or any other woman. This happened after he'd seen his mother's vagina. He walked into her hospital room just before she died, saw it with his eyes at the moment when the orderly was spreading her legs to clean her after removing the gurney from underneath. The sight terrified him. He covered his eyes and ran out of the room, stood in the hallway sweating bullets, his body on fire, his face turned bright red, and it felt as though his tears were going to ignite.

He was like that for a long time, feeling limp, imagining his mother's vagina right there in front of him whenever he had sex with Samiha or anyone else. He was overjoyed when he was finally able to sleep with Samiha again. He got up and started to pace around the bedroom naked, holding his lit cigarette high as if to show off his body, stealing glances at her in order to see whether she was looking at his cock while she lay on the bed. In the bathroom he stood beneath the shower, taking pleasure in the soap, in the hot water sluicing down his body, gleeful and proud of his dick, washing it with both hands, praising himself: There you go, you're the king. Bravo, player, you've saved my reputation, you didn't let me down.

Time had taken its toll on my brother Jawad, made a laughing stock of him as he got older.

He had once been the young and handsome Don Juan who Azizeh fell in love with, the one who melted her heart, the one who could make any of the most beautiful girls at university fall for him, the one who would leave every last one of them as soon as he slept with them. Nadine confessed to me that she had once had a relationship with him. He would talk to them about revolution and the need for liberation. At home he was a different person altogether. He was the master whose word was law. He prevented me from marrying Hani, got in my father's face and nearly beat him up when he told him that I knew what was best for me and that my life was mine to determine. My aunt Ruqaya used to dote on him, and my mother raised him the way she wanted, turning him into a powerful brother.

Jawad was sex-crazed his whole life. When he looked at a woman, all he saw was her vagina. Whenever he drove past the house of a woman he'd slept with, he would make a lewd reference to his dick. He wanted to sleep with every woman he was attracted to. He would get all feverish and fantasize about being with her even if he never managed to get near her. When he slept with his wife or one of his mistresses he would imagine a woman crossing the street who was going to sleep with some other man.

He seemed pleased with himself whenever he uttered the word 'mistresses' in the plural. It would be a sign of inadequate masculinity if there wasn't more than one of them. When he heard a friend say that big feet were a sign of a large dick, he began trying to exaggerate his large feet in front of any woman he found attractive.

College girls weren't that into him, so he lusted after the prostitutes he discovered so much pleasure with. He avoided his wife Samiha by spending his days in bars and cabarets. The odd thing was that when he fell for a woman, he became all fired up with romantic love. In his conception, love wasn't simply the desire for a woman of his dreams he'd never meet in real life. The woman who turned him on the most was the one he would never be able to touch or even imagine himself sleeping with.

Samiha endured more from my brother Jawad than any woman possibly could. She wasn't able to change him or even make him notice that she existed until she got sick and needed looking after, and then when his own strength left him.

Samiha was strong. He was persistent, though, and she finally came around to marrying him after having refused to do so when he first started pursuing her. She didn't even let him touch her hand, which really got to him as he had always thought of himself as being irresistible to women. After they were married she found strength in her chaste love, then in her children, the same way she would find strength despite his habitual trysts outside the marital home. She wouldn't forgive him and sleep with him until after he pronounced his repentance, kissed her hand, and cursed the devil who had messed with his mind as well as those women who were the absolute evil, who, as the saying goes, distracted the bear from his forage. Samiha was steadfast, swallowing her pride even as bitterness made her voice shake, perpetual raspiness became her trademark voice. He refused to discuss anything with her, only rarely talking to her at all. With time her powers were drained and she became weak.

Once she came over and complained to me in the presence of Suad and Hoda, then told me she was still steadfast and satisfied in the role of the victim, sighed and said, 'It doesn't bother me that he runs around with other women night and day. What matters is that at the end of the day he comes home and sleeps next to me.'

After Samiha had gone, Hoda said, 'You know something, Nahla, we women are cursed. In the name of power we become weak. In the name of patience we lose ourselves. A woman pretends to be weak so that her husband will show her mercy, so he'll promise that great things are in store. How can women behave like this? I mean, to just sit there in the image that's been laid out for them. What matters is that you should talk about it, girl. Sweetheart, don't wait until Judgement Day. Let other women enjoy themselves like that. What a bunch of bullshit, at the end of the day he prostrates himself and tells her, Oh I love you so much, honey. A woman is supposed to just wait her whole life for him to utter those words.'

Samiha no longer cared much for my brother. He tried getting closer to her ever since his erectile dysfunction, but she didn't respect him, especially after discovering those little blue pills in his trouser pocket. The only thing she kept doing with any regularity were some of his daily rituals: preparing his coffee in the morning, placing a single apple on the serving tray for him to eat after he'd had a shower and before he'd had his coffee.

One morning when he came into the living room to have his coffee, he found an entire basket of fruit instead of that one apple. Sitting down on the sofa he picked up an apple and started to scratch it, scoffing at Samiha's slight. Then it dawned on him that she was rewarding him with a basket of fruit for having slept with her the night before. Stroking the hairs on his chest, he burst out laughing and muttered to himself, My God, women. I know them all too well, they really know how to get under my skin. They're all a bunch of whores. I mean, they all want a man to profess his love for them and flirt with them.

Jawad had already popped a Viagra as he drove to meet up with a woman when she called his mobile to cancel their rendezvous. He turned around and went home to sleep with Samiha after telling her how he hungered for her in a way he had never done before. For her part, she knew full well that there was something fishy going on, she knew his body and the limits of his capacity all too well. He never took those blue pills for her. He would wind up humiliated around her, unable to show off his virility. That little pill couldn't burnish his image in her eyes the way it did for other women who were ignorant of his inadequacy.

Those blue pills my brother Jawad relied upon were the reason he descended into ruin on more than one occasion.

There was another time when he booked a room for the night in a hotel overlooking the sea in Jounieh after arranging a date with this woman. Before he left, the whole house reeked of his cologne. Samiha was perplexed, and grew more irritated by his patent happiness about having convinced this woman to meet him after long fantasizing about being with her. He slipped a Viagra into one pocket and a sleeping pill into the other, well aware that he would be unable to fall asleep without it on a different pillow in a strange bed. When the two of them got to the room, he waited for the woman to go into the bathroom so he could take the Viagra, in order to be ready for her when he started kissing and touching her. But in his rush to swallow it without her seeing him, he took the wrong pill. Within minutes he started yawning even as she sprawled out on the bed beside him, then he crashed and started snoring. When he woke up in the morning she was nowhere to be found. He was disappointed, confused about what had happened the night before. He only figured it out when he put his hand in his pocket and found the blue pill still there. He thwacked himself on the head and cursed the day women were created.

He called the next day to apologize, claiming he had just been extremely tired. She accepted his apology after he told her he felt safe enough around her to quickly fall asleep in her presence. She agreed to see him at her place because her mother was going to the mountains for two days.

Jawad slipped a Viagra pill in a small vial in his pocket, so that there would be no mistake this time, and headed over to her place. He opened the vial in order to quickly swallow the pill the moment she went to pour him a drink, but the blue pill fell from his hand onto a blue floor rug. It was lost. He couldn't find it. When the woman came back with the drink in her hand, she was surprised to find him down on all fours like an animal, pawing at the carpet with both hands, his face pressed down against it because of his poor eyesight. He staggered to his feet when she asked him what he was up to, what he was looking for.

'No,' he replied, 'it's nothing, sweetie. I'm just so impressed with this rug, it's really dazzling. I was trying to tell if it's silk or cotton. Holy shit I truly have never seen such a beautiful rug.'

He was saved in this instance as he got a phone call from a friend. After hanging up he said, 'I'm so sorry, sweetie. Something really important has just come up at home and I have to go.'

He wasn't able to calm down until he had left her apartment. He stood there facing the lift, waiting on tenterhooks for it to arrive, sweat pouring down his face before he was able to run off into the night. He was too embarrassed to call that woman ever again. Yet sometimes he would pop one of those blue pills before heading out at night to get laid at nightclubs or bars, and if he didn't manage to find a way to get off there, Samiha was always around to oblige.

In the autumn of his life, after the doctor had forbidden him from taking Viagra any longer, my brother Jawad the physics professor started frequenting bars in order to cheer himself up and have a good time with prostitutes. The funny thing was that he wasn't even interested in sex any more. When he was alone with one of those women all he wanted was for her to stand him facing the wall, his back turned and both his arms lifted, and to scold him the same way his teacher in the village used to do when he was a little boy. I have no idea why exactly he did that, whether this punishment sent him back in his mind to the first unforgettable pleasure he ever experienced with the Heartbreaker, or whether he took pleasure in having his body toyed with. His perverse sexual habits didn't stop there. One night he went out cruising in Beirut, stopping on a side street in Hamra for a young lady who appeared to be streetwalking. She got in the car, sat next to him and asked him for five dollars.

'Five dollars for what?' he asked, turning towards her with an inquisitive look.

'Anything you want,' she replied.

'No, I don't want that. Take the five dollars and show it to me.'

He fixed his gaze on her crotch and kept staring as she lifted her dress and pulled down her panties while he continued driving. Then she asked him for five more dollars if he wanted her to show him her chest. And he did. Then she pulled up her blouse. He parked the car in an empty dark alley. Before she got out of the car she gave him her phone number and told him, 'Call me anytime. I'll show you anything you want, sir.'

My brother Jawad swore off women when his penis started to betray him. He became a loyal servant for his wife Samiha when illness destroyed her and reduced her to extreme debility, so weak that a man could no longer look at or feel any desire for her. He began caring for her, bathing her, washing her, taking her to the hospital every day for dialysis.

He mourned her for a long time after her death. He didn't bury her in the village but in Beirut so that he would be able to visit her anytime he wanted. It was odd that he started to visit her grave and tell her all the things he never told her while she was alive. After her death he would start crying over the silliest of things.

One night he awoke to the sound of her voice disturbing his sleep, but it was just the pouring rain outside. He imagined she was calling him. He got up and began to think about how much Samiha used to hate the cold, how she would almost certainly be shivering in her grave right then from the freezing rain. Why else would she have called out to him at the top of her lungs while he was asleep? He tossed and turned a lot all by himself in bed thinking about her. Without even realizing it, he got out of bed, threw aside the plastic sheet covering the kitchen table and rushed off into the storm, towards the cemetery. He covered her grave with the sheet and talked to her even as he started to cry, his tears mixing with the rain.

12

The whole way to the Bekaa Valley, as we sliced our way through the fog clinging to the mountain road, Suad was her characteristically quiet self. Dense clouds like a giant white monster swallowed up my car and then slunk away to devour the villages, mountains and forests. I was thrilled by what I saw. I had the urge to shout, possibly to cry. It wasn't just that the beauty of the place was delightful but also painful the way pleasure can sometimes be. Suddenly I found myself crying out as I beheld the grandeur of fog and nature.

'My God, I love you so much! Nothing makes me love you more than beauty like this. I can see your face in it, my dear!'

Suad looked at me in surprise, then smiled slightly. It was the first time I had ever gone with her to visit her mother's village in the Bekaa. She had invited me to attend her cousin Mounira's wedding. I liked Mounira very much. The way I danced turned people's heads, made me feel as though I was soaring on wings made out of the gaze and rhythmic clapping of all those crowded around me. Suad's husband seemed to be dazzled by me. He danced with me and then flirted a bit, using words I didn't think were directed towards me as much as they had been buried inside of him which he simply needed to get out of his system.

We walked back from the wedding to her grandmother's house to spend the night, the house where Suad spent most of her summers when we were younger. There wasn't a trace of blue in the sky, just a thin layer of scattered clouds oscillating between brown, black and grey after having been dappled with waves of other colours just a little while ago.

The moon in the Bekaa Valley can melt your heart. You'd be hard-pressed to find such a beautiful sight anywhere on earth. As if it's some kind of ancestral homeland up there, calm and happy, beautiful and at ease. The shining light in the low-slung sky can soothe the soul, blocking out any worries or darkness. It seemed so close I wished my arm was just a little longer so I could reach out and touch it, snatch it and put it in my pocket.

It hung there as though it were following us as we made our way back along the dirt road that led to Suad's grand-mother's house, with yellow autumn leaves fluttering to the ground. Soft music played as we walked in the door. I can still picture her grandfather, that eighty-year-old dancing with a horde of young men crowded around him, staring at him even as they opened a path for him to walk through. Their feet pounded out the rhythm, storing the power of youth, but his dabke, expressed through the musicality of his body, his senses and his movement, contained all the secrets of masculinity and chivalry. His shoulders were raised in the air, as though the stars in the sky were shining down on him as his thin body swayed and danced to the rhythm of his bamboo drumstick. My eyes were captivated by his attractive body and the ten-derness that radiated from the wrinkles all over his face, and the bamboo drumstick thumped as if flaying air, time and boredom.

In the living room of her grandmother's ancient stone house, we sat on a sofa covered with an Oriental throw, backed by straw pillows covered with warm arabesques. It was the first time I saw her at her grandmother's house. The way she moved around, the way she spoke were unlike her usual manner. Here she seemed comfortable.

For the first time in a long while I felt that she was more like herself, full of joy, satisfaction and relief.

Those emotions came flooding in all at once, unlike earlier times when I'd have to make do with hearing myself talk about Hani and my romantic exploits. She would rarely talk about herself, and even when she did so she would quickly fall silent again. I'd kick her sometimes, urging, 'Go on. Then what happened?' She would hesitate for a moment, smiling, and remain silent.

On that day Suad's voice couldn't contain all her secrets and all her pain. Her blood was boiling through her body, from the tips of her toes to the top of her head, her face was flush. She had never had such an urgent desire to speak, not because our times together were monopolized by my own anxieties and secrets, but because she had always preferred not to talk about her relationships with her husband and her children, especially after developing her skin condition. Without warning, I heard her voice, clearly exhausted from lack of sleep, and all the signs of contentment and calm vanished from her face. I could sense that something was on her mind, and I wasn't wrong. She lay down by the sofa, as if she wanted to talk without my being able to see her.

'Have you noticed the way my husband's acting?'

'What do you mean?'

'He's obviously been hitting on you. I want you to know what kind of a man he is, he doesn't care whether you're my friend. He can't tell the difference between one woman and the next. My girlfriends, his students, they're all the same to him. All that matters is that they're female.'

'Don't tell me you're jealous. Quit thinking like that, Suad.'

'No, not at all. This isn't about jealousy or anything. I stopped worrying about that a long time ago. I wish I could feel something like jealousy. My feelings are a combination of acceptance and docility and disgust and surrender and despair. Everything feels the same to me. Now listen, don't say anything, just listen.'

And then Suad really started to speak.

'Sulayman would walk out of the house, leaving the smell of his cologne behind as he headed off to the university. All that mattered to him was winning the attention of his female students so that he could flirt with them. His eyes would float in a kind of honeyed happiness when one of them called. He'd talk to them for long periods of time in our bedroom that I had ceded to him a long time ago while I went to sleep in my son's bedroom after he had gone off to study in America.'

Sulayman played with the milky-white hairs on his chest through the gap in his robe, scoffing at her, 'What do you care if I talk to one of my students? Do you think you're so attractive? Go on, get out of my face. Go look at yourself in the mirror.'

For the first time she exploded in his face. Her entire body was an erupting volcano, articulate, as if her loud voice was dragging her away to slam her against the wall or a metal column. She shattered. Then it dawned on her that he was gaslighting her, that she had latched onto him thinking he would guide her to salvation. She felt as though they were both damned. She tried to frighten him with her screaming, hurling her fear at him in order to liberate herself from it. The screaming nearly broke her, but she felt the pleasure of unloading a burden. She promised herself that she would never again need to scream that way.

In order to draw strength away from her husband, to reclaim her own feeling that she was stronger and more important than him, she decorated the house with pictures of her younger self. As she hung them up, she told herself he could distort every period of her life except that one.

She spread those pictures out all over the house but he would pass right by them without even noticing. Once she spotted him catch a glimpse of one and stop to look, but she understood that he seemed to be looking at a picture of some beautiful woman he didn't know, someone he couldn't ever remember meeting, a perfect stranger. That made her feel even more estranged from herself and her old photos, like a denial of her past. She could not look at herself in those photos any more, so she gathered them up and hid them in a special drawer in her dresser. She no longer looked at them. Once she opened the drawer to clean and organize them, but her entire past seemed to have been spoiled, so she shut the drawer and never opened it again.

At first Suad had been the stronger one in the relationship. She forced Sulayman on her family, and they furnished her marital home for him. She paved the way for his professional life by introducing him to the professor who had supervised his PhD. Her family turned to a well-connected political figure who supported Sulayman in his bid to become a university professor. She had once been an activist, and I can't understand how she settled for such an unbecoming relationship. She used to believe it was a good thing that he would have her. Was that because she had been traumatized by the war, now trying to beat a path back into the organization he belonged to? Or because of her skin condition? Or had everything in her life and that of her family simply been turned upside down?

One day in the cafe where we met up with Hoda, who had become one of our closest friends, she told us that she had agreed to marry Sulayman. That was in the early nineties. She showed up wearing a big blouse over her blue jeans, her face bulging with the desire to speak, excitement radiating off her. Her irises were dilated, shining bright, dancing happily against the pure white of her eyes. She told us how Sulayman had taken to her, how she felt such chemistry with him, but also that she took that decision to marry him based on a supposition: marriage and children make a woman stronger. Sulayman was a simple man, good and suitable. I didn't get involved in their conversation when Suad started talking about marriage based on a formula.

'Come on, Hoda. Don't rain on my parade. I'm a grown-up now and I need to live according to a formula. I want to get married and I want to have kids. Besides, we're already engaged.'

'But marriage isn't supposed to be built upon a formula.'

'Sure it is. You and your husband Tarek have an agreement. If he cheats on you, you look the other way.'

'Yes, we have an agreement, and I may turn a blind eye to his mistakes. But I know that he loves me as much as I love him, even more. He treats me very well, and I love that.'

'I'm going to love Sulayman, too. He's great. I understand him even more, accept him even more. I have no problem with marriage.'

'There's a big difference between loving someone and accepting them.'

'There's a passageway between love and acceptance that one has to keep open. Sometimes you don't even notice that it's open. And with love, the other awakens something inside of you, something you nurture as much as necessary. Just like a flower, and you know that it only lives as long as you water it.'

'What are you talking about? I can't just decide how much to water my love. Love is as irrepressible and as undammable as a raging river. Maybe you're talking about one kind of relationship. There's companionship and affection, but there's a difference. The love that I'm talking about comes with passion and dizziness, with lots of words, true romance and real adoration.'

'Look, Hoda. I don't want to leave the window fully open any more, to let the curtains flap in the breeze. It's true that if you open a window the air gets a bit more pleasant, but everything can get all messed up, all your stuff can get blown around. You might get cold, too. No, I'd rather just open the window a little bit or else shut it and run the air conditioning by remote control, to just sit here and feel safe. It's much easier when things are clearly defined, when you know exactly where you stand. If you open the window just a little, you can count the stars, but if you go out under a vast sky, you can't count them all, you get lost, you get all confused.'

'But there are more beautiful things. If love leaves you exposed under a vast sky, can't you see how many stars there are up there?'

Sulayman used to watch Suad walk down the hall towards the kitchen from the same sofa in the living room where he would sit whenever he was visiting his brother Yousef. His face burned bright and his big eyes shone as she brought in the coffee tray and sat down across from him. He would steal a glance at her from time to time as he discussed politics and other national affairs with his brother, the fingers of his right hand mechanically tapping the wooden arm of the sofa. When she opened the door for him Sulayman started to flirt with her, blurting out how radiant she was in the red turtleneck sweater she was wearing on that bitter-cold winter's day.

Over the course of the first few days Suad got to know Sulayman, he didn't make much of an impression on her. She didn't really even notice he was there. Any relationship that might develop between the two of them would end the way all her previous relationships did since she broke up with her college boyfriend, Marwan. I can still remember the way she would sit on her knees, her hair pulled back in a ponytail, fawning over him, so delighted by the treasure of love she had discovered. But when they broke up she showed no willingness to even think about him. She never shared with me the secret of why it ended, saying nothing more than that he wasn't worthy of her affection. In every subsequent relationship she would come to find that the love she felt wasn't true, that it wasn't the love she dreamt about—that is until she fell in love with Sulayman. For the first time in a while, she thought about getting married. It had been a long time since she ended her relationship with Marwan and denied herself any such possibilities. At that time she was against getting married and having children in a country that went to war every ten or twenty years. Children are nothing but fodder for death and instruments of war and exile. Tarek agreed with her back then, on the day his wife Hoda invited us over for her birthday party. That day Suad said that the only thing that mattered to her any more was teaching philosophy at university, and that the academic dimension of her life had become much more important.

When Sulayman knocked on the door I let him in and noticed right away the lascivious way he was looking at her, not a predatory face so much as a kind of jubilation at being near her. Melting into the couch Sulayman started to rhapsodize about his dream of pursuing a doctorate in philosophy too. She found him humble and ambitious. He talked about his difficult financial straits. When he started discussing philosophy with her, his erudition seemed vast, especially his reading of Nietzsche, which she went back to read again after he had left. At some moment her impression of him shifted. No longer her brother's short, poor friend, Suad imagined him right there in front of her, standing tall, with love and ambition shining in his eyes, his pupils spiriting her away. She thought she was sitting there with him, locked in an embrace, feeling an unusual pleasure at being whisked away like that. It all happened in a flash, as if a long time had passed, a feeling she had not experienced since her relationship with Marwan had ended.

Suad was in her thirties when she fell in love with Sulayman and forced him on her family. What convinced her to get married after all that time was her conviction in Nietzsche's argument that motherhood increased the strength and authority of a woman. During the war she had been debilitated. Suad didn't give her family any reasons to reject Sulayman. She was their spoiled little girl. Sulayman changed dramatically, though, amassing so much self-confidence that he began to mistreat her and detest her, to be disgusted by her and refusing to sleep with her, especially after she developed her skin condition.

***

After months of not seeing her, and for the first time since she had got married, we ran into each other by chance at a literary gathering. Our friendship came back even stronger, and she became my closest friend once again, the way we were during childhood and adolescence. But when I first saw her I didn't recognize her at all. Of course I realized that a person changes but I had never dreamt someone could be transformed to the point that they lost all their previous traits and actually became a new person. It felt as though the old Suad had been born, had lived and died, and that she had been resurrected as an older woman with all new characteristics.

She was very thin, her facial features delicate, her gaze so childlike that she looked like an apparition. I couldn't understand why she gave off the impression that she might collapse at any moment, generating in me the desire to protect her, to take care of her, to fall in love with her, knowing full well that she wasn't going to break because she had an invisible inner strength that would keep anyone from ever controlling her.

If I was surprised by how much she had changed, I remained constantly astonished by the person she had become.

The wrinkles of her narrow face seemed to have slackened and become less numerous. Her thin, pink lips had grown engorged, brownish and less sleek. I don't know what kind of disease had turned her skin all scabrous and caused her veins to expand; her skin was turning a horrifying shade of purple and her veins were nauseating. Her face, which had once been wheat-coloured and attractive, turned the colour of rancid barley, pockmarked with large, splotchy discolouration.

What really frightened me was that Suad had developed a feeling of worthlessness she had never known before. I can remember how she used to chastise Azizeh for feeling that way when we were young. She lost her self-confidence after developing that skin condition, which may itself have been caused by her depression and anxiety, her pain and loneliness. She consequently cut off all sexual contact with her husband Sulayman.

On one particular day during the later stages of the war, it was hot and there was no electricity, so she put on a pair of shorts to cool off. Her husband stared at the splotches all over her legs and said, 'Get your sick ass away from me. Who would have a woman like you in their house? God curse my misfortune, sonofabitch.'

At that moment all of Suad's feelings towards him fell away, and this man, the one she had married and imposed upon her family so rashly, was the person she hated most in the world. At the same time she was totally incapable of letting go of her feelings of weakness and being unwelcome by her family and her children.

All Suad could think about was her aunt Mounira, whom she loved so much for her warmth and for how comfortable she felt when she was around her or when she went over to her house. She would place her head in her lap and immediately begin to feel better. When her aunt got tired it was an unmistakable sign that Suad had been cursed by the evil eye. She would stroke her forehead, her hair, and make her feel at ease until all the pain in her head went away.

Suad walked out of her apartment on al-Watwat Street in Sanayeh and headed towards Zuqaq al-Blat, along the green line, towards Aunt Mounira's. The streets had been emptied because of the shelling. She didn't know where her tears were coming from. She walked blocks and blocks without a care about the militiamen armed to the teeth with guns and grenades scattered among the alleyways, entryways and rooftops. The owner of a used clothing shop, whose door had cracked open, called out to her, telling her of some brand-new boxes he had just opened in which she was sure to find something she liked. The street was totally abandoned, all the shops closed except this one. Her tears had dried up, and feelings of emptiness and sorrow propelled her inside, now that the shopkeeper had opened up his wares to her. The young man was tall, bald, broad-shouldered. His complexion was leprous, his face pock-marked, his green eyes contained black dots, like dots of desire. The edges of his brown eyelashes were a lighter shade.

Suad had stopped walking down the street leading to her aunt's house to go shopping, slinking down another street instead. After that incident, Suad's betrayals only existed in her mind, she stopped talking to me about what she was thinking because, if she talked about it, that would amount to her doing it all over again.

**

Suad didn't talk much any more. She seemed totally devas-tated, distracted all the time. She was the spoiled daughter in a family of men, a family that had once been liberal and open-minded but which became religious and partisan after the war because of the sectarian circumstances and communal rancour that prevailed in Lebanon and around the region. Even her brother Bilal, who had been a Marxist and a leader in a leftist party, became an official in a religious party. He divorced his wife Rima when she refused to put on the veil. He had fallen in love with Rima while he was a student in Paris. They lived together for years, and then got married after a long courtship. She stared him straight in the eye and said she'd get divorced before wearing the veil. In his own way, Suad's brother Ahmad, the youngest in the family, a lawyer, went berserk when his two-year-old daughter showed her underpants to male visitors while she was sitting on the floor in the living room playing with her toys, with no attention from Rima; he threatened to divorce Rima if it ever happened again. Suad did veil herself for a little while. She imagined that the veil could render her body mute, make it die, but she discovered that while it may have been within her power to conceal her body, she couldn't keep her voice hidden. She kept on talking anyway, so she decided to unveil, choosing to wear long-flowing clothes that would hide her figure instead.

Everything about Suad's life made her feel estranged from her past and her present. She perpetually felt like she was alone, cut off, that she had never had a home in the first place. Her children began to behave just like her uncles as they got older and turned more religious, rejecting her for going without the veil. Her husband sympathized with the children, as though they were his kids alone. She didn't feel like they felt the same affection for her that she felt for them. She spoke with such awe about how they excelled at university, about their sharp intelligence, but she only talked about them the way she would talk about distant relatives, not the way a mother would, as if she were sometimes convinced that she wasn't actually their mother, which was just what her husband wanted. She began to hold back and conceal her feelings towards them. The one thing that made her feel most like herself was university teaching. After all, she had a prestigious academic position, she was an accomplished philosophy professor. Once we were all sitting in the Rawda Café, and when Hoda said that work was deathly boring, Suad smiled and said she was at peace with her job, which made her feel alive. She felt like she truly existed when she was doing it, to the point that she came to believe that her only source of power was her job, not motherhood which had disappointed her and failed to give her strength. On the contrary, motherhood forced her to put up with things she would never have accepted before, but she didn't have the strength to rebel twice—once through her belief in love and freedom, and a second time through motherhood. She believed Nietzsche: she had gone into marriage and motherhood and she no longer had anything else, outside of university classes she wouldn't speak to anyone. But Suad would always bend her ear to me, carefully listening to whatever I had to say. She would sit across from me, hike up her skirt, and stretch out her legs as though she wanted someone to accept her sickness, to love her, to recognize that she was a person and not just a spurned woman. She didn't speak with her family much any more. She would just listen to them, silent and apathetic. She only talked to her father after he fell into a coma that lasted several months; her father who had always been traditional and a believer was the only one she reconciled with. She would go visit him in the hospital and talk to him for a long time, just the two of them, he with his eyes closed and unable to hear her. She complained to him about her husband and her children and her siblings. She wouldn't stop talking until some point when she would hear the sound of her own voice and notice that she was talking to herself.

Suad could only stop talking to herself when she was with me, which felt no different to her than sitting by herself. The truth of the matter is that nobody could ever be as important to me as her. Often I would get the urge to tell her what a special place she held in my life, which could never be taken by any other creature in the world, not even my children. Once I told her she was integral to my life, a beautiful reason for me to stay alive. I told her how she and Hani and my children shared me. I love each and every one of them in a different way, but I really love her. The strange thing is that when I would sometimes talk to her about my desires and my body and my feelings, the way she looked at me made me feel I had said something that caused her to swallow her already-tied tongue.

Silence was Suad's constant companion.

Her thin lips looked to me like waves with words undulating on top of them, then dropping off. The same way I would tell my story in words, she would spin out strands of silence, a kind of silence that didn't seem to stem from sorrow or social exclusion, or one caused by ignorance, helplessness or lack of understanding, but rather a vague silence whose secrets I couldn't discern, as though she had swallowed her voice entirely, or run away from it and lost it altogether. Even while she was in motion I couldn't think of her as anything but a pile of ambulatory silence.

Besides me nobody except Azizeh and Hoda would even look at her. She didn't seem to care at all that men had stopped noticing her. She just laughed and rubbed her hands together approvingly when I told her about how two long-time women friends I knew got into a fight when some guy walking behind them on Hamra Street started flirting with one of them. Each one claimed that he had been flirting with her and they fought like hell in spite of them being in their forties. There was only one time when I sensed Suad might be happy. We were sitting at the City Café and the waiter asked with great interest, without even looking at me, what she was going to have. He always seemed to do that when the two of us were together, or even when I was there by myself. That waiter obliterated the notion that I was the most beautiful woman of all. Suad used to find it strange, the astonishment plain in her eyes, and I understood that she was wondering to herself about why he should be interested in her when he was basically her children's age.

Not even the things she used to do perfectly well could eliminate her constant feeling of loss—loss of whom and what, I had no idea. Mysterious feelings—I never understood their secrets, their meaning, their source, as though she had become accustomed to them and they had petrified. Freshness in her life never seemed to last long. Sometimes a view of the sky would give her a feeling of possibility, granting her small gifts, but then again turning miserly all of a sudden.

13

My body calmed down from a feeling that was akin to flying, the kind of pleasure I hadn't experienced for a long time. When I was younger I used to have this recurring dream of soaring high over the deep wadi in our village. I'd come out of my body, out of the bed, shoot across the gorges, swoop down and then fly back up, climbing in the air as I flapped my wings with pleasure. Many times I would see myself falling and wake up in terror, thanking God I had only been on the brink of death in a dream.

I forgot all about it as soon as I woke up. Hani's name was on my lips this morning, as if I was about to call out to him. He called yesterday and we set a time to meet. He had been busy so I wasn't able to see him much over the past few days. Even though he calls me every day, I'm inexplicably gripped by the fear of being abandoned. That old wound like merciless fire and torturous love reopened whenever he went away. Fear drove me to do things that could keep me from thinking about him. I went back to my village after a long time. I met up with Hoda who told me how in love she was with her husband, how desperately she hoped they would grow old together. As usual I spent most of my time with Suad even though I thought about Hani constantly. Only the birth of my granddaughter managed to bring me enough happiness and distraction to prevent me from thinking about him.

The morning was sunny and pleasant. The sun beat down on half the living room in a way that cleared my soul and my body of all the staleness of waiting. Showering was like bathing myself in the waters of happiness and hope. I changed out of my pyjamas, had some coffee and read the paper. Before Suad and Hoda came over I went to play with my oldest granddaughter while my daughter Faten was still asleep with her newborn in the same room that was once hers before she got married. Playing with her I imagined she was Hani's granddaughter, and from time to time I could actually feel him come up from behind to hold me. Just then the telephone rang and I picked up to hear Saleem asking, 'How many kilos of meat do you want today?'

I don't know why I thought of my grandmother Amineh while I was playing with my granddaughter. I had been thinking about her all week before visiting my home village. The fear that Hani was out of my life again made me want to visit my family. Maybe abandonment drove me to places that resembled me, familiar and cherished places, as bereft as my heart, as dried-up as my body. I unconsciously steered my car southwards all alone. First I visited the graves of my father, mother and grandmother. I recited the Fatiha for them, talking to my father's grave for a long time, then gazing at the silent tombs of all the young men that had sprouted up during the war. I thought about how wars sowed graves but also how graves contained silence and peace yet no enemies.

Storms of loneliness, longing and pain raged in my eyes as I stood outside the old wooden gate that enclosed a lifetime of memories for me, an entire life that had disappeared inside that house.

The place was deserted. All the doors on every house in the neighbourhood were shut tight, their elderly inhabitants had all passed on, and the children all lived in Beirut now or in other corners of the world where they had emigrated to after all the wars. When I was a little girl I used to love stepping inside their homes, making myself comfortable, and listening to their stories about the harvest, the wheat and the olives, about djinns, angels and jackals, about anything they were willing to tell me, really.

Everyone had passed away—Suad's family, Azizeh's family, my grandmother Amineh and her neighbour Jameela, my uncle Mahmoud and my aunt Ruqaya. The old life that once dwelled in my soul was gone. For me the thick dust that covered the house was a white shroud. I don't know why the ghosts of the house seemed hidden inside. I could sense their presence but didn't have the power to see them.

Everything inside the house was ancient: my mother's first dress, which bore the smell of primitive things, the outside and the inside were in perfect harmony, crumbling stone in some parts, cement in others, indicating that the place had been built in stages. I studied the house and the garden, then the rooms that had been painted light green or pink a long time ago, while other ones had been left the way they were. Fresh concrete coated my grandmother's storeroom.

As I stood in the storeroom across from the two pomegranate trees, images danced before my eyes. I rummaged in my ears for old sounds: as if my mother's empty chair would complain to me about her absence, about how much it missed her; my father's old transistor radio on which he used to listen to Umm Kulthum, her voice flapping towards his fingers and his ears. Right before my eyes I could see my father's fez and his cane; the way my mother walked in her knit skirt, and I could smell the aroma of her cooking. I began to recreate an entire life spent in a house that was now deserted and desolate, just like my heart. Departure swallowed everything, wiped it all away. I was gripped by the strange conviction that places didn't only long for their previous inhabitants but would commit suicide to avenge their disappearance.

The quiet of the place reminded me of Suad's stony silence and the mysteriousness of my mother's feelings, that arid vacancy in her eyes when she saw the sheikh to whom she had been consecrated. The walls seemed to have exceeded the necessary waiting period for the previous inhabitants to return. The rooms were parched with thirst for the footsteps and the warmth of those people, dejected by their inability to elicit a response from them.

I didn't feel homesick but I did feel as though the house had forgotten me, that it no longer knew me. It seemed to consider me a stranger, wondering who I was. The house seemed to be doing more than just scolding me. It seemed to not remember me at all. The fact that I had dreamt about it—a dream I had from time to time in which I was able to visit—wasn't enough to keep it from deeming me an interloper.

When places lose the sensation of their previous inhabitants, the way they receive people turns colder, just like lovers who have split up, one of whom no longer thinks about the other or even recognizes them. I wished that something would give me a sign: the pomegranate trees, for example, or the soil where I buried my poetry. I looked up at the sky, thinking I might be able to find the North Star my father used to see when he was listening to Umm Kulthum, but I couldn't find it. I imagined that he had taken it with him wherever he had gone, but I could still feel his old, warm breath in the house, his perpetually luminous, handsome smile that would make me feel a kind of magic that spread through the house and out into the village.

I gazed out at the new generation of olive and fig trees that didn't recognize me and all the other little trees that grew outside our house. I imagined they had inherited something from their mothers the same way I had inherited from mine, but now my and the trees' mothers had all departed for the void.

My old impression of the village dissolved into a new one. The castles on the outskirts that had been restored didn't seem to be rooted in the ground in quite the same way as the houses that were as old as the village itself. They looked ugly and undistinguished to me, without authenticity or vitality. The town square was also deserted, hungry for the old men and women of the village. Even the domesticated animals, the chickens and the mules, no longer came out the way they once did. Nobody lived in the buildings and they were all boarded up. Everything was hidden away except for the martyrs' posters that had been hung up all over the entrance to the village, photos of bearded young men who were not part of my memory. To me they seemed like new immigrants. But thinking better of that I asked myself: Who is the arriviste, I or they? Who is the foreigner, I or they? There seemed to be a new meaning of death, a meaning I didn't understand, one that my village had never known before.

After driving around the neighbouring villages my eyes filled up with that old light. My throat clenched in the loud silence. There was a pleasant chill in the air, and I wished that the sky blocking out the light wouldn't forget about me. Tears of longing for my father and my mother streamed from my eyes, and out of my throat came a silent prayer to hear their voices, if only in a dream. The whole way back to Beirut I couldn't stop seeing the face of my grandmother Amineh. I recalled the story of her lonely demise in the storeroom, which appeared before my eyes when I opened its ancient door.

My grandmother Amineh had nine children, but they all died suddenly for mysterious reasons. Some of them dropped dead while they were playing. The people of the village urged her to give her youngest the name of an animal in order to protect her male children. And that was how my father was named Fahd (Leopard) . . . and he lived!

My grandmother went blind after already having gone deaf. During her last days I would listen to her mutter to herself about every afternoon gathering in the storeroom, especially after her friend Jameela stopped visiting because my grandmother could no longer hear anything she said. I found it strange the way she would fall silent as soon as I came inside. One time I sneaked into her room on tiptoes, but when she sensed my presence she froze and went silent. After confirming that I was Nahla, I asked her whom she was talking to and why she had gone quiet when I came in, but she didn't respond.

'You never want to tell me whom you're talking to,' I said jokingly. 'But when you start talking to yourself, Granny, you're losing it. We're going to have to put you in a home.'

'I'm losing it, little girl? Shame on you. You're going to insult me as well? Fine, I'll tell you what's going on. It'll be our little secret, Granddaughter. When all of you go away and I'm left here all by myself and have no idea what's going on in the world, Saliha comes to check in on me. Sometimes she comes to have some fun, talk to me for a while, and fill me on the village news. I haven't had any other friends since Jameela stopped coming around, which she said is because I've gone deaf, may God forgive her.'

After she had told my mother and father and everyone else about Saliha, I didn't hear another word from her. Late one afternoon I went into her bedroom and found her sitting on her mattress all by herself, in sadness and silence. When I asked her what was wrong, she replied with milky-white tears in her eyes.

'Why does she treat me like this, Granddaughter? This one time she came to talk to me and joke around. Sometimes I can see her even though I'm blind, coming out of her room dressed in all white. Now she's gone and isn't coming back because you've made a mockery of me. Ali bin Abi Talib appeared to me in a dream and said, "Your secret has been exposed, Amineh, and that woman is no longer going to come and see you. Why did you disclose your secret?"'

Then she continued, as if talking to herself, 'O Ali! O Commander of the Faithful! Why are you punishing me? What has it got to do with me if Nahla told? And what did I ever do that you would keep me from her?'

I remembered my grandmother as I played with my own granddaughter that morning, how her broad grin could fan out to encompass her entire face when I did well in school. Then Suad and Hoda came over to congratulate my daughter on the birth of her second child. I behaved just like my grand-mother, chasing my granddaughter around, embracing her with a big smile, and dancing around with her in my arms.

Grandmothers take care of their grandchildren, although at some point they can become loathsome because it reminds them of how old they've become. The only time I can forget about the whole world and forget about me and Hani is when I'm with my grandkids. I said this to Suad so many times. I also told Hani the last time I saw him. He nodded in agree-ment, and the two of us laughed like little children with grey hair. He was giddy over having become a grandfather.

I don't remember getting as much joy from my own children as I did from my grandchildren, who simply delighted me. Was it because they're my progeny, my children's children? I was connected to them by love alone, without any maternal connection or immediate feelings of responsibility, without the kind of fear that would come over me if my children were concerned. Did that have something to do with my age? Or was it that I had been so much younger and bedraggled with the two of them that the pleasure of watching them grow up in front of me had been interrupted? Or was it because through my grandchildren I could relive my youth and my old relationships with my children when they were still under my wing? Or did we simply relive the past through them, reconnecting to a relationship with the life we might believe receded into the past as we got older?

When Suad she came over, I asked all these questions, with my granddaughter sitting on my lap. She smiled at me as usual, then spaced out, as if her soul had floated away, then stared at my body ambiguously, the way she would sometimes do just before taking off her blouse and wearing only a T-shirt that showed off her forearms. It felt like she was inviting me to inspect the scars left behind by her skin disease. I could sense how upset she was with me and I wondered why she would act like that, why she'd decide to let me see her hideousness. Was it because her husband had rejected her body and she wanted me to accept it, or was she disclosing a secret to me in order to be rid of it, without even realizing how much it disgusted me?

Feelings of shame returned and overwhelmed me as I recoiled from her. I was sickened by myself as well, irritated that I had only ever thought of Suad as being close to me when she was fully dressed. I think she realized that, because one time she asked me, staring long and hard to make sure she got an answer: 'Nahla, why do you smile all the time but then look at me so doubtfully whenever you see me wearing my long clothes?'

What really caught my attention was the fact that Suad had been wearing her large blouse when Hoda came over to congratulate my daughter on the birth of her child.

***

The house was boiling and my heart was pounding because I was scheduled to see Hani that evening. Ever since he called me my fear of losing him had dissipated. Faten's mother-in-law was concerned that she didn't want to breastfeed her new-born. Hoda, so full of feminine and maternal sensibilities, so very capable of taking care of others, placed her hand on her heart and welled up with tears when Faten cupped her left breast, which was bursting with milk, in the palm of her hand. Faten closed her eyes in order to staunch the tears, bit her lip, and let out a barely audible welp of pain.

Hoda was dying to know what was going on with Saleem and me.

The week before I had felt an urgent desire to be alone with her. She, Suad and I were in a shared taxi together headed home from the cafe, and the two of us went back to my house after Suad got off near her place in Sanayeh. I had been complaining so much to her about Saleem and now I wanted to hear about her relationship with her husband.

The truth is, I always thought about Hoda when Hani was away, when I got bored of waiting for him to come back, feeling empty and listless without him. Her happy marriage came to mind, her desire for her husband that hadn't at all diminished, the commitment she had made.

I often thought about trying to emulate the way she loved her husband so that I might be able to fortify my own commitment to Saleem.

Before telling me about their relationship, a single tear as thin as cigarette paper darkened her eye as she began telling me how Tarek had become cold towards her.

She confided in me that when he touched her vagina it felt like a place of safety, happiness and harmony, that the sex had improved in marriage as their bodies got to know each other better. Familiarity opened up all their secrets and hidden corridors of pleasure. Tarek helped her to accept her body as it was, to make peace with it after having gained a lot of weight. He would compliment her breasts even after they had started to sag a bit, kissing her thin and wrinkly cleavage folds. Hoda began to enjoy herself more because he was so generous towards her in new ways, making up for his premature ejaculation and his sexual weakness by touching her body more. He no longer entered her as quickly as he did before, using suggestive innuendo when she stood on the other side of the counter or behind the ironing board, or else shoving her up against the wall and suddenly starting to have sex with her standing up. She experienced more pleasure because she was growing more attuned to her own body and its needs. After all, a woman gets to know her body more profoundly in middle age.

Hoda wondered why she had begun to think about taking more than she gave, about how there was still so much more for her to give. Had she become more assertive because she was no longer ashamed to take? Had her relationship with her body deepened? Or was it simply the case that people become more self-centred as they get older?

But then Hoda shifted course and told me about how her relationship with Tarek was falling apart. He had closed in on himself, she had turned inward as well; he avoided making eye contact with her when they had sex, he couldn't get hard. Things went back to normal when she finally figured out how to deal with him, pulling out all the stops to help him get erect. She dropped her objection to watching porn with him, finding ways to work through her own hang-ups about a certain way of touching or a hot new position.

Clear signs of satisfaction appeared all over her face. She smiled as she told me about taking a more serious interest in her body and her health because the body, after all, can judge and punish, can abandon you altogether if you rebel too much against it, can even break you if you don't take good enough care of it.

After Hoda left I took a shower, then called Saleem to ask if he wanted to have dinner. I told him I'd cook a special meal for him that we could eat out on the patio, play cards, and then do whatever he felt like.

I fantasized about him so that I could stop thinking about Hani. I didn't find him sexually unattractive, reminding myself that he wouldn't necessarily want to sleep with me anyway. He hadn't come near me for a long time because of his sexual dysfunction. We did little more than roll around and touch one another but there's no harm in trying again. Maybe now that he was older he'd say the kind of things Hani used to say to me. Maybe I'd even feel for him a fraction of what I felt for Hani.

Saleem would constantly disappoint me because he was incapable of being romantic, even for just a moment.

'Ohh, ohh, what a delight, woman. What an incredible spread,' he said, admiring the food. Then he proceeded to dig in without even looking at me, plunging his hands into the plates as though he hadn't eaten for a thousand years. His wide eyes bulged out of their sockets from the pleasure he was taking in the food, as strange noises and murmurings came out of his mouth. It was like sitting next to a man who had lived his entire life in the forest or in some remote prehistoric village, but who still didn't fail to mention the health benefits of every dish—which one increased cholesterol and sugars and fats in the blood. When we sat down in front of the television, he raised his rear end in my face and farted, as he had started to do recently, without even excusing himself.

I had never complained the way I did yesterday morning, when a foul stench wafted throughout the room. I asked him why he couldn't go into the bathroom to do that.

'What?' he replied annoyedly. 'If you were my wife, I'd say you were a strange one. Besides, you'd be telling me, man, it smells like musk and ambergris because you're my wife. But you tell me to go to the bathroom to do it.'

Ever since he had lost his ability to get hard, he started doing distasteful things, wouldn't help out in any way that required the least bit of effort. He was never flirtatious, avoiding any behaviour that might attract me to him or show me any respect, not while he was unable to sleep with me, anyway. As far as he was concerned I was no longer a woman or even a person, just a piece of his personal property, nothing more.

***

Saleem looked at Faten impassively as she cried out from the pain of her milk-filled breasts before he left the house at the same time as Hoda.

I didn't try to convince my daughter Faten to breastfeed the way her mother-in-law tried to do. I didn't tell her about the pride I took when I was with Suad, Azizeh and all my girl-friends, wearing milking pads under my bra because I was producing so much milk.

She had decided not to breastfeed because she feared her breasts would sag as a result. She had watched too many nature programmes on National Geographic, which made her recoil from breastfeeding because she thought she would turn out like all the other female animals. That was what really nauseated her.

Her mother-in-law came to visit her at my house as soon as Faten was released from the hospital, telling her, 'What a waste of milk, honey. There's not a woman on earth who doesn't boast about her own milk or who doesn't love to announce to the whole world that she's breastfeeding.'

My daughter remained silent. She was calm and smiling after I had replaced the contraption on her chest and handed her the medication the doctor had prescribed. Satisfied that she was all right, I headed back to my room to get ready to see Hani. I pulled out of my armoire the fancy dress I had bought and promised not to wear for anyone other than Hani. As I got undressed in front of the mirror, my body seemed particularly attractive, in contrast to the splotches I had seen all over Suad's skin. A new sensation came over me despite the changes in my body. I thought about how true that old expression is about the freedom of women's bodies, about how much care they put into them, even if they are under the power of men—because Hani was present there as I gazed into the mirror and thought about how he would look at my body now that we had agreed to meet.

I touched my breasts, held them in my hands and squeezed them together, remembering the days when they looked like pomegranates, just like my daughter's, and how embarrassed I was when Hani and I reconnected and he saw the way they were drooping. When we had sex and he kissed my breasts with his eyes closed, I wondered whether he thought about how firm they used to be or whether he still found them sexy.

The question vanished from my mind when I learnt that he still had fond feelings for me. The present can never be totally separated from the past. When I went to see him for the first time after our relationship rekindled, I immediately remembered his smooth, olive skin and the smallpox scars covering his gorgeous thighs. I can still remember his hard cock bulging under his tight trousers, so so long ago, his shoulders that used to be much broader, his waist that had swelled quite a bit, his ass that had always somewhat stuck out but had now become even more prominent. That whole time I was sure that the changes in his body had done nothing to quell my desire, that my lust for him wasn't quenched. And I recall on the day before going to meet him I asked Suad whether the body articulates its desire in a different way as it gets older, whether any of us can learn new ways of talking about desire, whether the body forgets all its earlier modes of expression or simply changes shape because it is no longer capable of accommodating those old ways.

My daughter's breast pump was right there in front of me as I slathered moisturizing cream all over my breasts before heading out to meet Hani. I could feel the sharp pangs when I struggled to help press milk from my daughter's breasts. The feelings of happiness and pride that I experienced while breastfeeding came back. I only breastfed my son Ahmad for a few days because my sadness over the death of my father had dried up my milk.

My breasts are for both love and motherhood, just like my vagina.

Hani used his mouth and hands to write a document of love all over my breasts, kissing them and caressing them. The white marks that speckled them ever since breastfeeding my daughter were like a tattoo that reminded me of her mouth and hands that I thought would never leave my chest, reminded me that breastfeeding was a covenant between my daughter and me, cementing her connection to my body.

I discovered that breastfeeding is the most extremely narcissistic stage of motherhood, but also the most intense affection one can have for oneself. While I was breastfeeding her, I thought of myself as a god, that all creation was my dominion, as if my breasts themselves were the universe and my entire being. An image of the Virgin Mary nursing Jesus appeared to me. I communed with her, denying the world all around. She and I were all alone in the world.

I was running towards her when she started crying, and I called out to her, 'My dear, my sweetie, come here.' I'd slowly and gently cradle her in my arms as I nursed her, without pressing too hard on her soft flesh and bones. Then I'd look down from time to time to make sure she was still breathing as she latched on to my breasts. My mother-in-law would say, 'The woman's lost it.'

Breastfeeding was like being with her in a cosmic nook. I'd close the door to her room so that we could be alone and listen to some soft classical music that would calm her down. Breastfeeding was an affirmation of the time when I was pregnant with her, when she was an extension of my body and I was an extension of hers, and not just for eating and nourishment. The mystery of my relationship with her vanished the moment she came out of my womb; that also eliminated my occasional feeling that there was a danger of her being taken away from me. The moment of nursing made me feel we were bound to one another in such a way that we would never be able to undo, neither she nor I, and that the relationship was so deep that no one would be able to get in its way, no matter who they were, not even my husband Saleem. After months of breastfeeding I no longer knew how to talk to her, how to make her understand as she gazed up at me, suckling in glee and safety: 'My dearest, this is my body and I'm nursing you so that it will become part of yours, my treasure, and there's nothing that will ever take you away from me.'

Strange feelings rolled over me when I nursed her in the presence of Saleem. I don't know why but I felt he was sometimes jealous, even if he was just sitting there watching us. 'I want to nurse, too, Nahla,' he would often say. 'Squeeze out some milk for me.' The truth is that his relationship with my breasts grew stronger during that time. He would suck harder on my nipples during sex. And often while he watched, he seemed to be thinking about his inability to experience that kind of moment, neither with his daughter nor with me. I used to wonder whether he hated me for the fact that the act of breastfeeding was mine and mine alone. From the look in his eyes it was unmistakable that he hungered to be the third arm of a triangle but he knew full well he couldn't participate in the act. I'll admit that I felt some pity that he became so distant at that moment. And I wonder whether God has given women breastfeeding as compensation for patriarchy.

I used to feel that Saleem came near us much less while I was nursing than while Faten was still in my womb. I genuinely wanted to tell him, whenever he stared at me, 'What are you good for when you've got someone like me to produce milk and create a child? And my milk allows this child to live, gives her life.'

Ahh, how I used to anticipate her waking up so I could feed her, to get rid of the pain shooting through my breasts, the same way they used to hurt before getting my period.

Breastfeeding was the way I expressed my love for her. I'd hold onto her little fingers that rubbed along my chest while I nursed and kissed her, and she'd smile up at me and continue suckling. I cried and felt pain the way she cried and felt pain before she knew how to nurse. The struggle between her and my breasts used to wear her out, especially when my nipples were still flattened and hadn't yet returned to being pointy after she learnt how to suckle.

The way she grabbed hold of me while breastfeeding made me feel like I was touching all the pleasure in the whole wide world, something that surpassed sexual pleasure, giving me with the same kind of satisfaction that it also brought her. I would lean into those feelings of pleasure and try to control them, sustained by the understanding that breastfeeding was necessary for her to live.

Slathering moisturizing cream all over my breasts before heading out to meet Hani, I recalled the moment when my daughter rooted around for my nipples while clinging to my chest, the way she suckled and gazed up at me with those almond-shaped eyes that resembled my own, and I would yearn for her to latch onto my nipple once again whenever she let go and nodded off to sleep for a while.

The way she held me could make me melt, and the sight of her could whisk me away from the world, towards her mouth as it opened slightly the moment she let go of my nipple, her tongue lolling to the side as a sign that she was still nursing, that she hadn't had enough yet. At that moment I would imagine her little tongue asking me, Are you still here? Do you see me? Can you feel me? Do you feel the same way I do? I would squeeze her and pull her in close to my chest. Just then her smile would become a way to feel alive, her smile that drove me wild whenever I started breastfeeding her again. I wouldn't know what she was thinking about, or what the secret of that smile was as she clung to my chest and nursed . . . that intimate smile that would never be seen again.

The two of us had a strong physical connection. It seemed like more than milk was passing directly from me to her when she suckled at my breasts. Strange feelings of hunger would come over me when I was finished nursing her, like the craving for chocolate I had when Hani wasn't around. At the time she turned two I became horribly depressed. I got sick, had a fever, and would break down crying for the silliest reasons. It felt like she was abandoning me, like she no longer needed me, as though this were the first real separation, not the moment of her birth. My milk started to leak out and I would just throw it away. Bitterness percolated through my insides. It felt like heartbreak. But the sense that I was getting my breasts back came over me, reclaiming them from my two children and my husband whom I refused to let near them during that time so that they could become my own property again.

14

I was feeling down and out. It had been about twenty days since I heard a word from Hani. My girlfriends were all excitedly chatting and giggling and their happiness somehow made me feel more alone.

Before heading over to Azizeh's I got dressed distractedly as questions bombarded me from all sides: Was my relationship with Hani over for good? Or were there extenuating circumstances that required us to go through another period of separation? And what was Hani up to right now anyway? Was he picking up the phone to call me and then putting it down again the way I would, or had he forgotten about me altogether? Did he take me to bed with him in his mind when he went to sleep, falling asleep with an image of me before his eyes or was I just imagining all of this?

Before walking out of the hotel room in Jounieh, where I had gone to see him twenty years before, he held my hands and smiled as he said, 'Leave your hands here with me when you go.'

I drew nearer to him, caressed his nose and replied, with a smile on my face, 'Go on, take them. I'd leave my soul, my heart, and my body with you, my entire memory, too.'

He pinched my cheek and started to wax poetic, 'There's nothing better than love as it grows, don't you think, Nahla?

Nothing can stave off getting old the way love does. Just look at how luminous you become after we've slept together.'

'Yeah, you know, all my girlfriends tell me that being in love is making me more beautiful, that it's really having an effect on me, that it's made me look like I'm twenty years old again.'

I used to think that everything ends except for Hani and me and our love. So why wouldn't he call? Had something happened to him or to someone in his family, God forbid?

I didn't realize that Hani had had a heart attack. His cell phone was switched off or he wasn't picking up. Ever since we restarted our relationship the spring before we would see each other every ten days or two weeks, sometimes a bit longer, but he would call me every day, he would send me a text as soon as he got up in the morning and before he went to sleep at night. I never asked for anything more. I was no longer anxious about whether he would remain by my side all the time or whether the two of us were going to do everything together the way I had been when I was younger, not only because I had a husband and had become a grandmother, but possibly because to me love had become something like candy, the sort of candy that brought me the kind of happiness I had always dreamt of, the kind that had been taken away from me, the feeling that I was truly alive, and possibly also because I had been nurtured by him, as Hani became more and more present inside of me. His presence was no longer external to me. My relationship with him and with my body are different at this age, the same way my relationship with other things has changed. When I was younger, my main concern was to be the centre of attention, for him to show me how much he cared for me, how sweet and special I was. The sound of my heaving body could drown out all other sounds. Now I have my life and my girlfriends. Even Hoda, who loved her husband more than anything else, started to enjoy spending more time with her girlfriends, staying out late with them. I feel as though a lot of the gaps in my life have been plugged. The pace of my life has slowed. I have acquired an incredible capacity to focus, profound desire has sprouted in me, as if a cell that had lain dormant inside of me during my agitated youth had been revived. Now it feels like an entire lifetime wouldn't be enough to appreciate the beauty in fluttering leaves, the motion of the waves, shadows cast by the sun, my granddaughter's giggling, or anything else in this life, though I know full well that such observation of the pleasure of life is little more than a ploy to escape the idea of death, or to postpone it anyway. Despite all of that, I fully realize that I am headed towards decline, that I will truly die if I lose him again because my love for him has never ceased. I still tremble like a young woman when I'm on my way to see him but I don't know exactly what it is that is shaking inside of me: my hands, my heart, my womb, or my entire body. Nothing is off limits for us, we talk to one another for as long as we wish.

All sense of time and age evaporates when I see him. The only times I feel like I have aged are when I sense that I'm going to lose him. All of a sudden my age is written all over my face. My neck bunches up. I don't understand how it is that my muscles grow taut whenever I see him, how I become more youthful.

I would often ask Suad whether the powerful feelings I was experiencing at this age could be called love, after love had been subjected to murder, amputation and abortion, or whether it was because I was approaching death, whether the feeling I had every time I saw him was that it might be the last, or perhaps it was because I had come to know what it is that I want from a man, because I know my body and my desires better, or whether it was the case that love is whatever feeling remains after sex, or whether he's my destiny, as Suad used to tell me all the time.

The tension in my expression yielded as Suad scrutinized my facial features, and I smiled in order to allay her confusion and her concern for me. Azizeh had invited us and our other girlfriends over for the afternoon. The older women were still happy to have get-togethers where there wouldn't be any men around. Early-morning gatherings were also held. They'd stay out late together at restaurants and nightclubs, maybe because they felt like they were no longer desired by men, or maybe to create another world for themselves because of how they marginalized were.

Azizeh's laughing and joking never ceased. And her mobile phone played a song by Assi Helani on repeat. Suad was as patient as a silent statue, following me with her bewildered expression because she could sense how nervous I was. Nadine and Mirna went out early to attend an art exhibition they had been talking about, but the event didn't really speak to them and they ended up feeling out of place and uncomfortable.

The women who had been invited by Azizeh sat there looking like dolls with stuffed cheeks. Their lips were full, but the muscles didn't seem quite right because of their advancing age, which made them look weighed down and paunchy, especially at the corners. Life seemed disabled, as if time was frozen now that Botox had wiped away any trace of expression and excitement on their faces.

I had often been tempted by the desire to do the same thing to my face, anytime I felt the urge to recapture its tightness and suppleness I had lost. I was ashamed that heads no longer turned my way, as if I had been shoved out of the scrum of life and banished to the margins. The wish to be like those women was growing in me before I met Hani. I would ask myself the same question that always crushed me:

Wasn't Hani present throughout my body regardless of whether I was flabby or firm? And wouldn't he still love my body no matter how much it changed? After I saw him again I thought about how much I had always adored his saggy neck, how I loved its rolls even when it was still relatively firm in his younger years.

Hot flashes consumed me as the women talked about their physical relationships with their husbands. And I wondered whether they had ever experienced true love.

Their puffy lips started flapping as they chattered on about the women of Beirut, about which ones were still with their husbands, and whose husband had left her or divorced her or married someone else. One could see their shapely, silicone-stuffed breasts through their open collars even as they judged someone or another who showed off in some clothes that didn't befit a woman of her age. Their bodies emanated a longing to be desired and loved—it was present in the look in their eyes, in the way they talked. But out of fear, they were unable to physically experience anything, limiting themselves instead to avenging their empty lives through the stories of others.

I don't know exactly why I tried to be so honest with them, to reveal my confusion when I said, 'You know, after the last time we met, I was driving home and asked myself, what even brings us together.'

They all replied in one voice: 'We thought about the very same thing.'

'And what did you come up with?'

Their response was unexpected, different from what I had been afraid they might say. They told me that even though they had asked themselves the same question, they felt that the bond between us was strong because we were so similar. It was natural for us to hang out.

I smiled without saying a word, feeling that it wasn't on me to ask the same question a second time. Nobody can predict where honesty among friends might lead.

After steering the conversation towards the latest diet they were all obsessed with, but which none of them was actually following, they returned to stories of men and husbands. A friend of Hoda's said, 'Come on now, don't tell me that men are more tolerable as they get older. There's nothing worse than old age. At night they snore, they spit and fart all day. All I can do is run off to sleep in another room.'

'And what's your husband like?' somebody asked her.

'What do you mean?'

'In bed.'

'Well, he's slow-moving, like a slug. It's pretty easy for me to get away. Just imagine, I suggested he take some Viagra after I heard some guys talking about it. What, are you trying to kill me? he asked. If you don't like what I'm doing why don't you just use your fingers? How pathetic is that? He'd rather not get any than be even a little bit embarrassed.'

'Please,' said Azizeh, 'you made me think of my dead husband as soon as you mentioned your fingers. I hated my fingers as much as I had to use them when he was still alive.'

Suad, who rarely spoke, got all worked up and said, in a quavering voice that was unlike her, 'Yesterday I took a sleeping pill. When I woke up in the morning I was all wet. When I asked my husband whether he had done anything, he said, Yeah, I woke up with the sun and I was hard so I fucked you from behind. Are you serious? I asked him. He said thank God I did it for once without having to look you in the face. Otherwise I wouldn't have been able to do it. Why, did someone else do something to you?'

Azizeh had a friend in her fifties who had fallen in love with a man twenty years younger and spent a lot of money on him. She left unmistakable signs of amazement all over the women's faces when she said, 'Can you believe my husband doesn't know what a thong is? He doesn't know a goddamned thing. So now I get dressed up for my boyfriend.'

She bit her lip, nodded, and said, 'Mmmm, there's nothing better than making love. My God, the things he does to me, what we get up to together. It's something I never experienced with my husband. Now I can finally say I've experienced real pleasure.'

A friend of Hoda's raised her hand and said, 'No, no, don't say that. I love my husband. He's on dialysis now. He's become quite a burden. I'll be better off when he's gone, but still I get so jealous, even of the nurses.'

One who hadn't spared a single part of her face from plastic surgery said, 'It's unbelievable what these women will do, how they mess with their faces. There isn't a single operation they haven't tried.'

Then she started talking about how beautiful she used to be when she was younger, taking a picture out of her purse and saying, 'Look at how hot I was, ladies.'

As I listened to them I thought about Hani and me and how well our bodies worked together. I could be paralysed with pleasure. Every time we had sex we would slowly harvest the ecstasy bit by bit, not all at once. A lot of the time we would talk about a whole spectrum of topics, laughing together in bed, except one time he didn't laugh and changed the subject after I asked him, 'How come we women can have more than one orgasm but you men can't?'

It was the only question of mine he couldn't answer. It was the only time I ever saw a devilish expression appear on his face as I watched his muscles go slack.

Suad and I left Azizeh's together and went over to my house to smoke argileh on my balcony. I told her how much I was thinking about Hani. She promised to ask about him at the university the next day. Then I began to tell her how I was feeling since we had restarted our relationship at that age. Suad puffed on the argileh as she listened to me, filing away all of my secrets the way she always did.

I told her he was everything love meant to me. Now I'm sure I didn't only take pleasure from him. Pleasure isn't limited to one specific part of the body, I had always plucked it from all over, from his presence and caresses, his talk, his silence, his ideas, the way he looked at me and the way he walked, the warmth that filled my heart when he was around. I also confessed to her that I needed longer to get turned on, that it started taking me longer to get wet enough for sex even though my love for him hadn't abated, I hadn't stopped feeling desire and pleasure.

I told her about the first time we met, which I never forgot, even after our relationship restarted at this age.

At this age we don't judge each other based on our previous bodies. His kiss had a very particular taste that lingered in my mouth and under my tongue. It's true that he couldn't last as long as before, but his mouth tasted delicious, more so than when we were younger, back when our kisses would crash into one another like violent waves, as though they were winds that nearly blew us away. I could never forget his distinctive, warm taste.

As we get older our love grows larger as well, Suad, it becomes ripe and sweet, as mouth-watering as honey, it doesn't go bad, it's as if the soul is reclaiming its rightful place in both love and sex at this age, taking back the place where it had once been forbidden, pushed aside by the raging sensuousness of youth, as if arousal existed on the tip of the clitoris

243

and it shouldn't be casually touched. Just getting ready to touch it was enough to ignite desire, whereas in middle age desire seems to have descended to deeper places; the lair withdraws inside, as if the body's surface is a place of pure sensation while hills and valleys on the inside have become hiding places for explosive desire. Desire doesn't even mean explosions any more. Ignition results in warmth and pleasurable numbness rather than an inferno, as if desire has slowed down, not that it has disappeared or grown weaker or wilted but has become straighter, more mature.

That day I asked Suad whether our love had turned into the love of fear or of running away from endings that had never been available to us when we were younger, which always seemed like the peak of new beginnings. I said that as we get older touch comes to resemble a commitment to run away together, a desired and hasty departure that never comes, possibly because older lovers long for madness while the commitments of young people are always susceptible to being undone over time.

Our love, Suad, I said to her, is an ember that stays lit, one that started out as fiery and scorching as our young age, but which no longer torched us with the flame of desire but with its warmth alone. A kind of ecstasy that isn't simply caused by the contact between two bodies, but rather emerges from the embrace in which one buries her head in the arms of another, her eyes closed, inhaling their scent, listening to the beating of their heart, to the sound of their breath, and then whispering to the other: My love.

15

The house was mired in oppressive loneliness. Everything seemed foreign to me just before I left for the airport to go see Hani in Paris. As I looked up at my wedding photo hanging in the living room I imagined it was a picture of some other woman I had once seen in a movie a long time ago or perhaps someone who had drifted in and out of my life, someone I used to know but can no longer remember when or where we had met.

Everything in the house seemed alien to me, not my property, or if it was still mine it had become unrecognizable. Even the furniture that had seemed so familiar just moments before was now separated from me by a distance borne of estrangement and exile. Out in the street I felt very alone, as though the residents of the apartment, the building and the entire neighbourhood had vanished without a trace.

I couldn't remember my room number on the third floor of the hotel where we stayed, but Hani's room on the ninth floor was 903, that number was burned into my memory.

As soon as I arrived I called to make sure he was waiting for me and then went up to his room. We embraced just inside the door for a few moments. I nearly started crying from sheer desire and love. He immediately pulled me towards the bed.

I asked him again whether he was allowed to have sex and he told me, smiling proudly, that the doctor hadn't told him not to.

Suad sighed as she narrated to me what Nahla had told her about her rendezvous with Hani in Paris. She filled out the story for me as I tried to follow along:

He covered me with his entire body before I could even tell him how badly I wanted him to get on top of me, to smother me with his lusciousness. I want you on top of me so bad, to make love the way the first human being who ever discovered sexual pleasure did it. I want to return to the beginning, Hani. I want to try and experience it this time from scratch, in a new way, perhaps to determine whether I can make time turn around, to see if time is still under my control, within my grasp, or if it's possible for us to make our beginning together even more beautiful each time. Hani, make love to me as if I'm your first, as if my body is the first to ever awaken yours and to teach you to feel pleasure. My desire for you, my love, weighs tons that I cannot carry by myself. Fill me up with pleasure and let me drink in your body. Hover over me, fence me in on all sides. Shut me tight and come inside me so that all the water of the universe can fill me up. Tether me to you, let me give birth to you the way countless other women have done. Devour and ingest me so that I'll become part of you and you'll become part of me and we won't be able to tell where your body ends and mine begins. Cover me entirely, Hani, let me tremble and drown, take pleasure, and take flight.

In that moment, Nahla's face ignited, turned into a flickering ember. Her voice quavered, melting a little. Flush with sweat, I asked her to continue, and she did: Suad, I believed my words that were shooting out of my desire for him could switch on his listless body. Though, all of a sudden his body just went limp, Suad. His dick, too, obstinate and extinguished. His lips continued gliding freely over my body to the rhythm of his shaking hands as they tried to penetrate my most intimate parts, so hard that it hurt and made me scream in pain. Only then did his hands calm down and he stopped moving. As he closed his eyes, I started to get suspicious, Suad. Hani never closed his eyes while we were having sex. He always insisted on staring directly into my eyes. He'd hold my face, directing it towards him and burying his gaze in mine. I was assailed by disquieting thoughts. For a moment I contemplated that he might no longer be attracted to me, I mean, that he no longer loved me, Suad. And I thought the reason why might be found inside of me, that somehow I was to blame, that I had become old and disgusting. I was scared! I was scared and started to behave like a crazy woman. I felt like I had died or had been disappeared, like I no longer existed. Hani is the love my life, Suad. I mean, losing his life would be no different than losing my own. I struggled to say something, anything, but my tongue was dry, petrified like a chunk of firewood. I remained frozen where I was, lying down on the bed staring at him as he sat on the sofa after having dragged himself over there, resting his beautiful head that I had always compared to a Greek god. He curled up as though he were trying to make his body disappear or melt. This body that I had once worshipped, Suad, now seemed defeated, depleted and debilitated. His hands were wrapped around his cock, which I had called 'master' ever since our first time together. Maybe he wanted to conceal its flaccidness. I didn't dare get near him. I was afraid that if I did he would try and stop me, that he would think I was up to no good, that he would interpret my kindness as a futile attempt to entice him back into bed so that I would be able to finish off my unconsummated orgasm. Anyway, my feelings of guilt and concern for myself were stronger than my desire so I didn't want him to try a second time. It was enough just to be with him. I started thinking about all kinds of things. I didn't know how to behave. I don't know why I started behaving like such an idiot, Suad. I was completely paralysed. The only thing that could move were my thoughts, which started spinning in my head, shooting around at the speed of light. It felt like my thoughts had eyes that could see and ears that could hear. I looked hard at Hani and listened with all of my senses to his whispered thoughts. He seemed to be telling himself what he would always say to me.

Nahla, your eyes have such amazing powers—they can hear and touch and smell and even taste. Your eyes have always been able to read me, Nahla. I've never been able to hide anything from you or to lie to you. You always suss me out. You always know what I'm trying to hide, what I remain silent about sometimes. What am I supposed to do now? How can I justify to you what has happened? How can I get over the embarrassment, the disappointment, and the guilt oozing from my pores, scandalizing me? My sweat has run cold, Nahla, as cold as my desire. And now I feel like a traditional man who has lost the battle with his own virility, who has lost all sense of his own masculinity, who has lost all conception of himself. I feel like I'm shrinking and weak, down to the size of my own shrivelling cock. Now I'm just like that: defeated, depleted, impotent. How pathetic: this frustrated penis never used to disappoint me. Now I want revenge, to get as far away as I can. I hate it. I'm ashamed of it. I accuse it of being the reason for my weakness, I sever myself from it, as if it's no longer part of me, as though it's a sex toy I use when I get the urge, one that responds to me and obeys my animal instincts until I forget all about it once again. How easy it is to forget the way I used to scoff at men who were once stallions, how I saw their masculinity as no different than common beasts. Ah, the shame. How had I become one of them? I think just like them, I'm even worse than them. I think about my inadequacy, my weakness, my emptiness and my loss of respect all because my penis has betrayed me and won't get hard. Will you kiss me, Nahla, an inadequate man? Would you continue to love a man with a flaccid dick who hovers over you, except now more like a mountain of jelly? My God, dark shadows surround me. I thought that I had been spared the body and the rationality of a former stallion . . . Nahla's never going to believe me again after today, Nahla who knows me so well and can always read me. As far as she's concerned I'll never return to her bed like a knight just because I may possess her heart. My God, I've lost the heart and the bed. I've lost Nahla and that's the end of that.

There were so many other things I imagined Hani was telling himself, Suad, things that tore at my heart, but seeing him right there in front of me shaking like a bird whose wings had been clipped and who crashed to the ground caused me to lose whatever bearings I still had. I leapt out of the bed like a crazy person and sat down on the ground between his legs, held his freezing hands and started to kiss them, to warm them with my hands. But he avoided making eye contact with me.

In that moment his face looked strange, it was a face I had never seen before. No, it wasn't sallow or cloudy, slack or sad. There was something more terrifying about it. His face that I had once worshipped now seemed defeated. This was precisely the distinguishing feature that drove me to move my face closer to his, to graze my nose against his, to press my cheek against his, to drag my lips across his forehead and between his eyes, whispering to him, Give me back your face, Hani. Give me back your eyes. I'm afraid that if I look I won't find the sky and the sun and the sea and the moon and the stars and the light and the fields of the whole world. Your eyes are the whole world. Please don't let the world abandon me.

I heard his voice calling out to me as I went into the bathroom. I ran back towards him, and in a choking voice he said, Cover me up, Nahla. I'm not well. I grabbed the blanket from the bed and covered his entire body. I planted kisses on his hands and knees, then pressed my face against his and whispered in his ear. No, I didn't whisper, Suad, I knelt down and prayed to him: You're my man, Hani, my master, and you'll continue to be even if everything about you wilts. I've loved you throughout all the twists and turns of your life. No matter what happens, you'll always be my only love, my whole world, my paradise. Don't fret, Hani, don't blow things out of proportion. No doubt this is just a passing phase, and, besides, don't forget you've got medicine for this, strong enough for a camel. Look up at me. Just to look at you or to sit here in your arms, for your eyes to caress me is enough to make me come, something no other man can give another woman. Our love isn't temporary, Hani, it isn't a passing infatuation or some simple desire. Get up, get up, my love, so we can go out and walk along the Boulevard Saint-Germain. Didn't you promise me . . . but I couldn't finish, Suad. He wouldn't let me. Suddenly he took my head in his hands, pulled me up towards him, squeezed me, then pushed me away a little bit, asking me to stand up naked, just as I was, and he proceeded to look at me from the top of my head down to my feet. You can't imagine, Suad, the way his eyes regained their spark and their desire. His handsome face was no longer a suspended and sagging curtain, nor was his body. You wouldn't believe it, Suad. His body, which just a few moments before had taken on the shape of a crumpled heap of flesh, stood up straight and tall, returning to its solidity and strength, and along with that, of course, 'my master's' erection returned as well. Hani made sure, Suad, that I could see how hard he was, he even made me hold it, to say hello using its special name, before he moved his body on top of mine, whispering that there was no other woman in the world like me, that there didn't exist any love like my love. Sweetheart, you are my paradise, he murmured, his honeyed lips brushing past mine.

Once he had entered me I gazed at him, then he smiled as he said, proud and relaxed: 'Can you believe it, Nahla? God Himself wouldn't believe it.' Tell me, Hani, try, I know you can't do this with medication alone. 'You see, Nahla, you see, how love can conquer illness?'

That day I realized a lot of things about me and about him that I had never noticed before, Suad, things that helped me understand myself and get to know him better. I knew that love could transform weakness into strength, Suad. Either way our love only increases. Desire may fade away, Suad, if it fails to translate itself into physical form, especially as age gets the better of us or disease wears us down, although that doesn't necessarily mean the degradation or disappearance of love. With true love our bodies can learn how to be patient, accepting, satisfied, they come to know how to have compassion, how to be gentle, how to show mercy and how never to forget the beloved or take them for granted, our bodies become pure consciousness made of unalloyed love. This is the only way the body can become whole, capable, confident and unafraid of expressing itself . . . not only as a sexual instrument animated by the volcano of excitable desire. They become love, nothing else, otherwise little more than sexual tools handicapped by some kind of flaw, which makes them dispensable and so we exchange them for others that can provide a sense of well-being, under the pretence that love can heal us.

I know there is something inside of all of us that is ugly and inherited, Suad, something we remain prisoners of until it's revealed to us, until we acknowledge it so we that we may overcome it, and not make excuses about it. My ugly inheritance still seems to be buried inside me, radiating fear, terror even, throughout my body, of the decrepitude that has caused me to lose some of the vitality in my body, some of the health, fear of the wrinkles that have become so pronounced, which speak about me in ways that I don't accept myself, whether that's coming from me or anyone else. Deep down inside us, Suad, there's war and truce, but reconciliation is still a long way off. As women we might yield to the defeat of age, make accommodations and get used to it in spite of ourselves, only on the condition that nobody else should notice. Just imagine that I'm anxious and afraid, or rather embarrassed and frustrated by my fat belly and my saggy breasts, which only appear more prominently when I lie down naked. I thought that my breasts were the main reason for his fading desire. I couldn't tell the difference before, Suad, between desire and the capacity to act upon it in bed with the one we want to be with. I never thought for a moment, Suad, that he might be a cheat and a liar and a hypocrite and a coward, that he had regained his horniness for one reason only, namely, that he had conjured in his mind the image of a young woman who turned him on and who he wanted to sleep with. But at some point I sensed he was replaying before his eyes the vision of my body when I was younger, I felt that for a little while and then he snapped back to seeing my body the way it was just then. And I'll tell you the truth: I couldn't get rid of all of my doubts until I asked him to keep his eyes open, to stare right at me the way he used to do when we made love. I insisted that he call me by my name, once, then twice . . . four times . . . I can't recall how many times, Suad. Then I discovered, just the way I'm revealing to you right now, the fears I had of my ageing body being exposed in front of my lover, but the eye of love prettified whatever age had ruined, or maybe I was just seeing what I wanted to see. But when I got back to my room and lay down in my bed, the question that really ate at me was: Is it possible that Hani would lose his entire memory of my body if our physical encounters came to an end? And would it be possible for me to completely evacuate him from my memory—not because our love had come to an end but because he was no longer capable of penetrating me?

What brought me some comfort and allowed me to fall asleep was that our love hadn't yet ended. My love for him goes by many different names. I might even add another because of just how scorching and warm our love was on that day. The love that had been contracted between us was a new kind of covenant I hadn't yet been able to fully appreciate. It was enough for me to know it existed. Later on he would call me only by its name.

Now, Suad, I realize that what we feel about each other's desire, even if one of us is unable to translate that into sex, is a force more powerful than any aphrodisiac used by women or men.

If only you could have seen it, Suad, how radiant and thrilled I was as I walked beside him along the pavement on Saint-Germain while he held me as I stole a glance at him from time to time, then back at myself. I truly felt my body growing taller and prouder, as if it were becoming lighter and more elegant.

The neckline of my blouse made my cleavage more promi-nent, Suad, and I smiled like a wicked young woman, turned on by the feeling that my breasts weren't as saggy as I thought, that the flabbiness of my belly wasn't quite as bad as I had believed. I had no worries! I'd knead them into the softest, the most beautiful and delicate and proportioned in the whole world. My footsteps, ahh my footsteps. They grew confident as they stamped on the ground, Suad, sounding like a shout. I looked up at the sky and from deep in my gut I laughed out loud.

***

Nahla's laughter stung me, yanked me out of my protracted silence, pealing like holiday bells with the joy of a woman who had just experienced intoxicating ecstasy. She asked me, half-joking, half-scolding, when I would grace her with an interpretation that befits the magnitude of her great romantic encounter. My body started fidgeting once again, my worthless and silent body that had fallen into a coma for a long time. Sometimes I would wake up and then fall back asleep. Most of the time I felt as though I was falling into the infinite void, in a death-like experience. Sometimes it would feel like there was an open grave waiting for the hour of my burial so that he could be buried and rid of me, so that he would no longer be forced to carry me and maintain the bitter patience I forced him to endure. My silent, repressed and listless body was jealous of Nahla. Her scorching tales of love gave me some moments of vitality, and my body would become refreshed and revived in its early grave, struggling to awaken me, to bring me back to it so that we could live together the way people live with their bodies, sometimes despising them, sometimes making peace with them. Ever since I got married, my body had rarely been in a state of accord with me. I hated it and it hated me. It stung and I would sting it. It would bite me and I would bite it right back. It would slap me and I would claw at it, smothering it to my last breath. We would exchange the cruellest insults. I would describe it with the most demeaning adjectives and it would respond with twice the force, accusing me of being hideous and ugly. But I would always defeat it, emerging victorious, and it would retreat from me in fear, scurrying like a mouse back to its burrow, waiting for Nahla to gush with her stories until it would get aroused again, fidget and want to scream . . .

I couldn't understand why my body only had the courage to confront me when Nahla's body was in motion and talking to me about love. Her body would start to ooze words that spilled out of her mouth like sea foam. Nahla and her body seemed to suit one another, like lovers who were never apart. Each loves the other and they conspire to harvest whatever pleasures they wish to experience. Jealousy creeps over my body as I listen to the frenzied weeping that reminds me of the days of amity, the time when we were in a state of truce, love and concord, a time when I was proud of it and it was proud of me, when I wasn't ashamed of it and it wasn't ashamed of me. I wore it and it wore me the more I cried out, and it would cry out at the same time. My God, how our bodies change as we age, everyone's except Nahla's, which she never gave up on and which never gave up on her. She never neglected it, always tended to it carefully, listened to it closely. She slowed down when she got pregnant, and after she gave birth, acquiesced to it and showed patience, though not for very long.

Nahla was telling me about how much her body had changed, asking me if I felt the same way, about how it had become more mature, more aware, or perhaps it had lost some of its recklessness and wildness. In the old days it had been both the object and the obstacle at the same time, had its own special place, even during the most splendid moments of love with Hani in which she imagined her body was a volcano of pleasure and enjoyment in which Hani could immerse his own pleasures. She found in it a separate, self-sufficient planet that attracted the stars of Hani's desire, fusing with him until their two bodies became a molten mass of pure pleasure, a kind of pleasure that didn't mix with any other sensation, that didn't have space for anything else. Gradually there emerged inside her a new feeling she didn't know how to name at first, learning later that it was something like intimacy. When bodies get bigger, Suad, they shed their inconsistency and their arrogance, they lose some of their boastfulness and their self-satisfaction. It's only then that space opens up for the feelings that accompany pleasure. It's intimacy, Suad. Gentle intimacy in love as we get older, it can heal you, open your eyes to the wide and wondrous world of the body. As Nahla spoke, she sighed and chewed on her lower lip, as though she were resisting the discovery of something specific about her, or perhaps she was articulating the pleasant remains that she held onto from the time of pure pleasure.

Nahla's sorrow gave her pleasure and kept her body alive, pulsing with desire and responsive to love. My body smells like a musty wardrobe and sounds like the creaking bones of a lonely skeleton, which makes me jump and touch my legs and my arms and my shoulders and thighs and my vertebrae, which feels like I'm reassembling fragile bones, dry and hollow. I'm afraid they'd collapse and fall out of my body if I whispered to myself the way Nahla does, or even had a thought about love the way she does.

I deny myself my body, keeping it at bay. The more it tortures me or tries to get away from me, the more I try to prevent it from doing so and the more I remind it how fragile and hideous it is. Whenever I sit down with Nahla, Azizeh,

Hoda and Nadine I take care to stay as still as the Sphinx. I turn inwards on myself, roll up my bones, and observe how supple their bodies are, how they obey their sexiness and their desires, to the rhythm of traditional Arabic music or dance music that booms from the cafe where we always meet up. I secretly look at all of them, then let my eyes fall on Nahla's body as it folds and billows, light as a feather, swaying and falling as if the music were human fingertips that she was tickling, swinging back and forth and caressing. Then Nahla closes her eyes and starts to moan, raising her arms to wave in the air, unconcerned by curious eyes. My body flees into the past, remembers its gentleness, elegance, lightness and its ability to dance, and then I make fun of it. I remind it of how creaky it has become and it calms down once again.

God, my body has changed so much. It has become so ugly, a burden I carry around in spite of myself. How long has it been since I got any pleasure from it, since I played with it the way I like to do and the way it likes for me to do? I can't keep track of the years any more. Maybe it's been no longer than since the first month of my marriage. No, what I felt during that time wasn't pleasure, it was the illusion, a false mirage that wasn't anything like the pleasure I had experienced before. Ever since that time my body has been dying day by day. I'm disgusted by it. I blame it, and I don't think the pleasures of secrecy and fantasy are worth anything. My body has a story I don't dare to tell, a truth I'm careful to keep hidden. Nobody but Nahla knows it. Of course, she doesn't know all the details, or maybe she does and tries to pretend not to notice. Nahla took care of me, sometimes making me believe our bodies deserve love and confidence and recognition no matter how ugly or sick or even deformed they may be. The body is paradise. So why do we think of it as a coffin? she used to ask. How I wish I had a body with even a fraction of her pride and love. How I wish I was like her: capable of being kind to my body, of accepting it as it is.

Ever since she disappeared I'm sinking day by day, deeper and deeper into the grave, trying to get closer to her body, to apologize, to acknowledge her, to touch her tenderly and encourage her to be strong, to ask her to accept me and teach me the patience to be strong, too.

Take these, take these pages and read them. Nahla didn't leave behind anything she didn't write herself. I think she must know a lot more about me than I had ever imagined. Listen to me before I forget what Nahla said nearly a month before she disappeared: I buried a stack of papers under the pomegranate tree at our house in the village. The funny thing is I wrote about you, Suad. I wrote things I couldn't possibly have known. I swear I never knew these things about you. A strange kind of intuition was pulling me towards you, making me think about you and write some of it. Do you believe that writing can allow us to know things before they happen? Can writing propel us into the future? Oh, Suad, will anyone write my story and then find out things about me I don't know myself? I forget so many things, Suad. How will I be able to remember that these things are mine, that this is my story, unless Alawiya truly listens to me and writes about me, seeks guidance in my memory and my story? Suad, my memory feels like it's getting weak. I forget faces and names. Sometimes I even forget who I am.

16

I didn't want to put her in the corner or restrict her to this fate.

Nobody knew anything about her.

Nahla had gone missing. She disappeared during the July War after Alzheimer's had already consumed her memory. It occurred to me that she told me her story because she was certain her memory was on the verge of vanishing.

One morning Saleem woke up to find that she was gone. She must have opened the door, walked out and got lost. She could no longer find her way home. Or else she didn't want to come back. None of the attempts to find her or find out what had happened to her at the police stations or in the village or other places she used to go turned up any trace of her. At first her husband and her children tried to keep it a secret but it quickly became public knowledge. Suad combed the city, street by street, stopping at every spot she had ever been with Nahla, but it all amounted to nothing.

Suad called several times to ask if I had heard anything or if Nahla had called. She came over one morning, stood outside my front door without saying a word, her eyes all bloodshot and muttering something I couldn't understand, then turned her back to me and walked away. Then she called again but didn't say a word when I picked up. My throat constricted as I asked again who was calling, then I said, 'Now listen, who is this? Tell me or I'm going to hang up.'

'It's . . . it's Suad,' she said in a choked voice.

'Oh, hi Suad, how are you doing?'

'What kind of a question is that to ask me? How do you. *think* I'm doing with Nahla missing? Where do you think she is? Tell me, I haven't left any stones unturned, I've looked everywhere. You're a writer. Your imagination is supposed to be so vast, what do *you* think? And what are *you* going to do about it? What are you going to *write*?'

'I don't know,' I replied.

I never dreamt this could be her fate. She talked to me so much about oblivion, even if she called less and less after getting back from Paris. Still, her disappearance shook me. Suad told me how shocked Hani had been to hear about her illness. Nahla has Alzheimer's? he asked. Seriously? Then he found himself saying, Don't worry, Nahla, your memory's safe with me, our love will never die or disappear or be forgotten.

If she had a grave, I would have gone and stood by it, recited the Fatiha, and told her that her story would never disappear the way she did, the way other people's stories disappeared beneath the rubble. I would have asked her if she actually unearthed the old papers that had been buried in the ground with her when she went back to visit her village for the last time, whether they disappeared along with her, or whether she believed she had come to terms with the story of her childhood and that of Suad and Nadine and Azizeh . . . I would have asked her if she went back to her village when she lost her memory, but was unable to come back because of the war, if she had fallen under the bombs, had got buried beneath the ruins of her house or in the dirt alongside her old papers.

One day she told me writing is a portal to the future, and that she had written down Suad's life in her old papers. The truth of the matter is that I have no idea whether she had also written down the story of her disappearance or whether her hands had been buried down there for a long time, alongside the papers, making it impossible for her to write anything at all.

On one occasion, in the middle of telling me her story, Nahla asked why she had been so afraid of losing Hani, why she never shared the story of her own fear of losing herself, why she seemed to always have a million excuses.

Hani was lost. He felt her absence deeply, as though he had lost all memory of his own body. He felt weak, her love had kept him strong. His weakness should have been as light as a feather but it was a strangely powerful weakness, the kind that could move mountains. With her disappearance it seemed to him that the twittering had been ripped out of the birds' throats, that the sea had been drained of its water and its blue, that the air had lost its transparency, that the moon had lost its luminescence, that the stars were no longer in the sky. Sometimes he felt like he was being suffocated, as though she had sucked all the air out of his chest, strangulated him and then taken off.

Hani went over to Nahla's house for the first time since the news of her disappearance had spread. The house was full of family, friends and acquaintances who streamed over to find out what had happened to her. Nadine, Azizeh and Hoda were there, deep in silence. distracted.

Hani sat down beside Suad and asked her in a whisper whether she had heard anything about Nahla. She shook her head, then went back to staring at all the things and the furniture in the house, as if she were just waiting for her to get home. When he laid eyes on her daughter Faten, who looked so much like her when she had been that age, all the colour drained from him as his heart started racing. He got hung up on the fact that she could be his own daughter. He got disoriented and agitated, the way he did whenever he met her downstairs and rode up the lift with her. Pain immobilized his knees and confusion filled his eyes because of the uncanny resemblance between Nahla and her daughter.

After taking a look at the plants on the balcony that she used to talk about, Hani gulped hard when he looked at the portrait of Nahla hanging on the living-room wall. He had gifted it to her for her fortieth birthday, after they got back together and he read *Love in the Time of Cholera*. He had asked a famous Lebanese painter, a friend of his, to paint it based on a photo of her. She was smiling in a way that was somehow both sharper and narrower than her usual smile, which could extend out into fields and suns and moons and birds and trees and a whole country. There was life in her eyes, luminous and generous. Her inner beauty shone like a star. Her affecting habit of truth-telling was plain to see in her eyes and on her face, her loving expression seemed to be tinged with sadness. It looked as if she had a big lump in her throat. The collar of her red dress showed off her shoulders. Hani hadn't seen her wear that dress, which she had bought before they got back together. When the Alzheimer's started to eat away at her mind he asked Suad to go into the armoire and help her try on all the dresses Hani never saw her wear.

Hani went back to her house one more time. The electricity was out so he had to climb the stairs all the way up to the eleventh floor. By the time he finally made it up there, he was dripping with sweat, his heart pounding. He stood on the edge of the stairs and started to shiver, then went right back down-stairs without even going inside. Suad had done the same thing numerous times. She hadn't been to Nahla's since that time when she went there one morning to find her husband wearing strong cologne for the first time since Nahla had disappeared. Nahla's neighbour's spinster sister was in the living room, wearing a ton of makeup, and sporting a skirt similar to the ones Nahla used to wear. She was having coffee with Nahla's husband, who had a robe on over his pyjamas. She could see his concern for her, and when she came out she looked incredibly sad. She felt like someone was chewing on her heart. She thought that Nahla being gone for a few weeks wasn't enough time for her to forget her, and that someone would have to forget her before she herself would be able to do so.

Hani was no less tormented than Suad when Alzheimer's started to attack Nahla. She forgot who Hani was, then forgot who she herself was. When she could remember once again she would start to cry and get depressed. Before her memory went she told Suad all about her childhood, sometimes calling her mother or father or grandmother, then she'd forget all about them and call out for her children. She would often for-get her husband's name and call him Hani.

Nahla suffered so much before finally losing her memory for good. It was equally painful for Hani. He'd cover his mouth with his hands in order to remain silent. Confusion would take hold of him if she looked at him suddenly without recognizing who he was.

Hani avoided seeing her after the two of them got back from Paris, afraid that his body would betray him, though he remained in constant contact with her. And when she got sick he lost it. He began seeing her in the company of Suad.

Nahla was being tortured, aware that she was in the midst of losing herself bit by bit, the entire record of her life, her memories, everything she loved. She felt like she was all alone, suspended in air: no past, no present, no future. Her eyes filled with tears when she told Suad, with a brave smile on her face, that she was afraid to leave the house by herself because she might get lost in the street, that she was thinking about storing her home telephone number as well as Hani's and Faten's inside her purse along with a note indicating that those numbers should be called immediately if she ever forgot who she was. Then she smiled once more in order to hide her sadness.

But she never took that precaution, however scared she might have been of getting lost one day.

Nahla was well aware of her condition before things got bad. Whenever her memory came back after a period of loss, she would fall silent fearing she might say something inappropriate, that she might not be able to focus. And when she started getting confused, she would sometimes feel she were a little girl or a university student, and she might start behaving with Hani like a twenty-something brimming with vitality, optimism and high energy. She lived out a kind of love she could believe in. Yalla, she told him, get up and take me to the Orange Café, a place near the university where the two of them used to go in the sixties. Come on, she said, I want to go see Suad and Nadine, they're waiting for me there.

She insisted with intense enthusiasm. Hani looked at her and actually saw that young student, the girl he had fallen in love with. His heart skipped a beat, and then he noticed how lost she was, how she was losing him, but he didn't like to disappoint her, and maybe he even enjoyed reliving those experiences and those days.

264

All the same, it hurt him to find himself laughing like that when she was unwell, and he started to get lost amidst her confusion.

Once he and Suad actually took her to the Orange Café, which had changed its name as well as its orange furniture and décor, and just about everything inside, including the owner and the staff. They walked into the place that had once been packed with students and young men and women. Hani glanced over at a couple sitting in the corner that was laughing and hanging out. He felt as though the two of them were living out his and Nahla's past, and they likely had no idea that the two of them would one day wind up just like them, perhaps one of them would develop Alzheimer's. Nahla laughed loudly that day, attracting the attention of the students who were there, and Hani and Suad felt bad and embarrassed for her.

Once again she wanted to go to the School of Education in order to see her friends. She ran ahead of Hani and Suad, though she had difficulty getting down the small step leading to the cafeteria. Nahla felt drawn to those old, forgotten places, as if deep inside her there was an unquenchable nostalgia for the distant past.

'Where's Asad?' she asked loudly.

Hani remembered Asad's booming laughter, his edgy humour, loud voice, and the delicious sandwiches he used to make. And he remembered the sound of Fairuz singing, which always echoed through the large cafeteria hall.

Nahla was behaving like a little girl. She asked about George, the old owner of the restaurant, but they couldn't find anyone with that name. Her enthusiasm dwindled as disappointment set in. Hani tried to comfort her but she retreated inside her shell, like a spooked and cautious turtle. After a long stretch of silence, her features changed as her memory came flooding back. She stared at Suad with sorrow and pain in her eyes.

'How did I get here?' she asked. 'Please, come on, take me home.'

When Nahla suffered a bout of forgetfulness, her eyes would get all cloudy and she'd seem distracted. She'd start jittering, sometimes she'd cry. Hani could think of nothing better to do than hold her close, squeeze her with love and in pain. The last time she ever saw him she cried and asked him whether he thought her love could make miracles happen. His eyes welled with tears. Then she refused to see him any more, stopped returning his phone calls, started to feel ashamed of her condition, entered a tunnel of depression and sorrow that she never came out of. In those moments when she plummeted into oblivion, Suad would recite the love poems she had written to Hani and the letters Hani wrote to her, but she used to just stare back blankly at her in a silence that was unlike any other on earth. And when she felt like giving up, Suad would motivate her to keep her faith, to take hold of whatever aid God could provide in order to calm her down so that she could reclaim and renew her lost hopes. In these moments of weakness, she could grab hold of her faith and be convinced.

***

Nahla disappeared and Suad lost her mind. Throughout the July War and the weeks that followed she searched for Nahla without knowing where to look.

Where are you? Where can I find you? I can hear the sound of your voice in my ears. My whole life disappeared when you did, Suad told herself as she aimlessly wandered the streets, stopping at intersections, her eyes darting in every direction. But it was all in vain.

The war went on for weeks and Suad had no idea where to find her. She marched up and down the streets of Beirut one by one, in excruciating pain. She was drenched in beads of sweat. She wondered whether Nahla was among those who had disappeared beneath the rubble or into one of those coffins she had seen on television the night before, covering the main square in the southern city of Tyre. She could see the features and hear the voice of that woman standing alongside those coffins and wailing. The Al-Jazeera correspondent asked her whether people lacked food, medicine, water or anything else, and the woman replied, 'The only thing we lack is coffins, so go ahead and send us some more.'

Suad walked and walked without knowing which way to go. She regarded men's shoulders as if they were nothing more than a platform for carrying coffins. She seemed to be hunting for scattered bodies that she had lost. Eyes weren't like normal eyes, as if they were redolent of death and blood and loss and glory. On their transient bodies she could smell all these different scents blended with the odour of sex. Early in the evening she wondered why it should be that such pungent aromas of sex should hang in the air during wartime. She saw men passing through the streets, scratching their crotches. She turned towards the cafes on Hamra Street that were packed with people having the same conversations over and over. She stood at the intersections as her eyes hunted Nahla, scrutinizing passers-by, hoping to spot her. Darting across the street from one side to the other, unconcerned by the oncoming traffic, she thought, Do any of these people know where they're going? Have they got a specific destination in mind? Or are they like me, do they not have a clue? Rushing along those streets, she felt as though she were searching for her own shelter, and she asked again, Where are you, Nahla? You used to talk about the streets in wartime, how they seemed like skeletons when they were deserted, how the pavements were like naked bodies. Just like a human being, the street is afraid, it groans and feels pain. You used to say that they felt just the way you did throughout the wars, all alone and abandoned just like you, and you used to say that the street was waiting for Hani to arrive, for lovers to show up in order to become active and behave badly and to waste time.

Suad walked down alleyways that were covered with tents set up by people who had fled the south for Beirut. She heard the din made by some people and the silence created by others. The sound of her own footsteps alerted her to the emptiness of a desolate street. She knew that the pulse of life would return someday. The sound of her solitary footsteps might be enough to make that happen. She thought about the earth down below. Was it soil underneath or something else? Everything she had once taken for granted was in doubt. Ever since Nahla disappeared she started thinking about what was beneath her, ever since the wreckage of decimated buildings started piling up. She stared at the mounds of earthen asphalt in front of her, appearing like a whole other world that unexpectedly collided with the pavement that was no longer a pavement as much as heaps of pedestrians.

Suad also went to all the places where refugees had wound up. She thought to herself that maybe she'd find her there if she had forgotten her name, had got completely lost, even to herself, and no longer knew who she was. She thought perhaps she'd find her there barefoot and filthy and stinking to high heaven, or perhaps she would have hidden her hair under a kerchief, or perhaps she'd be dressed like a beggar. The tears she swallowed were like ropes wrapped around her neck that were going to strangle her, and she imagined she was perhaps lost. Her senses felt endangered. She told herself to be on high alert when it occurred to her that this might be her condition. Things got even more mysterious for Suad when she went searching for Nahla. Whenever she noticed someone crying she imagined those were Nahla's eyes, and whenever she heard crying or laughing she believed it was her laughter or her tears, as if she were seeing her scattered among all the people. And she thought about how if Nahla had been there she would have asked her who was going to write the stories of all those people who had perished beneath the rubble and whether their stories had perished along with them. She smiled for the first time since Nahla's disappearance when she saw some young women and men in the Sanayeh garden walking around and flirting with one another in spite of their tragedies. She thought about how life carries on in spite of everything.

Even though he hadn't slept with her for two years she also remembered the way her husband would sleep with her despite her sadness over Nahla's absence. She smiled in spite of the sorrow, telling Azizeh, 'I'm telling you, I have to wait for a war for this animal to get it up and sleep with me?'

Azizeh was also distraught over Nahla's absence. She sighed. She was nervous, a bit yellow, and she had pain in her body and in her head. Azizeh had never been concerned with politics or war but she remained glued to the news night and day. When she complained to Suad about how sick she was, she told her she needed to watch less of the war on TV, to listen to the news less, because that was surely making her sick. But Azizeh surprised Suad when she raised her eyebrows and answered back, 'No, Suad. You may think I'm sick from watching the news but it's not true. Honestly I'm annoyed because I want a man.'

As she said that she put her hand on her vagina. When she came back later that night to have a drink, she lost her composure the way she always did when she drank. She forgot all about Nahla, forgot about the screeching planes overhead and the bombardment. She doubled over laughing, then asked Suad, 'You know what the most wonderful thing about a man is?'

'What, Azizeh?'

'The most wonderful thing about a man is that he has one,' she said, by which she meant his penis.

Suad got up and left.

Throughout the war she continued to roam the streets every day in search of her, and at night she'd plant herself in front of the television, staring deeply into the screen. Whenever somebody pulled out a shirt from beneath the rubble, or human remains, or a loved one, or their children or their memories, it would occur to her that it might be Nahla. Then she started seeing her in everyone who had perished beneath the rubble, believing they irrevocably carried down with them something of Nahla's forgotten memory. She feared that one of the corpses being exhumed might turn out to be Nahla's. She waited anxiously for morning when she could scan the papers for her name and picture among all the victims and martyrs. She spent a lot of time beating herself up whenever she caught herself thinking about Nahla and forgetting all the other death, displacement and destruction. Most of the time she had the unbearable feeling that she had been shredded into strips when thinking about the innocent victims besieged in their villages. At the same time, whenever she thought about them, she felt there was no point.

Once she asked herself how she could possibly be so fixated on Nahla's fate when there were so many other tragic ends confronting her. My God, is it possible that Nahla epitomizes all of the disappeared? Could just one of them become the battlefield for me?

It was as if the July War took away Nahla's fate as well. She tried to calm herself down so many times, to think about how reality is so much larger than Nahla. Where was her compassion for all the others? But a voice inside would insist that Nahla had taken all of her sentiment with her.

***

The television gorged itself on Suad's face, devoured her eyes, not just her ears. She followed news of the fighting throughout the July War. One night after pacing through the streets in search of Nahla she came back home and found her husband playing cards with his friends. She went into her bedroom to relax, and when she opened her wardrobe to put on her pyjamas, her eyes fell upon a dress that Nahla had given her as a birthday present well before her illness had become terminal. She shut the wardrobe and went into the bathroom just as her body gave out. She cried a trail of tears longer than herself, and when she tried to wash her face her tears dissolved in the water. She went out onto the balcony and gazed up at the sky as Israeli warplanes zoomed past to bomb the southern suburbs. She felt like her insides were being torn apart by the bombing, and by the pain over Nahla. That night the moon was white and full, its silvery light luminescent. She thought about going over to her neighbour's house—only in wartime do neighbours open their doors to one another—in order to assuage her fear, as if the feeling of community and familiarity would be sure to drive away the spectre of death and lighten its weight. She entered her neighbour's apartment and sat down with all the other people crammed into the living room. The news broadcast sounded like wailing, and she felt the whole world going mad as the names of the martyrs and the casualties were read incessantly while fierce resistance prevented

Israeli forces from advancing along the front lines. The shouts and the voices of the women sitting there were like gunfire blasting at the screen. Their eyes seemed to be popping out of their heads, their hands were flailing, and they were wailing as well. But when Sayyid Hassan Nasrallah began his address, the women fell silent, waiting with bated breath to hear what he had to say. Their bursting eyes grew calm, their gazes seemed to sigh the same way as their chests. They looked hypnotized and sleepy. As he raised his fist, one of the women asked why the Sayyid was always wearing a button-down shirt under his robe. Another woman replied, 'Hey, you're right. He's always dressed like that, he keeps it buttoned up perfectly. And what about you, ladies? People are preoccupied with each other, while the cat is busy giving birth, as the proverb goes.

Then they all let out one big collective sigh, expressing their envy of the woman who had asked for and then received his robe. Their voices followed one another: Good for her. I just wish I could smell it, let its smell waft over me. Good for her, good for her heart and her fate.

When her neighbour asked his wife to bring coffee for all the guests gathered there, she said she wouldn't move until the Sayyid had finished his address, but then he shouted, 'What do you care what the Sayyid has to say? Get up and go make coffee for our guests!'

She dashed to the kitchen in fear, muttering to herself: I care what the Sayyid has to say. How come the Sayyid appears in my dreams and not he? If only he knew the way I hold on to him and how to keep track of him on my fingers and toes, he matters so much to me, more than him.

Suad went straight to her bedroom as soon as she left the neighbours. Her body was freezing despite the July heat, so she covered up with a light wool blanket. She was having trouble breathing, as if she was suffocating beneath the rubble, like the dirt and the dust and the gunpowder and the melted metal and the scattered stones from houses that had once stood upright all filled up her chest, and the colour of gushing red blood spurting from her eyes made them resemble two burning embers. She switched on the television again so that she could watch the news of the fighting, then she fell asleep for a little while even as her mind kept racing, talking to herself after she saw the ruins of an entire village and massacres and mass graves and the rescue of wounded people from beneath the rubble.

As she dozed off she dreamt about the Prophet Moses dressed in a robe and holding a cane, waving it right and left, using it to smash the planes and the tanks, then wiping it against the ground as he crossed mountains and villages, which were standing upright once again with their houses and trees and people and birds. When the dead saw his staff they came back to life. She awoke from her slumber, the sight of the Prophet Moses from behind up in the sky, painted across her eyes. She was unable to cry despite the fact that she felt like she was on fire, like a burning flame. Just a single mute tear fell from her eye. She felt like her body was falling, weighed down despite how extremely angry she was. Previously she had shut all the doors leading to her anger. But the dream about the Prophet Moses brought her peace in just the same way as the dream she once had about Our Lady the Virgin Mary after the Qana massacre. She saw her standing there before her, holding baby Jesus, who was reaching his hand out to every child that was waving their hand like a leaf for him to come back and greet them. The virgin was smiling, and she saw with her own eyes how the killed children got their little lives back, had their amputated and severed limbs sutured back together, and sensations restored in their bodies. What really astounded her was that she was seeing the Virgin's smile in her own eyes when she gazed into them, whereas when she looked at her lips she would find that they were sealed shut. She found this secret odd, asking herself how the Virgin could smile without moving her mouth. After inspecting her face she realized that this was no ordinary smile. She was simply expressing the satisfaction of a mother with her son as she returned life to all those children.

Suad kept following the TV, the newspapers and magazines until weeks after the war had ended. Perhaps she had found a trace of Nahla among the casualties of the war who had disappeared beneath the rubble, but there was none to be found.

***

Suad felt completely naked in the face of this disappearance, the nakedness of the sky and the earth and everything in-between. One sunny autumn morning on her balcony, she asked herself, gazing up into the void, Isn't disappearance one way to melt into the sun and the wind and the water and the trees and the songs and the music and the kind of beautiful poetry that Nahla longed for?

Is it possible that Nahla disappeared into the wind or in the roar of the surf? Or into the light of the sun or the moon? Or into the scent of a flower? Into the tears of lovers and the smiles of children?

Had she become a bird, or a tree, as she had so often longed when she was a little girl?

Maybe she disappeared into the tree with which she had come to cultivate a deeper relationship in middle age. She used to tell Suad that one lifetime wasn't enough to properly regard a tree. And when she went to her village for the last time before Alzheimer's entirely consumed her memory, she meditated on the trees in the valleys and the foothills, all those crops growing outside most of the houses and the benches out front. When she stood at the foot of the tree, beside her grandmother Amina's bench, it felt like she had taken some part of her spirit and some part of her smell, especially since she wouldn't leave her side when they were sitting on the bench.

One her way back to Beirut her attention was drawn to two trees that stood alone on a little unpaved, uninhabited road. One was taller and larger, its branches extended over the top as though it were reaching out its arm to cradle the other one. She imagined the two trees had fallen in love with each other. She wished that she and Hani would turn into two trees just like those, making love, holding one another and exchanging kisses. Most people don't notice love among trees, they don't believe that trees can fall in love, don't believe in their profound ability to love, invent another name for love that has never been fully captured by the human lexicon. She fantasized about Hani and her becoming two trees having sex, intertwining their roots under the soil, beneath the grasses that were familiar to both of them. Together they would see how winter and spring were all around them, how they became so beautifully naked in the autumn and suffered pain together during the winter, enduring the same fate, while the same thing that happened to the grass happened to them.

Maybe Nahla had been transformed into a tree. Perhaps she became a star.

Suad remembered telling Hoda once before she got married that whenever she looked up at the sky, she was comforted by the existence of all those stars but that she never tried to count them all because she certainly would have failed. She preferred to try and count the stars through her window. But it turned out she was never as comforted by the existence of stars in the sky as she was after Nahla's disappearance.

On the balcony outside the living room, opposite the couch where she typically liked to sit, she noticed a single star in the sky. This happened again and again during the nights following Nahla's disappearance, and she became increasingly convinced that her house was in the exact spot where she'd be able to see it. After she imagined seeing many different figures, the star took on the shape of Nahla's face. She used to scrutinize it on a daily basis, taking comfort and feeling at peace as she became more certain that it was Nahla. A few days later, several stars appeared all around her, and she got lost. She tried very hard to find her but she failed. When the stars disappeared she felt the sky was lacking something, that now it was abandoned, just like the earth after losing Nahla.

Wherever Nahla showed up, there was love, Suad told me when I met her one day after Nahla's disappearance. Her formidable physical strength could make places, even those that were small and isolated, more spacious in order to absorb the joy that was created by this energy.

Her presence opened up all the closed doors and windows that looked out on the universe. She wasn't only full of life because of how much she loved her, but life, too, had been made full with her. She had different kinds of smiles that never seemed to end, and the expressions of love that appeared on her face were boundless. She could make her girlfriends laugh for a moment when they were sad, and then make them cry in the blink of an eye.

Her life was a poem that she lived but never wrote down, Suad told me.

She used to think of all of the texts she wrote outside of the obsession called publishing were real writing. She felt as though she was reclaiming time through writing, with a real sense of being created and growing up again. But from time to time she would get overcome with feelings that this writing, however much it pulsated with life, would never be completed, despite the fact that at the time Nahla was hardly thinking about her being forgotten or about her disappearance or death. She thought about that because all the real things, those that she did with the same sincerity and passion, had left or were lost. She wasn't able to get them back because they had been buried in the ground.

It's as if real things are incomplete, unfinished, Suad said.

***

Nahla didn't shut up, even when she was silent. She spoke through all of the pretty things, if not with her tongue then with her eyes, her hands and her heart. Confusion shone in her eyes when she gazed upon all the pretty things around her, as if she wanted to drink everything up with her eyes. Suad often noticed that confusion when Nahla was out on her balcony, when she talked to her about Hani, her grandchildren or her girlfriends. She would pull back her bangs as she looked out at the sea, at the birds in the cage, at the seedlings, at the beautiful paintings hanging in the living room opposite the balcony, and at the amazing traditional textiles that she planted in the corners of the house.

Oh, how Nahla adored such beautiful things, how free she was, Suad told me. Even though her family had forced her to get married, she lived out her feelings in the deepest and most transparent way possible, through love and motherhood and marriage. And she cherished her freedom so passionately that she would show off her body in every situation, more so when it came to love. She didn't believe in obligation, she was liberated from all restrictions, and her love for her children and her husband was not the same as her love for Hani.

She used to tell Suad how she loved Hani because 80 per cent or even more of him was 'sweetness' while the rest was bones and flesh, blood and skin.

Suad believed she knew her body so it would surprise her that she was constantly rediscovering it. Whenever Nahla talked about how her sense of her body oppressed her when she was in her fifties, Suad would ask her for clarification about the details of her relationship with it, and those feelings that she was being inauthentic would spread. It was confirmed to her that her desire arose from her body, that it was present there, and that she wasn't repelled by it.

She loved to have other people understand the way she felt about her body.

My God, Suad said, remembering the first time she went to her house after she got married. She arrived as planned, around 5 p.m. When she rang the doorbell, the cleaning lady opened the door and said, 'Madame told me to inform you that she's waiting for you in the bedroom.'

Suad stood bolted in place, astonishment written all over her face. How could she just go into the bedroom when she was visiting her at home for the first time since she got married, and why would she want to receive her there anyway?

She found herself trailing behind the maid as she walked down the hallway, leading her to the open bedroom door. Nahla stood in front of the vanity mirror, stroking her hair and swaying right and left. She saw Suad in the mirror, turned round and approached her from the edge of the mirror where she had stacked up her beauty supplies, smiling and welcoming her. Her open robe revealed her body, naked except for a thin wine-coloured lacy bra and panties of the same colour. Suad was stunned by the way she was acting at first, but then came to understand this juvenile behaviour. Nahla wanted her to see her shapely breasts, her smooth belly, her muscular legs, and the prodigiousness of her chest. She opened her robe to show Suad her body, smiling at her with her fleshy oval eyes almost the colour of pistachio, made even more attractive by their pitch-black lashes.

Suad's surprise notwithstanding, Nahla's feelings for her were uncomplicated, even if she sat down in the living room and started pulling aside her robe a little bit from time to time, stroking her legs. It was clear to Suad that Nahla wanted to hear from her, or perhaps from anybody, what she already said to herself, the same words with which she used to flatter herself.

Suad never thought this behaviour was an indication of Nahla liking women. She was sure that Nahla never had any such inclinations, and that she never would. In contrast, Suad could see those feelings in Nadine's eyes when she met Mirna for the first time at Nahla's house. Her eyes told the whole story of her desire—as bright as if they had siphoned away all the energy from her other senses and gathered it there; they radiated her desire; her gaze made it seem as though her irises had become hands reaching out for Mirna's body. When Mirna passed away, that light in Nadine's eyes went out. They receded inside, as if they had only ever been present so that Mirna could illuminate her last light. She cried when she told Suad that cancer is vicious and horrible. It ate her, devoured her, and she shrivelled up like a fist. This disease is awful, Suad. A fantastical monster consuming the body with its horrible teeth. When Suad went to her house for the mourning session, Nadine's eyes were hollow, as if they were staring at something invisible, as though she were trying to discern the eye of death, to ask who and where he was. She wanted to see him. The line between death and life seemed quite flimsy at that moment. Nadine couldn't seem to get her bearings after death snatched Mirna away from her. Sorrow pooled in her eyes, which had lost their spark and were now saddled with confusion and distraction. It was clear from how she slumped her shoulders and the way she walked. Suad felt as though her lips had become thin, had lost their fullness.

If Nahla had been able to see her, she would have lost it. Nahla always had a bigger heart than me, she told me, she was more forgiving when it came to those she loved. Suad found strange the kindness she showed Hani's wife and kids. It was hurtful for her when Hani's wife Sawsan needed to undergo a mastectomy. She asked him to kiss her there, to rub and caress her. She loved Hani even more when he spoke affectionately about Sawsan in her presence. She was never jealous of her, even though Nahla loved him so much and had such a perpetual desire to be close to him that she was almost violently jealous of all the things that touched him or got close to him, of the air that entered his chest, the cologne that got mixed up with his scent, the light that fell on his cheek, the shirt that rubbed against his body, the collar that was wrapped around his neck in place of her hands. Suad found it so strange that Nahla took stock of the household goods that came to Hani's family from the village.

'Nahla, aren't you jealous of his wife?' she asked her once.

'No, not at all, Suad. I love him, my friend, and I love his wife and kids. I enjoy being able to feed them from our land.'

Nahla often said that we cannot avoid heartache our entire lives. We might never succeed at that, Suad. But Hani was both chronic pain and perpetual warmth in her body. Suad realized she had had a few brief relationships because she had never been able to hold on to the one true love of her life. Nevertheless, she often asked herself whether Nahla ever longed for the scent of a man.

She would ask that question when she saw her body writhing because of a virile smell wafting from a man. But she was confident that her body wouldn't express any desire on its own. Her fantasies about male longing were what incited her own body to feel desire. Everything was different with Hani, though. The storm that whipped through her words and her eyes whenever Suad talked about men who had come on to her would subside when she talked about Hani, as though her voice were ransacking its vocabulary from a well of tenderness deep in her heart, as if it were floating in a boundless sea of love, an very particular love, exceptional, unbounded by the body or the heart.

She used to tell Suad that Hani's love was her destiny. Her body knows his body, and his knows hers. She loved her body even more when she was with him. Once she proudly told her about how Hani admitted to enjoying being with so many other women, but that the pleasure he experienced with her was the most beautiful, the most complete.

Nahla used to share all her desires with Suad. But Suad rarely talked about her own desires—whether she ever noticed her excitement and the glimmer in her eyes when the waiter at the City Café came to take their order. The same glimmer shone in Suad's eyes when the doorman at the university would run over to make her some fresh coffee as soon as she entered the faculty lounge.

Suad would often resolve to acknowledge her suppressed feelings towards those men, but that acknowledgement only ever amounted to small openings within the walls that separated her from her body, and they didn't stay open long because she would hurriedly shut them. The only thing she wouldn't tell Nahla about was her need for love, not because she had lost all desire but because she didn't want to feel socially inferior, especially with the filthy feelings she had after having sex with the used-clothes shopkeeper. After Nahla's disappearance she wished she had told her all about her desires, and she blamed herself for not noticing how Nahla would drop those confessions when it came to matters of love.

Before the July War broke out, about a week after Nahla disappeared, Suad had a strong desire to go to the university even though all the students were gone. This urge was surprising even to her because she had felt abandoned that whole time without Nahla, as though the university were icy cold. She couldn't explain why she felt like going there, though perhaps in her subconscious she knew it would lighten the weight of her loss. The closed university seemed even icier when she went in, and she felt more strongly that the universe had abandoned her. She wanted to go inside the faculty lounge but stood outside the door for a moment. She smiled bitterly before turning around and heading back home. All through the drive back she remembered the familiar feeling of how the students never interrupted the flow of her lecture, how none of them ever cut her off. She also thought about how the wall that she had put up between herself and her colleagues was the only thing protecting her. She imagined the scene as she sat in the faculty lounge listening to their discussions about the war without ever chiming in. She could see how it might seem that she wasn't even there, in response to her feelings, not because her colleagues were uninvolved in those conversations, and she imagined her laughter and how she must have looked when a colleague approached her at the end of the academic year and jokingly whispered in her ear, 'Doctor Suad, you're avoiding talking to anyone as if you're afraid he's going to hit you or that you might fall in love with him.'

She thought he might be right. She closed the door and refused to open it for anyone so she wouldn't fall into a trap.

When she made it home, she took off her clothes and let her hair cascade down on her shoulders in front of the mirror. A single tear would form in her eye from time to time. Right in front of the mirror, she began to tell herself that there was nobody as talented as she at squandering opportunities to live the life she desired. She started rethinking the nature of her relationship with Nahla. As she rubbed her face and wiped away the tears with a towel, and then lay down in bed on her stomach, she asked herself why Nahla had always been the axis on which her life spun.

She remembered when Nahla went with her to her grandfather's house in the Bekaa Valley on the day her cousin got married. She noticed how interested she had become in all the places that connected her to Nahla, and she was no longer dispassionate towards them. She asked herself why she enjoyed everything that had some connection to Nahla, why she was the only lens through which she could look at the world. Nahla lived her life out loud, authentically, and she gave herself the right to live according to her desires. She wondered whether there could exist another creature who also believed her desires could be fulfilled through friendship even if that other person's desire had no connection whatsoever to her fundamental desires. Was it reasonable for the other's desire to become your own, and for you not to gain anything more than the satisfaction of observing the world around you? Was I vicariously satisfying my desires when I participated in them by watching and listening in order to preserve my purity? she wondered to herself.

My God, the whole thing has always been so mystifying to me, she said.

Repeatedly she gazed into the mirror and proclaimed, This is my body, not Nahla's, my moans aren't hers, and my bravery isn't like hers.

Without any feelings of maternity or guardianship, Nahla would ask her, with a sly smile, 'Why are you so hung up on me, Suad? Tell me. Why don't you do something that you honestly think is yours to do?'

Nahla was always telling her that their relationship was indulgent. She would protest that she was stealing too much of her ear and her time. And when the two of them walked places where they would be with other people, Suad seemed not to be there at all.

'Please tell me, Suad,' she asked her several times, 'Where do you think this relationship is going?'

Sometimes she would say she didn't know, other times she would sneer at her.

***

Suad started to look unwell a few months after Nahla disappeared. Her pupils shrank; they now looked like two grains of lentil on her face. Everything about her became more frail and hollow. Despairing of ever finding Nahla, she no longer saw anyone, until one day, Nahla's daughter Faten called her and said, 'Tante Suad, my husband's out of town, I'm sick and want to go sleep at my father's. God, I miss you so much, come stay with me for a bit. When you're around I feel as though mama's here.'

Suad tensed up and her eyes filled with tears. At first she thought about not going at all but she couldn't refuse when Faten asked her for something.

In Nahla's absence the house had gone ice-cold. When she first walked in, she noticed the dry and dead leaves, as if their spirits had been expelled just like Nahla's. It surprised her to see a pile of basil, rose, gardenia and jasmine leaves mixed together with other leaves on the ground. It seemed they had been shaken and fallen from the plants owing to all her chattering about losing Nahla's touch and voice. Suad said the speech of plants can be more truthful and even more articulate than the yammering of human beings—for plants love unconditionally, expecting nothing in return, because they know that their survival is contingent upon the existence of the other. Absence hurts plants, too, makes them sad, stirs up their appetite for talk. And in plant talk, she could also hear something about her loss of the voice and the tenderness of their owner.

Suad missed the smell of basil in particular because it's the most pungent of all the flowers and plants on Nahla's balcony. She asked herself where all her scents had gone. It was as if all the plants had packed up their scents and set off in search of Nahla's smell.

That night she went to sleep in Nahla's room. Everything in there was still the way it had been, her smell hadn't dissipated yet, at least that's what Suad thought. But that night was the most difficult of her life.

Beside the bed that picture of Nahla was laughing the same way she used to laugh when she started talking to her, or when the memory doctor would flirt with her.

Who else am I supposed to listen to and talk to besides the picture that's talking to me? she said as she wiped away the tears, then got up and opened the armoire to look at the clothes that were still hanging there. She inhaled the smell suspended in there, which mixed with the smell of Nahla's perfume, the one that she used to love so much, that would cling to her skin long after she had put it on. She shut her eyes and deeply breathed in the smell, then shut the armoire. She laid back down on the bed and stared at the picture once more. Nahla's features seemed harsh, her face distant and absent because of how forgetful she seemed. Then Suad found herself saying, Ooof, ooof, Nahla, your face is so harsh the more I forget about it. And as she gazed more deeply at the picture, those features started to soften, she felt herself remembering more, and without paying much attention, she said, You're back, Nahla, you came back. It's as if you're back. By the time she noticed that she was raving, she already felt as dizzy as someone who had fallen into a trance. She could no longer tell whether Nahla's face in the picture was there or not, just as she didn't know where she was: was she in Nahla's room or her own? Was the face she saw in the picture hers before Nahla disappeared or Nahla's face after she had disappeared? Was Nahla trying, while she was away, to ask through the picture if she still had a face, or was she also asking about her face that had disappeared as well?

Nahla had also lost her face when she could no longer see me, and I can no longer hear her, Suad said to herself, then fell onto the bed and felt as though she were disappearing, that her eyes could no longer see anything but Nahla's absent face. Without even noticing, she opened the bedside table drawer and found Nahla's memory pills. She opened the vial and swallowed one. It felt like her memory was biting her, as if she were covered with lice. She slid her hand across her face and remembered Hani without understanding why she had just thought of him. Was it because she was sleeping in Nahla's bed, because her body and memory had been sprawled out there, or was it because she yearned to love a man the way Nahla had once loved Hani? Could it be that she once lusted for him just because of what Nahla said about him? She remembered the letter that Hani sent with her to Nahla after she lost her memory; it was still in her purse. She got up, opened the letter and started reading what he had written: *Forgetfulness is death, Nahla. I beg of you, please don't die. You are my memory and my body, my whole life. Your womb is my home, and to your womb I wish to return.*

Suad read the letter Hani had written to Nahla before she disappeared, but Nahla started staring back at Suad as if she couldn't hear or see her, as if she couldn't tell who was talking to her or what was being said.

Suad put the letter back in her purse. She stretched out on the bed and switched off the light.

In the morning, Faten was shaking her, calling out to her, but there was no life in the woman she was calling. She went to sleep for the last time in Nahla's bed, and never opened her eyes again.

Suad was dead.

Every one of her stunned friends had something to say about her death.

One day Azizeh, Nadine and Hoda met at the Rawda Café. They sat there without Nahla's and Suad's chairs at the table. Azizeh left the two of them and came over to me. I asked her who she was and she told me her name, and said she was a friend of Nahla and Suad. She told me a lot of things, some of which I knew already, others that seemed fishy. But the one thing that wasn't a lie was Suad's death.

With great sadness I asked her why she had died, and how.

'She flickered like a candle and then went out entirely,' she replied. 'Every day she would come to see one of us, just stand there at the door crying and then leave without coming in, until she finally died in Nahla's bed.'

'I understand, but what killed her?'

'I don't know. Every one of us has her own opinion. One person said it's a ghost story, that she was following after Nahla. Someone else said Nahla couldn't go on living without Suad's ears. Another person said she disappeared as soon as Nahla had gone missing, that she couldn't live or even feel life without Nahla. And somebody said she followed after her so that they could finish the conversation they were in the middle of . . . '

17

Nahla disappeared.

If I knew where she was I would have gone and found her and told her everything. Who knows? Maybe her memory would have come back as soon as I read to her what I'd written about her. But I'm afraid that even if I did run into her she wouldn't recognize me. Perhaps she'd stare at me with confused, lost and vacant eyes as I narrated her own story. Then she'd continue on her way into oblivion without even realizing that the story was hers, that her name was Nahla, and that she had added another name to the many names of love, one she couldn't take with her into her forgetfulness.

The truth of the matter is I don't know whether Suad would rather Nahla be dead or disappeared before going to look for her.

She came to see me once after Nahla had disappeared, at the seaside cafe in the Raouché neighbourhood where I would sometimes go to write. Her complexion was the colour of death. She smelt funny, a combination of cold, clammy silence, sorrow, loneliness and confusion. I set aside my pen and paper so that I could greet her as soon as she came in and sat down across the table from me. She asked me straight away whether a disappearance is anything like death, and which is worse.

I didn't know how to respond and, in any case, she didn't wait to hear what I had to say. She rested her cheek against the palm of my hand, pressed her elbow down on the table, and said, 'No, death is a period, a full stop. That's it. Disappearance opens up every possible punctuation mark: comma, ellipsis, exclamation point, question mark.'

After saying that, she turned to look at the sea, got lost in the waves. Her face rippled with shades of desire to go looking for Nahla. She said that death contains at its core a kind of amnesia that swells with time, that it sweeps off the chest those shards like broken glass that are created by sorrow, eliminates deadly thorns. But the idea of Nahla being dead made her feel as though a part of her own life had departed with her, if not her entire life altogether. In response to that absence she felt constantly unsettled, in suspension. Absence dangles you there, dizzyingly, leaves no space for sorrow to settle or be set aside to cool down.

I remember her saying to me, after a long sigh, 'Oof, nobody should give their opinion about anything that doesn't concern them, anything they know isn't their business.'

It was strange for her to ask my opinion about Nahla, to be so hung up on her. Then she repeated her question about whether I believed Nahla was dead or disappeared.

She put the question there on the table for me and left.

She didn't ask too many questions any more but when her longing for Nahla and their conversations overwhelmed her, she would open the door and come out. Sometimes she would walk the streets, turning right and left, as if she were searching for something she had lost. During the times when she had once been accustomed to going over to Nahla's, she would head to Azizeh's or Nadine's or my brother Jawad's instead, or else to Faten's. No matter where she went, though, she would just stand there in front of the door after they opened up for her, her eyes brimming with tears, and then turn around and leave without going in. If all the windows were closed, she wouldn't be able to think about anything but Nahla's window, from where she had been able to look out and watch life without any worries. In those moments she would stumble over obstacles and walls, she wouldn't be able to distinguish between herself and Nahla, those feelings of emaciation and weak bones would vanish, she would feel she had become stronger, she would attribute to herself a capacity she only enjoyed when Nahla was by her side. It was only in those moments that she thought about how the people we love give us our strength and our abilities. The idea rattled inside her head that her yearning for Nahla might also be for an ability she had lost. She could no longer bear the walls standing in front of her. She would often find herself shutting her eyes all of a sudden, believing that if she did so the walls in front of her would just disappear. In those moments she could see Nahla's eyes, always laughing, like a raging waterfall with nothing standing in its way, eyes that were capable of eliminating every barrier and every wall. But ever since Nahla's went missing she shut her eyes so often that she feared she wouldn't be able to go on living without her eyes closed.

It seemed to her that after Nahla went missing it was her fate not to see life with her eyes wide open. The last time she shut them they felt like Nahla's eyes, that they looked at life as if they were closed.

Had Suad intuited her death or had Nahla hinted at it in her papers? Why had Suad handed them to me and then asked me to read them so quickly? Questions appeared all over my face and I asked her, 'What's the rush?'

'Nobody knows when . . . ' she replied, then adding after a brief silence, 'Those papers are the past, and one can't always return to the past, one can't just face it whenever they feel like it.'

I assured her I would read them. I didn't hear another word from her as she left, closing the door behind her. When she came over to my house one day during the July War, I was thinking about the raging conflict and everything that was happening.

That day she told me she had brought me those papers because she knew Nahla hadn't told me everything, that she had only shared with me what she was able to remember before entirely losing her memory. She told me that's not the way people's stories are related, that the hero has to tell their whole story, and that when a writer writes about heroes she must know everything about them.

She handed me the papers and left. But doubts and questions tugged at me whenever I recalled the look on her face at the moment when she gave them to me. It's true that she had stated her desire that I write down Nahla's story but, at the same time, I could discern in her eyes a hidden desire I couldn't quite name.

Reading those papers wasn't easy. The words seemed to have been written in moments of raving madness. After finally managing to get through the diaries and the stories with great difficulty, I realized that Suad's story is bound up with Nahla's, but I still wasn't sure who had done the actual writing, whether it was Suad's handwriting or Nahla's. On some pages there were two different scripts, and no definitive evidence of which was which. It's possible that Nahla had written it, and that this is why she shook me when she said, 'Even if you know me, who told you that you're ever going to find out everything about me? Just write and you'll find a way to understand.' Had Suad written it in order to add things Nahla never said in the first place? Or did she have a buried desire to write in order to commune with Nahla the poet? Writing was her dream, which was why it was up to Nahla whether she wanted to hear everything she had to say. Did Nahla ever imagine her fate and Suad's? She believed writing was like peering into the future.

I'm not sure which one of them did the writing. I don't know anything about what happened to Nahla, whether she was disappeared or dead. I started to doubt the entire story. I had a feeling I was going to find her. Maybe she was living out her life somewhere. Still I had to believe Suad before she too went away; after Nahla's disappearance she was the only one with whom I maintained a relationship. At the same time I also believe what Nahla told me: 'Write and you'll find a way to understand.' I'm certain that writing leads us to knowledge, and not the other way around. Suad told me that Nahla had gone missing, and the papers say the same thing. The papers say Suad went home to sleep at Faten's. She got into Nahla's bed and fell asleep. She slept late the next morning, and when Faten came in to wake her she found her dead in Nahla's bed.

***

'Why aren't stories known or written down until after their tellers are already dead or gone?' Nahla asked me one day even as she was telling me her own story.

She talked in order to break the rule. She affirmed her right to tell her story, demonstrating that she had the ability before being immersed in forgetfulness. She told me how Mahmoud Darwish said that the one who tells their story owns the land of talk. She also wanted to own the land for her talk.

There are many things a writer doesn't write down until after the heroes are dead or gone so as not to bring them harm. Maybe the writer does this in order to retain some measure of poetic license after their heroes die, in order to shape their lives and destinies however they wish. But I was sad when Nahla went missing, beyond my sadness from the war, beyond losing my mind in the war that sent me raving and the void that was swallowing me as I wrote, no longer able to know for sure whether I ever actually knew a woman named Nahla and was writing her story or whether I had confabulated the story I was writing about a woman who perished beneath the rubble. Things are jumbled in my mind the same way they are in Suad's. The line between writing and speech seemed more and more flimsy as she grew despondent searching for Nahla, as her last dream of finding her died. The last time I saw her, she came over to my house and stared at me with a strange expression on her face, as if she were asking me for help. 'Think about what you want to do,' she said. 'The story's in your hands. I've given up on finding her. You're the writer, you're the one who's hidden her away. See if you can find her in the novel.'

She asked me to find her, to determine her fate. Then she left and I never saw her again.

I was annoyed but didn't respond, didn't tell her how much fate bothered me, how much it frightened me. I'm more interested in writing about lives, which is like swimming through life, whereas fate sends me flying out of the sea. Neither did I want to play the role of the judge, or simply accede to the fate my characters wanted; I can't write unless I'm immersed in life, unshackled from everything they ask me to do. And I don't want to write about inevitable fate. That's the space of tyranny. I have never believed that in writing freedom can be achieved by expropriating the fates of others. Writing events that have a beginning and an end is just filling in the blanks. But the irony is that the writer writes, and may imagine lives for their characters that aren't their own. It's odd that the writer never questions the extent to which the power he grants himself and imposes upon his characters clashes with his beliefs when he expropriates their fate and guides them along certain paths that might invalidate their lives, or perhaps dissolve them in death.

The truth of the matter is that I don't know Nahla's fate, whether she lost her memory and went missing, whether she had been kidnapped, or whether she was dead—all of those are nothing more than faces of death. If she returned, reappeared, came back to life, she'd realize that I steal the lives of characters, not in order to write them down but in order to gauge my own fearful ability to tinker with fate. She'd find that despite her and Suad's long and intimate friendship, the two of them didn't know each other at all. And that's what really scared me.

'Write and you'll be able to understand,' she told me.

Her story would tell her many things she didn't know about her own life.

And in spite of my certainty that no person's life resembles anyone else's, I'm not sure exactly what I took from each of their lives and attributed to the other's. Maybe I did that in order to find out what would happen if I swapped the roles, what each of their fates would then become.

One day Nahla told me that a writer is a thief, that writing is like a game, warning me not to mess with fate.

She didn't want me to alter her fate the way I did in my previous novel *Dunya*. She asked me if I was planning to run away from her fate because I'm so afraid of endings. She told me she knows Dunya, knows about her life, and asked why it became a different story when I wrote it. And she told me Dunya read the novel and got lost, that she no longer knew whether the fate she had been handed by the novel was real or whether it was the fate she knew and experienced in real life. But she cried when she read the novel and discovered how harsh and unstable life is, how weak and imprisoned and paralysed she is. She ran away from the text, took revenge on her fate and her destiny in the novel. But when she finally came out of it she no longer knew who she was. She discovered that she was in a new kind of prison that was no less brutal because she didn't know how to stand on her own two feet or how to enjoy this life of freedom. 'Try and you'll be able to understand,' I told her. But she was afraid to try. It began to dawn on her that the fate I had created for her was fully independent of the life she had refused to recognize in the novel, like lip-syncing where there is no possibility of animation or existence. And so she returned to the text in order to live and reconnect with herself.

Dunya had grown alarmingly addicted to antidepressants and anti-anxiety medication. She asked for a divorce in exchange for giving up her children and then she left Malek and the house. She worked in a hair salon and studied cosmetology, which she loved, so that she could apply her own and other women's make-up the way she saw it on the faces of models in advertisements on TV and in magazines. At the salon she met a man named Joseph who was six years younger. They fell in love. She started wearing halter tops and miniskirts so he could appreciate her beautiful body. She told him she was divorced but didn't say that she had children so he wouldn't be able to tell how old she was. Joseph loved her in a way she could feel in every fibre of her being. She began to see the world filled with colours and joy. When Joseph decided to ask her to marry him, her family was furious. She couldn't impose her will on them the way she used to do with me. She was afraid that her family would abandon her, as they threatened to do, the same way she had abandoned her own children.

In order to stanch her own desire for Joseph and to make herself off-limits to him, she began to put on the veil. There was nothing that could come between them quite like the hijab and her return to Islam, which forbade her from marrying him and which could send her straight to Hell.

She left the salon and then called him, promising to meet at a cafe in Beirut. She got dressed and carefully did her make-up to leave him with a beautiful impression of her. He was on tenterhooks waiting in a corner inside the cafe when she walked in wearing a dull headscarf and grey make-up mixed with bright pink. He was shocked to see her, his eyes froze in their sockets. She told him they needed to end the relationship, to stop seeing one another because she had started veiling. Her eyes welled with tears when he told her he no longer had any feelings for her because he had started to look at her the way he looked at the Virgin Mary.

Dunya started to cry as she told me about the end of her romance with Joseph.

But I found it strange that she would tell me, 'The thing that really bothers me, Nahla, is that he never got to see how beautiful my breasts are. I considered letting him see them. It still makes my heart sad. To tell you the truth, I wish I had shown them to him before I started veiling.'

Even stranger than that was the fact that Dunya went to visit Malek in the hospital before he died. She asked him to forgive her for leaving him, then asked, 'There's still one question in my heart, Malek, please answer it truthfully.'

'What is it, Dunya?' he asked, his eyes aflutter.

'Did you ever cheat on me when we were married, before we broke up? I have to know, if you cheated on me, just say so.'

'No, I never cheated on you,' he lied after a brief silence, before his eyes shut for ever.

'May God forgive me for everything I did to you,' she said, as he closed his eyes for the last time and exhaled. This was the answer she had wanted from him, even though she was lying to herself because she knew full well he had always been cheating on her. Then she went and reread the novel, discovering the fate that writing had laid out for her.

I remembered the ending of *Dunya* as I approached the final moment of this story. I never wanted it to end because I'm as scared of endings as I am of fate.

I felt surrounded as I came closer to the last part of the novel. Nahla, Suad, Azizeh, Nadine and all the characters in the novel are wrapped around my neck, nearly choking me to death. I can't bear to sit at my desk any longer. I left the papers there and ran out of the house. When I found the lift was in use I couldn't bear to wait for it so I went skipping down the stairs instead. I hopped in my car and headed to the sea, my refuge whenever I craved wide-open space and an infinite horizon. My head was pounding as I sped towards the water. It was 5 p.m. during early autumn and a light rain was falling. The rhythmic drizzling on the glass resounded in my ears. The question of whether I was tyrannical in the way I imposed the destinies of my characters was lodged in my brain, preventing me from seeing or hearing anything else. The amazing thing is that, despite my own fear of fate, a vast inner happiness spread through me as I described theirs. What worried me more was the final, decisive climax, after which point I can't change anyone's destiny.

Just then I remembered what Suad had said about the harshness of loss and death, but also about the difference between the two. Whenever I tried to write, my thoughts were as dishevelled as my hair. I never felt the same way as someone who finishes telling a story, I didn't feel as if completing a text was like giving birth, I didn't find myself singing or crying spontaneously the way I sometimes would after I finished writing a novel. Simply put, I was at a loss, my characters' eyes were swirling all around me as I drove down towards Raouché. I arrived at an intersection, I turned right, then left. To my surprise I suddenly spotted a steamship on the coast alongside the road, where the pavement I used to know was now gone, there were no guardrails to separate the road from the coastline, as if the city were a different one than it had been in the 1940s, and the street as if I were seeing it in a *carte postale* showing the Beirut of those years. There was no trace of the military beach where it should have been. The French had built it over the olive groves between the Saint Georges and the Ajram Café. There was no trace of the lighthouse either, which was still in the Koreitem neighbourhood across from the Protestant College up on the hill. Things got jumbled before my eyes, time was caving in. I looked at my wristwatch, it was broken, I couldn't tell the time or the date. And just as I turned towards the front of the ship that was pressing up against the road, I saw something unbelievable as my car drew closer. Standing on the prow of the ship was a woman in a red dress, staring at me and smiling. I looked long and hard at her in order to be sure who she was, and I couldn't believe my eyes. It slowly dawned on me that this was Nahla, in her very flesh and blood. At that moment I truly felt as though I had fallen precipitously in the opposite direction of writing, when I return to the past, pretending to tinker with it. I continued to stare at her and where she stood, then examined my car and saw what I was wearing—and everything got even more confused: what time period was I in? Was this actually Nahla I was seeing in front of me or had I read about this scene in the papers that Suad gave me? Had Suad called me and told me that Nahla would be arriving on the steamship or had Suad died and was I hallucinating all of this?

* * *

Questions crashed down on me. Astonished to see Nahla right there in front of me, I started talking to myself: is it possible Nahla would come back after disappearing, just reappear like this? By God it's she, though, I have no doubt that it's she. But why is she coming back in the 1940s? And my God, how could she come back with her body the way it was in her youth, and at different times in her life?

My eyes darted towards her again in order to figure out whether I was hallucinating or it was actually she, but there was no room for doubt. Her pistachio-coloured eyes were locked right on me, and her smile eliminated any hint of suspicion I may have had. I was afraid to get out of the car and walk towards her. At the same time I didn't have the strength to move my head, to move even a muscle. The eerie thing was that it looked as though she were standing beside me just outside my open car window.

In her long dress, make-up, her Marilyn Monroe–style hairdo, Nahla looked like she had stepped out of the '40s. She bent over in front of me, then crouched down as if she were picking up something she had dropped. I had the feeling she was picking up the letter Hani had written to her when she started losing her memory as well as the love poems and other writings she had given Hani instead of publishing them. When she turned her back to me in order to look out at the sea, I noticed the folds and the tail of her dress that looked like wings trailing her. I don't know what made me believe that Nahla could fly at that very moment and that she was about to do so. She spun back around to look at me and smiled. Just then I heard her voice. She seemed very close, as if she were standing right next to me despite the distance between us. She started speaking in a soft voice, which then started getting louder and louder. I paid close attention to what she was saying:

My God, how many windows lead to love, there's a window to passion, a window to lust, a window to ardour, a window to rapture, and a window to affection . . . and I'm looking at you through all those windows. There are so many different windows of love with so many different names! But Hani and I have opened our window and it's never going to close again.

Then she started talking to me about desire:

So this is desire. I'm now in the heart of desire, Alawiya. Can you understand? My desire keeps me alive because I live inside of it and stand completely in its depths. I don't ever chase after it, there's no need for the chase. When you chase after your desire you begin to doubt whether you're actually experiencing love. I don't live in this kind of ambiguity, I'm alive, believe me. I'm alive. Everything you all call my disappearance was an exercise in drowning myself in desire. Why do others believe that a person has disappeared or died or ended when they immerse themselves in their desire?

Anyway, you don't matter any more, whether you're dead, absent or disappeared. I know that you're running away from the future and that Suad is dead. Poor Suad. She thought I was dead, and she stripped off the body she hated so much and went to join me, where she thought I could be found, in the hope that she would find me this time with a new body, so that she wouldn't look at my body with so much of the disappointment I used to see in her eyes whenever we were together. She chased after me so that I would hear her the way she used to hear me, as Azizeh once said. You shouldn't worry about my fate or hers. Just write down what my body says, and listen, I'll tell you something strange: I don't need to have a houri's body or a human body because I'm not outside of my body, a woman without a memory. I always used to say without any shame that my body knows all the names of love, that it was true and devoted to Hani, because he was the one who taught me or perhaps we learnt together this thing they call love.

Poor Suad, she chased after me to hear me talk about love. I wish you knew what she was talking about. Whatever the writer knows about their characters, and no matter how hard she tries to understand, there are many things she can never know, and even if she did know she wouldn't write them all down. We talked together, we relived our entire lives together, relived everything that already happened together. I talk to her and she talks to me in our absence and in your papers and in your dreams. We laugh a lot, sometimes we cry. But the interesting thing is that our crying is like swimming. Crying invigorates us because even in our ostensible absence that you all impose upon us, we're still human beings living through all our experiences, and in some of this absence there is a palpable presence. Would you believe that I see Hani even though he can't see me? I talk to him in my mind, sometimes he imagines that I'm walking behind him or in front of him or at his side. When I gaze at him he can smell my scent, he opens his palm and feels as if it's getting moist with my sweat. Write this down, Alawiya, write this down. Write love. And believe me, when you express my desire you're going to be speaking the truth, not something out of a novel.

I didn't know how to respond. I was in a state of shock that felt permanent. I couldn't believe my eyes and my ears when I saw her and heard her. It was her. The voice was her voice. But why had she come back in the '40s? Had she come back to determine her fate in the novel or had I done that for her?

I got lost trying to answer this, I no longer knew anything for certain. All I knew was that she seemed happy, seemed about twenty years younger. I didn't ask her anything but she could tell what was running through my mind. She looked at me again and smiled:

You witch, you know how to bring me back to life. I'm even more of a witch than you, I knew how to make it back with my body the way it used to be, the way it was when I was still alive. When you write a novel about somebody, they come back young and start to be alive again, as if they were coming back to seek guidance in life, to learn how to live it. When an author writes the lives of her characters, it's as if she's opening for them the door to life. That door is wide open when you're in love.

Alawiya, I don't know how to tell you this. I've been following everything you write, I've considered every last detail. I've heard the sound of your ink and your anxiety and your confusion. I've heard the sound of your thoughts while you're writing, while you're running away from the war in order to write down my life so that you won't get lost like me or that your name won't be written on a body bag among the war dead and not in a novel. I would have bet that you were trying to find meaning in my memory and my life. There's just one thing you don't know that has everything to do with what's happening right now. What you've written might be my story or the story of another woman you imagined beneath the rubble. It doesn't matter. You must be asking yourself: Is this Nahla standing so close at the front of the boat and talking to me, or is it only Nahla in my mind and my imagination? There's not such a big difference, this doesn't matter anyway. I want you to know, as you get closer to the end of the novel, that I'm not certain that everything in it actually happened. What I told you might not be so accurate, and you may have doubts about everything you wrote. But the one thing I know for sure, that I'm sure actually happened, is the talk about this thing called love.

As she said that her voice started to grow soft again. And when her voice was gone the sight of her vanished, too, as if her voice had been projecting her in front of me. When the last bit faded away, I wondered to myself: Did I just see Nahla or had the whole thing been an illusion?

Now the question of fate alone continues to hound me, makes me imagine things despite my certainty that I had really just seen her.